The Origami Deception

David Wickenden

Published by David Wickenden, 2024.

This is a work of fiction. Similarities to real people, places, or events are entirely coincidental.

THE ORIGAMI DECEPTION

First edition. July 24, 2024.

Copyright © 2024 David Wickenden.

ISBN: 979-8227491558

Written by David Wickenden.

As always, I am nothing without Gina and my boys, Adam, Daniel, and Ian. My dad, Dick, is still one of my biggest fans at 85 years young.

Huge thanks to Robin Carson, editor extraordinaire, for all his help and friendship. Thanks to Scott and Brianna for sharing the long, and sometimes wet tent at all the markets we attend, selling our wares.

I was blown away by the awesome coverwork by Juan Pardon of Argentina. I look forward to collaborating in the future.

And finally, to all those readers who faithfully follow me into breach and help me fight the good fight. Your trust and devotion to my stories keeps me hitting the keys.

Prologue

Novo Metals

Minas Gerais, Brazil, 2022

The high-pitched scream of a jungle animal drowned out low groans emanating from the hillside. The animal cry was cut short, as the unfortunate prey had its life ripped from its throat. Once again, the night hushed itself until the usual jungle sounds of insects and reptiles resumed their nocturnal symphony.

Had any of the creatures understood the source of the periodic groans and wet tearing sounds coming from deep under the soil, they would have fled, slinking away in fear. The tightly grouped ripples radiating from the downward slope of the man-made reservoir would have startled them. In the daylight, they might have witnessed tendrils of mud mixing with the surrounding clearer water, or the gurgle of bubbles that surfaced from the depths. Not that anything lived in the still waters.

A tailings pond was a common sight at major mining sites. Mining companies dumped waste material from mining into lakes, swamps or, as in this case, a man-made basin holding back billions of gallons of water and toxic by-products with a dam built of the same waste it contained.

Arsenic, copper, and other heavy metals created a toxic slurry of waste material. As the tailing material grew, so did the dams, looking like massive, tiered rice-fields cut into Vietnamese mountain sides. Depending on the size of the mine, the tailings pond could rise hundreds of feet above the terrain.

Mining companies, in general, tended to ignore waste, since it made no profit. And at the hillside where the animal had screamed, because it walled a pond that did little but contain waste, the company, Novo, gave very little attention to the structure. Only the annual rainy season proved a problem.

FRANCESCA woke, her skin cool and damp where her new kitten, *Gatinho*, had slept against her as a warm replacement for its mother and littermates. She groped across the single mattress for her fluffy companion but found herself alone.

Sitting up, she rubbed her eyes and squinted in the gloom for the wee animal. The house was dark; and what little light bled through the draped blanket that acted as a curtain, did little to illuminate the room. She was alone, which meant that her tiny friend was loose in the house.

Sliding off the mattress, her feet touched the hard, packed-soil floor. By feel, she moved to the curtain separating her sleeping compartment from the common room. Another, similar room across the rough hut sheltered her *Avó* or grandma. Usually, she would hear the deep snores of her father, mixed occasionally by a deep, racking cough. Her *papai* blamed the chemicals used to separate iron ore from base material at the mine for the harsh bark that would leave him breathless and weak. He scoffed when *Avó* mentioned his love of cigarettes and the homemade *cachaça*. But tonight, he would be at the mine, she remembered.

Francesca's eyes swept the room, spotted *Gatinho*, and watched with dismay as the kitten leaped from the window into the darkness outside. She imagined the spotted *onça-pintada*, the jaguar, attacking her defenseless pet, and she bolted to the door, bare feet silent on the well-trodden dirt floor.

She took care to ease the door open, so the wood didn't rub and make the familiar squeal. If *Avó* woke, she would tan Francesca's backside for going out at night. Night was dangerous. Both her father and *Avó* had warned her since she could first remember; but now, at eight years old, she knew enough to be careful.

The night hid animals that still preyed on those foolish enough to wander out. Not even the floodlights of the village could protect the unwary. The lights could push the jungle night only so far back, and the shadows were close enough to hide any number of carnivores, all ready to pounce.

The kitten was nowhere in sight, and Francesca's eyes filled with suppressed worry and fear. The cat was helpless, and it was her responsibility to fend for it until it grew old enough to take care of itself. Papa had been adamant about that. She had to find her pet before anything happened to him.

Across the road, she heard something fall between the two company homes. There was a plaintive feline cry of surprise, and Francesca sprinted forward.

She caught sight of the of the kitten's pale rear quarters as it scurried up the hillside towards the railbed. The tracks ran parallel to the gravel road leading to the mine.

Moving through the deep shadows, Francesca chased after the small bundle of fur, almost crying with frustration. *Didn't Gatinho understand the dangers? She needed to reach him before the claws of* da onça *found him.*

She swallowed a shriek of terror as a flock of birds thundered over her head. The flap of the wings nearly drowned out the terrified cries of the kitten.

Birds flying at night?

AS IF SOMEONE FLIPPED a switch, all noise surrounding the tailings pond ceased. No croaking of frogs. No buzz of insects. It was as if nature held its collective breath.

Low clicking broke the stalemate, growing in volume and speed so that it sounded like a crazy author abusing a high-speed typewriter.

The clacking and snapping stopped abruptly.

The sudden silence was deafening.

With little warning, the entire face of the soil and rock-waste dam slid forward and downward, like a theatrical curtain being cut, releasing the equivalent of seven-thousand Olympic swimming-pools of toxic mud and water. Gravity pulled away tier after tier of water-laden soil, gaining speed and force as it fell.

Four massive, articulated dump-trucks—yukes—sat at the bottom of the grade, waiting for the next day's labor to begin. When the crash of mud and water collided with the roadway they'd parked on, it lifted the two-hundred-ton Caterpillar heavy-haulers and tossed them aside like children's toys. Two rolled over and were swallowed from sight. The other two actually floated for a while, like massive, cumbersome canoes, bobbing and spinning where the current willed them. They, in turn, slammed into and carried away a mobile lunch-room with a snap of electrical wires and brilliant arcs of light. Muted screams from inside the structure were cut short.

The watery mass spread outward at the same time as it plunged down the valley floor, picking up speed, burying or tearing loose anything in its path to add to its mass. Then, as the lower tiers of the dam pulled free, toxic sediment from the pond's bottom crashed forward, first filling the valley to its far side, a quarter of a mile away, before following the valley contours to add its weight to the massive river of mud.

The waning moon gave little light and offered less sign of the juggernaut pushing southward at over a hundred-twenty kilometers an hour!

FRANCESCA WHIMPERED as she stumbled on an exposed tree root that caused her to fall and scrape her knee on a hidden rock, tearing the skin. But she heard the rumble that came from the direction of the mine, two miles away.

She could now hear her kitten mewing loudly somewhere ahead of and above her. The poor animal sounded terrified, and Francesca imagined it at the mercy of some nocturnal predator. So, she pushed aside her own safety as she pulled herself up the steep slope with the help of tree branches and trunks.

Now she could hear a growing roar coming from up the valley, raising fine hairs on her neck and arms. Her young mind tried to imagine what the noise might mean. It was tender mercy that the night was so dark that she could not see what was bearing down on her. It saved her a moment of terror.

EXHAUSTION, AS MUCH as the mud, made volunteer firefighter and miner Jaren Pinheiro stop to gain his breath. The sucking, wet muck pulled at his boots as he followed its flow upstream, searching for living victims. Since they got the call of the burst dam, he and his crew had located seven corpses: among them, a man and a woman still in their bed—and a massive bull. The rescuers had painstakingly pulled all victims from the mud, both the living and dead. Only then could a helicopter transport them to the base camp. The bull they had left where it was.

So exhausted were the living survivors they had found, that they moved almost as little as the dead. It broke Jaren's heart, and he knew instinctively that today's events would haunt his dreams for a long time to come. He had lived in the valley his whole life, but everything had changed in this flood. The valley and most of his village no longer existed.

He took a small sip from his canteen, reminding himself to conserve the little water that he had. Company representatives cautioned that chemicals and heavy metals in the tailings had made any groundwater in the area poisonous to drink. How far the contaminants would travel was for others to determine, but he knew that life in this area of the province would change forever.

Having been at the mine, and leaving soon after the tailing pond's collapse, Jaren's group found their way blocked by a wall of mud that stank of death. Their long, circular route back to the village was completed in silence as each man prayed that their own families had somehow escaped the rushing waters. Every time Jaren's rational thoughts tried to prepare him for the inevitable, his heart pushed the images of his little girl and her grandmother to the dark corners of his mind. They *had* to be alive.

He looked over the sea of mud, as a breeze traveling down the valley dried sweat from his face. He took off his helmet to allow the wind to cool his drenched head. With his eyes closed to enjoy the gentle relief, he tilted his head to a sound upriver.

A child's cry?

Slamming his helmet back in place, he moved with purpose, stopping every dozen paces to listen for further sounds. Within minutes, there was no need to pause, as he could hear the steady cry. Almost at a full run, Jaren followed the railbed until he found the bundle of fur clinging desperately to a slender, leafless tree-trunk.

He laughed and shook his head at how something so small had saved itself from the deadly flood. Reaching the tree, he called to the scared little cat. "It's okay, little one. I'll get you down." He slid a gloved hand up the trunk of the slender tree and pulled the branch towards him. The wood bent easily until he could reach the kitten and grasp it with his free hand. He slid the bundle onto his chest and his eyes widened as he felt sharp, tiny claws reach through his coveralls and take root in his skin. The terrified animal quivered in fear.

"Easy. You're safe, little one."

The cat hung from his chest; all four sets of claws dug in. He pulled out his canteen and carefully filled the cap with water. Balancing the canteen on a rail tie, he held the kitten with one hand while presenting the water-filled cap with the other. It took only one sniff of its contents for the cat to respond. Lapping enthusiastically at the fresh water, its nails relaxed with each flick of its tongue. After three caps of water, its sides bulged like a live water bag.

Without warning, the cat leaped from Jaren's arms and scurried among the trees. Jaren shook his head, figuring he would have to rescue the animal a second time, but the animal stopped mere paces from him. The creature began rubbing its face and side against something sticking up from the mud, as if to satisfy a burning itch.

Jaren moved forward and reached for the cat. As he pulled the kitten to him, he saw what had attracted the animal and fell to his knees in horror.

Rising from the mud, a small hand protruded as if grasping for help that hadn't come. He quickly scooped mud from the face.

And that was how Jaren found his daughter, Francesca.

IT WAS LATER THAT PEOPLE who hadn't moved away after the flood stood with bowed heads as the priest gave a final blessing for the dead, and another for the survivors. Everyone had lost someone.

Now, it was only a matter of determining if there was enough to re-build, or they'd have to start fresh somewhere else.

To Jaren, there was nothing left to put together. He had lost everything.

Again.

His wife, Bruna, had died four-and-a-half years ago because of the drunken ministrations of a traveling doctor. But Bruna had left him his beautiful girl, Francesca, who he would have died for. His wife had also gifted him with her gentle and giving mother, who had taken Jaren and Francesca into her care and had run their household for them.

Now, he had lost them both, as well.

He squeezed his eyes tight to hold off a deluge, but it was wasted effort. He was alone.

Now, what was left of his small community had joined to say a final and formal goodbye. He looked around the little church. A line of rescuers, fellow miners who volunteered as the town's firefighters, stood at the back of the chapel like an honor guard. They and Jaren had searched day and night since the dam let go for both living and dead. All had lost members of their families. And sitting by them-selves in the last pew were two men, representatives of the company, Novo Horizonte Internacional, looking scared and uncomfortable.

Rumors were already floating that the company had been aware of the poor condition of the pond, but felt it was too expensive to address. Everyone called the company just 'Novo', and Novo was be-coming a pariah. Lawyers and prosecutors were lining up behind outraged politicians, screaming about loss of life, and loss to the en-vironment—and economy.

Jaren felt anger rise, both at those who screamed for justice on behalf of the people and at this company that refused to accept re-sponsibility. *Those in the government may feel guilty, but not one of those sanctimonious bastards was here for those who were left behind.*

Where was o presidente today? He is silent on this day of all days, when we say goodbye to a mass grave filled with those we love. And the company sends only two representatives when they lost hundreds of employees?

He ground his teeth together to control his temper. Today was not for accusations.

Today was for goodbyes.

As the progression exited the old stone church into bright sunlight, Jaren squinted at a man he did not recognize. As he descended the steps, the man approached him. He was tall, with light-brown, almost blond, hair. Dark glasses hid his eyes. A sweat-stained shirt and a dark blue tie covered his wide chest, his suit jacket hanging from a finger at his shoulder.

"Senhor Pinheiro?" the man asked with a tilt of his head. His grasp of Portuguese seemed strained, so Jaren switched to the good English he'd learned from the American priest.

"I don't know you." As he spoke, Jaren allowed his eyes to search the crowd; but no one else seemed to be concerned with the stranger.

"No sir. This is my first trip to your country." The man looked relieved to be speaking English, and extended his hand. "On behalf of my employer and myself, please accept our deepest condolences for your loss."

Jaren shook the offered hand, trying to understand what it was the man wanted. He didn't have to wait long for an answer.

"My employer, who will remain anonymous for now, represents a group of businessmen who are tired of the way companies like Novo and others work with no consideration for anything other than their financial bottom-line. They take, but give back little to those who have served them faithfully."

"What does that have to do with me?"

The man looked at the crowd that stood hesitantly around the church, as if they did not know where to go or what was next, now they had committed their family members to the Lord. He handed

Jaren a business card. "Now is not the time to dwell on it; but when you are ready, we will be there to help you make Novo pay for what has happened here."

One Year Later

Chapter 1

Fox Lake, Ontario, Canada

The massive superstack rose into the few puffs of brilliant white clouds marring the summer sky. The chimney dwarfed everything around it, including the smelter nestled at its base, a testament to man's industriousness. When built in the late 1970s, the stack was boasted as one of the tallest freestanding structures in the world. Not quite as tall as the Superstack in Sudbury, but close enough. Now the company no longer needed it.

Situated five hours north of Toronto, the city had sprung up around the mine site. For over ninety years, since a lumber company discovered high-grade ore near Fox Lake, the city had grown as a mirror image of its southernly neighbor, Sudbury.

A late afternoon breeze cooled Lucas Kucher's damp neck and head, eliciting a delightful shiver. The bite of the July sun was easing gradually as it sank towards the horizon.

Even though he was wearing shorts and a golf shirt, the day's warmth was over-bearing. He looked forward to the coolness of night. If only the breeze would remain steady ...

He raised his Canon EOS and centered its lens up the road leading into the Novo smelter complex toward the striking workers. Behind him, vehicles slid past him, either entering or leaving the town of South Shore that stretched around the mining complex and originally was a company town.

Settled closed to the stack was the smaller community of Alta Italia. It got its name, Lucas knew, from the first settlers in the area. Its houses were built along narrow streets, one on top of the other, as in the old country. One of the oldest and closest section of the town to the plant, no site plan in the early 1900s could have predicted a superstack that could so easily affect the community. At different times of the day, the stack carved a shadow across the neighborhood.

With the strike in its sixth week, Lucas made a daily trip to one of the strike lines around the city to photograph and speak with the strikers. What the local paper didn't buy, he'd upload to his cloud-based gallery that syndicated media organizations could purchase as they saw fit. It was the only way to put food on the table since his newspaper's downsizing. Still employed, but in a semi-piecework arrangement, his managing editor tried to throw him any story he could; but it was less than a part-time role.

After the sale of the founding company to Novo Horizonte Internacional—Novo—the honeymoon between Novo and its union turned out to be short. The union had met with their new employer with open-mindedness, but it did not last. Used to third-world conditions, the company found itself unprepared when facing a workforce that could not be threatened, coerced, or intimidated to fall in line with management's will. The company's board of directors was shocked that the Canadian and Ontario governments would openly interfere and hold them accountable to the labor laws of the land. They had never encountered this in any other of their mining holding in Africa, South America, or Indonesia. Those countries fell into line, fearing loss of jobs and massive taxes.

The local USW was a force to be reckoned with, Lucas knew. Highly educated in labor relations, negotiations, and Canada's "Three Rights of Workers", they were also very active in the community. Because of that close link to the city of Fox Lake, during any work action, like the current strike, the people backed the union. Support entailed trays of coffee, fresh baking, and monetary help for the striking families.

Lucas aimed the lens of his camera at the massive smokestack rising 1,250 feet over the plant. The sun, which still lit up the roof of the smelter, lit the stack itself, highlighting it against the darkening eastern sky.

Huddled against the left shoulder of the road was a makeshift camp for the strikers. A sturdy, but roughly built hut tarped in plastic to ward off rain also boasted a lean-to for a spot of shade. A ring of chairs under the awning was filled by striking miners putting in their time.

One union member was using his legal right to explain the contentious issues to the driver of a delivery truck that was planning to cross their picket lines. Lucas knew the worker had the right to delay entry for twelve minutes, and the strikers enforced this right religiously.

He moved a step to the right to center the stack, the strikers, and the stopped truck at the picket line and pressed the shutter, taking multiple shots. He tried a few different settings and caught several more shots before he lost the light.

As the shutter clicked one last time, a massive hand clasped the front of the lens and yanked on the camera. Only the strap saved the delicate tool from striking the pavement. But it pulled Lucas off balance.

"What the ...?"

"No pictures," growled a voice so heavily accented it was almost indecipherable.

As Lucas caught his balance, he whirled around to face his assailant.

The man—or mountain—towered above Lucas's six-foot-one-inch frame. His chest stretched the navy and white golf shirt. The word, 'Security' was cut off and disappeared behind one of the chiselled pecs muscles, but the ball cap that shielding the man's bald head mirrored the word over the brim, which was pulled low over eyes that seemed too close together. Lucas immediately pictured a pig's small eyes on this fellow's face and had to suppress a laugh.

"I'm Press." Lucas said, reaching for his press ID.

The strikers had risen to their feet and surrounded the pair.

"Heel, Spike." said one striker. The man walked right up to the security guard and thumped his enormous chest without fear. "You can't mess with Press, my man. *Entender*?"

Two of the union men had their phones extended, recording the confrontation.

From behind the behemoth, Lucas heard a car door slam.

"*Abilo*," said a man's voice. "*Calma!*"

Abilo grunted and turned away from Lucas as if he didn't exist. Lucas relaxed slightly as the big man moved away. He eyed the man who strolled from the yellow Novo First Aid car, leaving the driver behind the wheel. He knew First Aid was comprised of both Health and Safety, and Security. "I'm sorry for my partner's enthusiasm, Mr. Kucher. He's still fitting into the job. I assume you weren't injured?"

Lucas eyed him. *Obviously Canadian. Fit. Looks like he could handle himself, but doesn't flaunt it.* The fact that the man knew his name spoke volumes. Novo, or at least its security, had been keeping tabs on his visits to the different picket lines. Although his managing editor suggested he might be more interested in photo and video content rather than reporting, Lucas had been making the rounds.

Lucas nodded. "No harm done."

The security guard gave him a quick smile, and without a backward glance, returned to his vehicle. Lucas could see silhouettes of the two men in the darkened car. He figured the man was entering a report to his superiors of Lucas's attendance on the line; but because of the low light and shadows, Lucas could not tell for sure.

A hand came down on his shoulder, making him jump.

It was the striker who had confronted the giant. "Don't mind Spike," he said, as the strikers who had recorded the confrontation gathered around. "He doesn't speak much English and sure as shit doesn't know Canadian labor rights."

"Or the rights of the Press," Lucas said.

The man shrugged. "He's just one of the Brazilians the company brought in to intimidate us. Not that it's worked."

That's a story in itself!

"Spike?" Lucas asked with a raised eyebrow.

The strikers all flashed bright smiles. "Spike and Chester, from Bugs Bunny."

Lucas chuckled at the reference. "How many 'guard dogs' have they brought in?"

"About twenty-five to thirty, so far as we can tell. They keep rotating them."

"Any real confrontations?"

"Not since the first day. It took only one phone call and both the police chief, and a Ministry representative paid them a visit. Novo backpedalled as fast as they could."

Lucas laughed. "I would have loved to be a fly on the wall for that meeting." *Why is it those in power figure they can sidestep basic rights?* Like most journalists, he loved to uncover stories of rights abuse by those in authority. It sold papers; but to Lucas, it was also about accountability and responsibility. Many of his top stories had dealt with corruption in local politics or of police turning a blind eye to the most desperate and vulnerable people in society. Lucas championed the underdog. *Someone has to.*

The man nodded. "Now, Novo has assigned a handler to each Spike to keep them from crossing the line."

With the sun set, one man dragged a forty-five-gallon barrel forward while a woman carried over an armful of three-foot lengths of wood cut from wooden pallets. Within seconds, tongues of flame lifted skyward, making shadows dance around the group. It left only one lane of the road open for vehicles, causing those crossing the picket line to wait until the other lane was clear.

Offered a folding lawn chair, Lucas sat near the fire with the strikers. It had a cozy feel to it; and if he forgot where he was, he could imagine being on any regular camp-out in Northern Ontario. The smell of burning wood only enhanced the feeling.

"How's everything else?" he asked, indicating the picket line.

He already knew the issues, but as a reporter in a pared-down newsroom, you never knew where a tidbit might be found. So, asking open questions became part of the norm, rather than the exception.

"We hear they might look at bringing in a mediator. Don't know if it'll help, but we can always hope."

Lucas nodded. He had covered numerous strikes and was aware of the hope these men had for a quick settlement. Strike pay was not a living wage; and the longer they were on the line, the harder it would be for their families. Mortgages and loans still had to be dealt with, and lenders were not sympathetic, and even less so if the strike lagged on.

The last strike with the previous owners had dragged for almost a year, and this strike seemed to be heading the same way. Novo was looking at cutting benefits—including retirement and health benefits—that had taken two decades of bargaining to gain. The fact that the company held record profits made the demand that much harder to swallow for their workforce.

As the sun set, the mining complex behind them was lighting up, looking like a city all on its own. Even the huge stack harbored rows of blinking white strobe-lights to ward off aircraft. The site held a strange beauty at night. Gone were the day's dust-covered buildings, rust-covered machinery and grimy dirt of the mining world. At night, bright lights lit up the complex and only showed the enormity of the industry and the resourcefulness of mankind. Lucas longed to capture this magnificence through his photography.

He raised his camera to the men. "May I?"

The men exchanged looks and shrugged with indifference.

Standing back, he was able to capture the mining complex with both the burning barrel and the strikers in the foreground. Using the sparks coming off the fire, he focused on a spot deep within the mining complex and clicked a couple of shots before moving to another location. As he scanned the scene through his eyepiece, he caught sight of a sudden glare of light. His finger depressed, causing the small motor to capture a series of images. He watched in wonderment as the light grew in size and intensity, pushing back the night. In the split second it took to realize he was looking at an explosion, the sound wave hit the striker's camp. His ears were assaulted as the blast rolled over them. Lucas kept the camera trained on the site but turned the camera's setting so the unit captured video.

Around him, men clambered to their feet and swung around towards the noise.

Lucas jumped from his spot and sprinted wide so that none of the men blocked his line of vision. He barely registered the yellow First Aid car whiz past him carrying the two security guards, missing him by mere inches, and heading towards the fire.

He kept his camera trained on the ever-expanding plume of flame. Raw fuel must have fed the flames as they rose up in ever-growing volume. He registered yellow, orange, and white flames, the night hiding black smoke that rose into the clear sky, a shadow that blocked the plant's lights in the background. And, even before they had time to recover from the shockwaves of the primary explosion, the strikers flinched and cried out in alarm at unexpected *whumps* of secondary and tertiary explosions

Lucas captured all of it.

Then, all at once, there was little noise—the fire burned silently in the distance. The only sounds were the hushed voices as the men spoke to wives, colleagues, or 911 operators through cell phones. In the back of Lucas's mind, he knew he had to call his editor, but he didn't want to miss any part of the growing conflagration in front of him.

This was an exclusive.

Chapter 2

The phone buzzed at his hip, and Mike Burgess stifled a curse. He had just put a rack of back ribs on the barbecue and snapped his second beer. He knew without looking at the display that it was someone from the union office.

Pulling out the phone, he dropped onto the lounge chair under the sunshade. Normally, his backyard was his only sanctuary, and he berated himself for not leaving the phone on charge in his den. Even so, the gurgle of his koi-pond waterfall, partially hidden by foliage that had been strategically placed, gave off a soothing vibe; and he closed his eyes as he swiped the answer button.

"Burgess."

"Mike? Nick. Sorry to bother you with this, but I figured I'd give you the heads-up, in case things escalate."

"What's happening?"

"Just got a call from the main gate at South Shore. Seems as if there's been some kind of explosion in the plant."

"What? ... Anyone hurt?"

"No idea, as yet. Fire department's on the scene; but of course, none of our people are inside the plant."

Burgess raked his mind for anything else to ask, but other than the safety of his people, the problems inside the plant were beyond his control or concern. If the fire caused part of the facility to be closed, affecting the workforce, he'd have a reason to get involved.

"Any indication whether the explosion was deliberate or an accident? The last thing we need is Novo pointing fingers at our people."

"I'm hearing nothing, but I'll pass the word to the other stewards to keep their ears on."

So, it was the company's problem. And he had to admit, it felt good that Novo might have bigger issues than taking advantage of his people.

"Okay, Nick. We'll have to wait to hear from the fire department. I'm sure the media will demand answers before long. It'll be interesting to find out what happened. Was it a real accident or is this something Novo will try to blame on us?" He considered for a moment. "Maybe open a line to the company that we might be interested in helping them if our expertise can help with the situation in a way that is beneficial to both parties. If you can also leak our offer, in a subtle way, to the press, it'll go a long way for the public-opinion campaign. Don't send a press release or anything. Just mention something off-camera that our members are eager to help protect the plant for both the company and the workers."

"Nice. I know exactly who I can talk to," said Nick. "Lucas Kucher was at the gate when everything went boom. The boys say he got pictures of the whole thing."

"Perfect. And could you see if we can get copies of his shots? Promise him an exclusive, if he needs any schmoozing."

That was the nice thing about a city the size of Fox Lake. There was only so much news happening. It's not like it was Toronto or Montreal. In landmass, Fox Lake and Sudbury could swallow the entire Greater Toronto Area, the GTA, but had only a small percentage of its people. The Press in the north was always open to news stories; and most times, a phone call was faster for setting up a news story than a formal media release.

"That won't be an issue. I'll take care of it. Sorry for disturbing your evening."

"No, no! It's all good. Listen, make sure you have a steward at the main gate, in case things escalate. And have our people keep a running log of who comes and goes."

"Already on it," Nick said.

"Perfect."

He clicked off and stood to check the ribs. He allowed the situation to roll through his mind, trying to figure how the company might use it against the union, or if there were any opportunities that the union itself might capitalize on. Depending on what exactly had exploded, it might be a maintenance issue that could be blamed on his people not being on the job, or it might point to the company's habit of cutting costs to line the pockets of its shareholders and pay executive bonuses.

Of course, all anyone had to do was compare Novo's earnings, which had risen dramatically even though the world had been in the lockdown from Covid-19 that had crippled the world's economies. In their non-stop fight for every profit dollar, Novo had no interest in those people who worked on the bottom rung of the company. These were the people who actually got dirty and took the risks, and who dealt with hazardous processing systems that gained those heavy dividends.

Production had never stopped during the pandemic, even though there had been outbreaks at the different mines throughout the area. Novo Horizonte Internacional kept that information quiet. So quiet that most locations didn't even know what was happening at other locations across the city. More than once, his members entered infected sites with no knowledge of the dangers involved.

Despite all Novo's talk of safe working conditions, more and more miners suffered after a lifetime in the dangerous environment of mining. Heart and lung diseases—and cancers—were the main issues. Yet, health benefits for retirees remained one of the first things the company wanted to cut.

This time, though, we're not pulling the punches, Burgess thought. No more of the 'take the noble road' mentality. The Steelworkers of America were going to show the world what kind of monster Novo really was. Now, these mining companies could not hide in the jungles of Brazil or New Caledonia. It was time the world saw how dirty they really were, and how they treated their employees.

The union wasn't stupid. They knew they needed the company to be in a strong financial position to compete in the world market, but it could not treat its chief assets, its workers, like slave labor. A healthy workforce was a productive workforce.

But it was an uphill battle to convince the greedy bastards of that.

LUCAS PULLED HIS OLD 2006 Honda Accord to the curb and gathered his camera. He grimaced at the fading green paint and reminded himself again that he had to take the time to search for a new set of wheels. Of course, affording it was another worry altogether.

Since its big reorganization, the paper carried few full-time reporters, or, in his case, photojournalists. He had been one of the fortunate ones to be kept on, but he knew it might only be a matter of time, before some bean counter decided his fate with a ledger sheet. The specter of the axe hovered over every monetary decision he made.

The change to digital publishing was happening to every newspaper in the world. At first, using the internet was great for collecting background facts on stories that Lucas was assigned to follow; but as print news grew less and less profitable, Lucas's paper had begun carrying fewer and fewer full-time reporters and photojournalists.

Vowing to find some time to search for a new ride, he pushed his way through the doors of the *Fox Lake Journal*. Ignoring the unreliable elevator, he took the stairs, two at a time, to its news editor's office who, now with the cutbacks, also was the managing editor. The growing excitement of this news story spilled out in an excess of energy that did not even allow Lucas to be winded as he topped the stairs.

The newsroom, once filled with reporters, photographers, graphic designers, and many editors rushing to meet deadlines, was quiet with less than a handful of computer stations in use. Reporters mostly filed electronically now, and Lucas usually filed his own copy by email with his photos being uploaded to the paper's cloud service. But the explosion story was huge, and he wanted to ensure he'd be the lead moving forward.

That meant a face-to-face with the paper's news and managing editor, Felix Cameron.

The two went way back. In fact, Felix had taken a chance twelve years earlier and given Lucas his first full-time job. Felix was only nine years older than Lucas's twenty-four, and had risen in the media field because of his no-nonsense editorials that held nothing back and gave an honest opinion of the political scene. More than a few city councillors and even a few provincial premiers, had suffered from his honesty. He was honest, yet fair, and had become well-respected within the community. Many sought his opinion in different areas of expertise, and there were very few doors closed to him.

Felix looked over his monitor with one eyebrow raised. If the man was tired, only his rumpled shirt showed it. Dark-blue eyes were alert and ready for anything. His dark hair held no gray, though now he worked double the hours of most of his people. Even sitting down, the man held a larger presence than his height of five foot nine.

Lucas handed over the memory card and said, "This is huge."

The editor said nothing as he slipped the card into the hub beside his laptop. With a few clicks, the first images expanded onto the screen. He flipped through the group of photos until the images of the explosion made him sit upright. He glanced at Lucas before downloading the slideshow file and handing the card back to Lucas. From his backup, frame by frame, he examined the growing conflagration.

"I heard the call go out with my scanner. What do we know?"

"At this point, not much. The fire department knocked down the flames quickly enough once they arrived, but there's been a steady stream of police ever since. Platoon Chief Reilly told me that there were no injuries, but they were treating the incident as suspicious."

"Union?"

Lucas shrugged his shoulders while raising his hands. "If so, the guys on the picket line sure knew nothing about it. They were as shocked as I was. I have about fifteen interviews with witnesses to the explosion, but only from outside the picket line. I've not been able to get hold of anyone from the company."

He watched as Felix glared at the screen, but he knew the man wasn't even seeing the photo on it. Lucas had seen his former boss like this in the past. The man's mind was racing through a hundred questions that needed to be answered before they had a story.

Lucas knew better than to interrupt the man's thoughts. He leaned against a filing cabinet, eyes flicking to the now-familiar photos of Felix with a variety of local influential movers and shakers, influencers and entrepreneurs. There was even the shot of Lucas when he had earned an award from the Canadian Association of Journalists for breaking the news of a Fox Lake city councillor accepting a bribe from a developer for his support in a controversial building plan. It had been the highlight of Lucas's career, and Felix had made sure everyone knew it.

The explosion at the smelter might even be bigger.

"Okay," Felix said finally. "You're not going to like this, but I want you to pass all you have to Jamie Coleman. As you know, she's been covering the strike for us since the beginning."

Lucas took a deep breath. "Come on Felix. She doesn't have the experience for something this big. She's been with the paper for less than a year."

His editor leaned back in his chair. "Don't you remember when you started here? I ignored the complaints that I was giving you choice assignments. Like you, Jamie is going to sink or swim. With a little luck, guidance, and some time, she could be as good a journalist as you are."

Lucas had to force himself not to say anything about Jamie Coleman. The fact that her father was a long-time friend and supporter of Felix and the paper—and a key advertiser—was not lost on anyone.

Unlike how Lucas had begun, the minute she showed up, Felix started her with some important stories. Lucas had ground away for four years working for both the *Toronto Sun* and *Star*, working as a cub reporter on less exciting human-interest stories, before working his way to landing a post as an investigative journalist here at the paper.

He had put his time in. She hadn't.

"Before you get bent out of shape," Felix said, sitting forward. "I had been planning on getting you to look into another story."

Lucas waited, mainly because he didn't trust himself not to say anything he might regret.

"Got a call today from a source inside Sudbury District jail." Sudbury, an hour south, was much bigger than Fox Lake. The city boasted many mining companies and had a competing smelter. Because Sudbury was considered the hub of the northern Ontario, most government offices were situated there, including the jail and courthouses. "A guard overheard a couple of inmates talking about someone going around kicking the hell out of some sex traffickers."

"Probably a turf war."

"That was my first thought, but then my guy tells me that the kickers wore heels."

Lucas pushed away from the cabinets in surprise. "Are you saying a couple of women beat the shit out of their handlers?"

It was Felix's turn to shrug. "Listen, Lucas. You know half the players out there. And they know and respect you."

Lucas relaxed as the comment reminded him how long it had taken to convince three sex workers to trust him enough to tell their story. It was a heart-wrenching, but unfortunately familiar, tale of exploitation, and of physical and substance abuse. One community group in particular had convinced the women that they had a chance at a normal life. A life without constant cravings for the next bite of the needle and without the fear of violence from drunken customers or a greedy pimp.

That group gave the three women the needed support to break free of their drug addictions, and the police put two traffickers behind bars. Social services stepped forward to help house and clothe the women—helped them step out of their former lives. It should have been over, Lucas reminded himself.

Lucas's newspaper series went nationwide, and Lucas was once again applauded for a job well done. Two of the women continue to thrive; one even got married. But the last one, a young woman who had not even reached twenty, was found dead of an opiate overdose. Just another dead junkie—unless you knew the rest of the story. She left behind no one, and only a note explaining that her family would not forgive her for her transgressions. She died broken and alone.

And with that, Lucas lost something of himself. He went to the young woman's funeral, and the only others there were two social workers and a representative for the women's center. Christine. Not even the other two women that the dead woman had broken free with had bothered to attend.

A few days later, the street corner where the woman had solicited men had different girls working it.

He had changed nothing.

"Lucas?" Felix said, his tone soft as if could sense Lucas's pain. When Lucas looked up, he asked, "Can I count on you?"

Closing his eyes, Lucas nodded.

Chapter 3

Lucas angrily flung the entrance door open so hard that it bounced back and nearly took him out. Only a quick dodge saved him a world of pain and humiliation. It did nothing for his mood though. His gut told him this might be an enormous story. That even with his photos and first-hand experience of the explosions he'd got passed over in favor of a debutante whose only claim to fame was her daddy's deep pockets was even more galling. The squeal of his tired Honda's tires helped a bit, but he eased off the gas pedal.

By the time he pulled into his driveway, his anger had dissipated to mere annoyance. He had to admit that Felix had never treated him unfairly. He had always been honest, sometimes brutally, but he was never flippant. If Felix felt this was the best course of action for both the story and the paper, he, Lucas, would have to suck it up and accept it.

He was reaching for his house key when his phone vibrated in his jacket pocket. Snatching it, he read the screen, closed his eyes, and groaned. *I can't get a break.*

Jamie Coleman

Taking a deep breath to calm himself, he swiped the screen and said, "Hi Jamie. I'm just getting home. I'll email what I have in a few minutes."

There was a pause on the other end, and for a moment, he thought she had disconnected.

"Thanks, Lucas. But I wasn't calling about the photos. I knew you would pass them along to me when you were able." She paused, and he was about to ask why she called, when she said, "I'm wondering if it's too late to get together for a drink or a coffee."

"Tonight?"

"Yes. I want to run something by you, but I would prefer speaking face-to-face."

Though he didn't know her well, she didn't strike him as the type to gloat about getting the choice assignment that should have been his. They had only exchanged pleasantries when he had visited the office to see Felix, which didn't happen as often as it might have a couple of years ago. Not that it had done him any good.

Whatever her motive, he was curious. Her serious tone intrigued him.

"Tim Horton's on Centre and Alford, say in twenty minutes?"

"That's perfect. Thanks, Lucas."

LUCAS ARRIVED FIVE minutes early, only to find her waiting inside for him. He stood there for a moment, studying her. She was dressed in a fashionable cream suit: skirt, with an open jacket over a white blouse. She looked like a successful businesswoman or lawyer. Her long legs were folded under her seat, ankles crossed. Dark hair was wound in tight braids that framed her face, and her ebony skin glowed.

She rose when he entered and met him at the counter.

"How do you like your coffee?" she said, her smile genuine, reaching up to her startling, pale-green eyes.

"Black, one sweetener."

She placed the order, and they took their coffee back to the table in the far corner. She wrapped her hands around her coffee cup as if her fingers were freezing. He noticed and reflected that he needed a sleeve on his cup because it was always too hot.

There was the awkward silence of two strangers trying to get a read on each other. While they weren't exactly strangers to each other, they'd never traded more than a hundred words at work. Lucas used the same tactic he used when interviewing people to help them relax around him. He asked about her.

"How are you enjoying working for the paper?"

"I'm loving it," she said with enthusiasm. "I mean, I'm still learning the ropes and finding my way around, but it's so exciting. There never seem to be enough hours in the day, but I'm burning the proverbial candle at both ends. As it were." She began ticking each of her fingers as she listed all she was busy with. "Felix has me doing a weekly interview with some of the region's most successful female entrepreneurs, covering the mayor's Opiate Crisis Committee, and I'm writing about the strike, of course. I'm also taking a weekly photography course and tackling an online course towards a master's in journalism."

"It's a good thing you're young. It sounds exhausting to me."

"I'm not as young as more people think. I'm twenty-nine."

"Twenty-nine," Lucas said, surprised.

She laughed. "Just because I just got out of school, most people figure I'm around twenty-two. I have to thank my parents for good genes, I guess."

"If we're being candid, I'm thirty-six," he said, sipping his coffee. "But you better get down to business so you can get home and get some sleep."

She laughed, and he realized he enjoyed hearing her laugh.

"Okay. By the way, nice job getting me to open up."

"Busted," he said with a smile. "I've been doing this for a while."

She nodded. "And I haven't," she said in a matter-of-fact manner. "Listen, I got the message that you want this story. I've known Felix long enough that I can read between his lines. However, the last thing I wanted to do was piss you, of all people, off."

"Why? You don't even know me."

She leaned back and appraised him. Taking a sip of her coffee, she placed it on the table and resumed warming her hands. "You're wrong about that. I've known you for a long time, only this is the first time we have actually gotten together."

He tilted his head, perplexed.

She smiled at his expression. "Years ago, you wrote a story about a mother's grief as she watched her young child die of neuroblastoma."

The story jumped to the forefront of his memory. The story had, of course, been a tragic story of love, loss and letting go. It was another of those stories that ripped him apart. It was one thing to report the story; it was another to empathize with the family and actually feel their grief.

He nodded.

"That story turned a spoiled brat who was going nowhere in her life to journalism. It was *the* changing point in my life. It may sound corny, but your writing put me right there in that hospital room. I could not read fast enough, even when the final, tragic end came. I wept for that poor little girl and the family that was left behind. Your words pulled me into their world; and as hard as it was, you showed me how important it is to share human experience. That's when I first thought that writing was something I wanted to be part of."

He sat back in surprise, not knowing what to say.

"After that, I followed every story you put out. I even read some of your past stories when you were at the *Toronto Star* and *Sun*. Then I had a long talk with Uncle Felix."

"*Uncle* Felix?" Lucas said, raising an eyebrow.

She laughed. "He's been Uncle Felix ever since I can remember. Our families are tight. But being a newspaperman, I figured, he'd be the best one to talk to about becoming a reporter. He guided me through school, mentored me when I graduated, and now here I am."

"I'm flattered that you think that I started that ball rolling," he said, slightly embarrassed.

"Trust me, it's not hero worship or anything like that; but your writing—your stories—helped guide me to where I am at the moment."

He threw his hands open. "What? Not even a little hero-worship?" he said with a smile.

Her eyes crinkled as she sipped her coffee. She held her fingers an inch apart.

"A guy has to take what he can get. Insecurity and ego, you know?"

"Yeah, right?"

He leaned forward on his elbows, his chin on his hands. "So, what did you want to talk about?"

Placing her cup on the table, she looked straight at him. "I got the distinct feeling from Uncle Felix that you wanted this story about the explosion at the Lake Shore complex and he shut you down."

"He probably had his reasons," he said, keeping his face neutral.

"Oh, knowing him, I'm sure he did. But the last thing I want to do is make an enemy so early in my career and lose an opportunity to learn from someone of your experience."

"I'm not that petty."

"Maybe not, but I really do want to learn from you." She wrapped her long, tapered fingers around the Tim's mug. "I want to learn how to write stories that move the reader as well as inform them. Felix told me about the story he assigned you. I want to experience that world like you have. I think it's important to compare what you see and how you write it. I have read your series on human trafficking, of course. But I'd like to see it from your perspective. I would really like to work with you on this story. At the same time, I sure could use your guidance with the explosion at the smelter, if only be-cause you know all the players."

Lucas's mind whirled at the implications and opportunities she was offering. Surprisingly, he had never worked with another re-porter; but having a second perspective might be a good thing. Of course, it was a way of staying on the strike issue, something his gut told him was only the tip of the rock he had stumbled on. As for jumping back into the human trafficking story, Jamie might serve as a buffer to the pain that still haunted him.

She was staring into the dark liquid in her cup, evidently giving him room to consider her proposal. He felt a surge of appreciation for her consideration. He was warming to her.

Feeling his eyes on her, she looked up, her expression empty.

"So, what are the ground rules?" he said.

She smiled. "We share everything."

He nodded.

"Including by-lines."

He gave her a sly smile. "Like, Kucher and Colman. Obviously, seniority based."

She gave him a sarcastic look that told him she could hold her own. "No, if I'm assigned to the story, I lead. Same goes for you."

He stared into those unflinching eyes and liked what he saw there. "Deal. Who gets to tell Uncle Felix?"

"Don't worry about him. I did say I've known him for a long time. I'll have no problem selling him on the idea."

Chapter 4

"Hello," croaked a sleepy voice, and Lucas felt a sense of satisfaction at the thought of having woken up the paper's future star. He knew he was being childish, but to hell with it. He was due.

"Good morning, Sunshine. It's Lucas."

"Luc ...? What time is it?"

He could picture her groping in the dark to turn on the light and find her clock, in a panic, thinking she might be late for an appointment.

"It's five. The jail guard who brought the story to Felix works at eight this morning, but has agreed to meet for breakfast at seven before his shift. We're to meet him at Shirley's Diner, if you're game."

"Yeah. Sounds great," she said, but it sounded to Lucas that she was still trying to play catch-up.

"I can pick you up, if you prefer. We'll be together most of the day. Novo is issuing a statement at eleven; so, if you meant what you said last night, we can follow both stories."

"I meant it, Lucas. I'm not here to screw you around."

She gave him her address, then hung up, and he recognized it as an apartment building on Elbow Road overlooking the Spanish River. It was in a triangle of land on the northern end of the city that was contained by the river on two sides and Fox Lake on the other. For Lucas, the river was where he'd performed his certification scuba dive—he could still remember how cold his lips became as he had struggled to hold the mouthpiece in place while fighting the current. As a young teen, he had learned the finer skills of canoeing through a summer camp, shooting white-water rapids through the chutes all the way to Lake Agnew.

The price for an apartment in that location was way above his own salary, so he felt another jolt of jealousy for the little rich girl. He had worked for everything he had, and he resented anyone who skated through life because of who their father was. On the other hand, would he have not done the same if the opportunity offered itself? Either way, it was time to man up and concentrate on the story—stories.

On time, an hour and forty minutes after the phonecall, Jamie exited her apartment building. Wearing a light blouse and slacks, she looked professional, yet comfortable. He also noted that she had on sensible walking shoes rather than high heels. A green silk flowered scarf accented her green eyes. She carried a backpack, which she tossed onto the back seat before opening the front passenger door.

"My kit," she explained before he could ask.

Lucas had moved his laptop from the front seat to the seat behind him to make room for her. He gave her an apologetic smile as she pushed empty coffee cups aside to make room for her feet.

"Sorry. The car is my office, and the janitor is away."

She kept her expression neutral, but he cringed, seeing that she had used the time since he called to create a perfect image of a professional reporter. Self-consciously, he ran a hand over his two-day stubble and thought of the wrinkled sports jacket that he had thrown into the rear seat.

Class act!

He pulled out of the drive to cover his embarrassment and said, "The fellow that we're meeting is named John Rocca. According to Felix, he's been a guard at the Sudbury Jail for eighteen years and has seen pretty well everything inside. He's been throwing stories our way for about five. Felix had originally thought it was for the fifteen minutes of fame, but now thinks it's just because the guy is bored with his job. Especially since the guy stays firmly anonymous."

"Dealing with society's worst elements can't be that rewarding."

"You wouldn't think so, but any of the corrections officers that I've dealt with are all business. They make a mistake and people get hurt, including themselves. I don't think they get enough credit for the job they do."

"Might be a story there."

He considered her response. It was exactly the way his own mind worked. He had lost out on more than a few relationships because his mind was always on a story rather than on the person in front of him. He was constantly looking at different angles and developing follow-up stories. Twenty-four/seven.

He turned off Elbow Road to Main Street, which was the center of the original city and what remained of downtown. As the city had expanded, the town center slowly became less important as shopping malls opened up in other areas. There was little to draw people downtown, and the area deteriorated regardless of the money thrown at it. Now, with the opioid and homeless crises, it was an area to be avoided rather than celebrated. And in that, it didn't differ from any other municipality.

In fifteen minutes, they turned south on Highway 144 towards Sudbury. Forty minutes later, he turned into the tight parking lot of a local diner that had been in business since he had been a child.

"Have you ever eaten here?"

"No, I don't think so."

"Food's great and the service is fast. Almost every lawyer in town eats here."

"Well, location gives it an advantage."

As their eyes adjusted, Lucas saw an arm raised in a booth near the windows. The man attached to the arm wore a stereotypical jail-guard uniform: dark shirt and pants with the black and yellow 'Corrections' patch on the shoulders, and black tie. On the table beside the breakfast special—two eggs, toast, home fries and (because it was Wednesday) peameal bacon—was a pair of puncture-resistant black gloves.

Considering what he did for a living and the exposure those gloves might have had, Lucas eyed them with disgust. The man caught his look and smiled over a mouthful of eggs.

Swallowing, he said, "Don't go all clean-freak on me! They're brand new; took them out of the case this morning. No way I'm going to catch what the cons might be carrying."

Lucas and Jamie exchanged a silent glance but slid into the booth across from the guard.

"Thanks for meeting with us, Mr. Rocca."

"Call me John."

Nodding, he said, "I'm Lucas and—"

"And I'm Jamie," she said, shoving her hand forward with a little too much enthusiasm.

Lucas paused uncomfortably, wondering if he had unconsciously done or said something wrong. Maybe this partnership was going to be more trouble than it would be worth.

When the man's eyes flicked from him to her, he knew he hadn't been the only one to notice it.

Lucas waved a hand at Jamie to continue.

"Our editor, Felix Cameron, gave us your name and said that you might have some information about something you heard in the course of your duties."

"Lady," he said, in a horse whisper over another mouthful of food, his eyes angry. "Why don't you hold up a fucking sign saying 'snitch.'" He looked around the crowded diner to see if anyone was paying any attention to the conversation or had overheard her. Seeing nobody, he leaned forward conspiratorially. "Felix and I have an understanding. And over the years, my name has never been mentioned or even *hinted* at. I don't mind throwing some tidbits his way, but not enough to risk my pension. So, let's keep this between ourselves."

Lucas kept his eyes on the guard, not looking at his partner's reaction. Even from the corner of his eye, he could see her nodding quickly. To be honest, he wasn't sorry for her. She had done it to herself. Her inexperience was clear, or maybe it was that she was trying too hard.

The waitress came by and Lucas ordered coffee, while Jamie requested a fruit platter, yogurt and a bottle of water. John allowed the woman to refill his coffee. The three avoided speaking until the server left.

John turned to face the two. He leaned low over the table and kept his voice even lower, causing both reporters to bend towards him. "As I told Felix, I overheard these two guys talking about a couple of *women* kicking the hell out of a pimp over on Kathleen Street. From what I heard, the pimp—they called him Kebede—got himself fucked up really bad."

As he spoke, Lucas pulled out his phone and opened a note-taking app. Beside him, Jamie also pulled out her phone.

"Stow it! No recording." He leaned back, eyes crossing the room, looking for threats. Lucas thought the man might bolt.

Lucas turned the phone around to face the guard. "Just a note-taking app. It records nothing." Tilting his head to include Jamie, he continued, "Neither of us would record you without your permission."

The guard seemed to relax a bit. "Yeah, but this is all off the record. Otherwise, it'll be the last story I pass on to Felix. And you two will be the reason." He glanced at both of them. "Got it?"

"Loud and clear," Jamie said with a nod, and exchanged her phone for a small notepad. "Please go on."

"Anyway, this Kebede is up at the hospital right now, but for how long, I have no idea. These guys say the girls really messed him up, so ..." He shrugged his shoulders before shoveling the last forkful of hash browns into his mouth.

"You mentioned Kathleen St. Can you narrow that down for us? It's a long street."

"I've heard about this guy before. His girls work the corner of Pine and Estelle. I'm betting they dragged the guy into One Pine Road. Nice and dark there. No streetlights, and off the main drag."

The server showed up with the coffee and Jamie's order. "Anything else, John?"

"No, just the bill, Sarah. My shift starts in fifteen minutes. Just enough time to walk down and punch in."

"Be a minute," she said, grabbing his plate before retreating towards the kitchen.

"And you're sure they mentioned it was two women attacking this guy?" Jamie asked.

"That's what they said. Remember, I wasn't part of the conversation. These two dudes probably don't even know I was there listening. It's part of the game, you know, finding what the idiots are up to before all hell breaks loose. Preventive, y'know? It's routine to walk up to a corner or ahead of a cell and just stand there listening. If you're lucky, you might hear about some contraband that's being smuggled in. Hell, we stopped a breakout once, just because two idiots couldn't keep their gums from flapping. We're not dealing with the sharpest knives in the drawer, here." He wiped his mouth with his napkin after slugging back the last of his coffee. "Most of our guests are on the bottom end of the pay grid. Desperate people trying to get out of the shit-hole life handed them. The smart ones don't get caught."

Lucas pulled out a business card and looked at Jamie, who produced her own. "Thanks for the information, John. If you hear anything else, give either of us a call. Off the record, of course."

Sarah showed up with the bill and placed it on the table before the guard's plate. "See you tomorrow, John."

The guard pushed the bill across the table towards Lucas. "Thanks for the breakfast. I'll call if I hear anything." He grabbed his gloves and jacket and slid out of the booth. Pulling on the jacket, he smiled at the two reporters. "Tell Felix I said hi."

As the man left, Lucas rose and slid into the opposite seat so that he faced Jamie. "So, what do you think?"

He had swallowed his irritation at her attitude with the introductions. He let out a long sigh. *Give her a bloody chance.*

"Look, I know I'm new to this, but I'm not your assistant or your sidekick. Do I have a lot to learn? Well, yes. But I can speak for myself and stand up for myself."

He ran his hand through his hair. He didn't have time for this. Leaning forward, he said in a low voice, "Look, you wanted this partnership. You came to me, not the other way around. I don't care about your feelings, feminist bullshit, or any other crap you want to throw my way. I only have one agenda—the story. That's my only motivation. If you can't deal with that, then take a walk and learn the ropes the old-fashioned way by fucking up and learning from your mistakes." He leaned back and took a pull on his coffee. "But decide now, because we have a busy day ahead."

He looked across the restaurant, but not to see the other customers. It was just a tactic to avoid looking at her hurt, yet hostile, eyes. She was definitely not used to being talked to like that.

It took almost a full minute before she said. "Yeah. You're right. The story has to be the priority."

He noticed she had not offered an apology, but figured he had gotten as much as she was willing to give. He turned back. "So, what do we have?"

"Well, we have the victim's name now and might have an opportunity to interview him. We also have the possible location of the assault, so we can canvass the neighbors."

He nodded. She wasn't some wide-eyed intern. She could put together a course of action from what she had heard. But did she have the tenacity to continue with the story when the simple stuff dried out so there are only new avenues that hadn't even been considered before? Time would tell.

He glanced at his watch. "We have time for one more stop before we head to the press conference."

She looked up from her phone. "Oh, *Daily News* announced on their app that the fire service has determined the explosion at Novo is definitely suspicious. Novo has handed it over to Sudbury police and the fire marshal." She handed her phone to Lucas.

Lucas looked at the announcement, then handed back the phone. "Do you know anything about arson investigations?" When she shook her head, he continued. "The office of the Ontario fire marshal had a distinct division of investigators that specialize in arson investigation. You might want to draft a question or two if they're at the press release today."

She nodded and made a note on her phone.

"Where do you want to stop?"

"There's a local group who helps get women off the street, called The Second Chance. Their office is just down from where this Kebede was allegedly beaten. If anyone knows about the assault, they should."

Chapter 5

Lucas pulled his car to the curb. The neighborhood had a tired look to it. It was more than the peeling paint, and the rust-covered wall anchors that held together one side of a crumbling brick building—it was also that the people here all seemed to have given up trying to pump life into this old area.

He saw a group of men sitting along the stone wall of a planter once installed as a futile attempt to beautify an otherwise-ugly street. The group sat in ragged clothes, cigarettes dangling, with bloodshot eyes that showed no signs of hope or opportunity.

A young man, pants drooping close to his knees, and with long, dirty-blond dreadlocks, staggered towards the group. He suddenly veered towards the entrance of a credit union. On one side of the entrance, he dropped to his knees, pulled off a stained Toronto Maple Leafs ballcap, and dropped it open-side-up on the sidewalk in front of him. When the door opened and the emerging patron ignored his pleas for a handout, he cursed, angrily snatched up his hat, and stalked over to the guys perched on the planter.

Farther up the street, a scrawny woman with a 'Jesus loves us!' t-shirt was waving at passing cars, yelling out greetings. She walked back and forth between two corners with jerky, nervous motions, looking like a chicken ever-watchful for a fox. As Lucas and Jamie watched, a pimped-out, electric-blue Corolla Sport slowed; and some unheard conversation must have set off the woman, because she spun on her heel, middle finger raised high in the air. Rough laughter came from the vehicle as it drove away.

Shutting off his old Honda, Lucas turned to Jamie.

"Second Chance is a non-profit that tries to help get women and girls off the street. Christine and her people have their ear to the ground and have been a great source for stories over the years. If anyone knows anything, it'll be this group."

"How successful are they?"

"Depends on who you talk to. Their fight is an uphill battle. Because most of their clientele suffer from substance abuse, the police treat these women and the crimes surrounding human trafficking as a joke. Of course, the cops will never admit it. Unfortunately, even those who can kick the habit are never seen as reliable witnesses because there's always a pretty good chance for relapse. But the main issue is the lack of funding."

Jamie shook her head.

They left the vehicle; but instead of crossing, Lucas looked over the area, reminiscing.

"What is it?" she asked as she followed his gaze.

"My grandparents lived just up the hill," Lucas said, pointing up one side-street. "My grandfather emigrated from Ukraine after the second World War to work here in the mines. He lived in one of the many rooming houses, with twenty other men. Each guy had a room big enough for a bed and a chest of drawers. Common bathroom. That third building—the one with the white stucco—used to be Edvin's Sauna, and it cost two cents for a shower after work to wash off the filth and sweat from the mines and smelter. We just referred to them all as "miners," even the smelter workers who had never been underground.

"The men would then go to one of the town's many communal eateries for their supper. Big, hearty meals were needed because of the hard work and long hours, before they headed home to bed. They'd return at five o'clock in the morning for breakfast before heading back to their jobs."

He smiled at the family history.

"After three years, Grandfather had saved enough to rent a house, which he eventually bought, and then sent for my grandmother. She had her own adventure, because by that time, Ukraine was part of the post-war Soviet Union and travel was restricted. But she escaped and arrived in 1949. And that's another story!"

He saw that this was all new for her. She obviously had not heard about his past.

"It must have been difficult back then."

"Not the way my parents explained it. You just did what you had to do. Simple as that. They were hardworking and very devout in their religion—Ukrainian Catholic. As more kids arrived, the family home expanded a few times. It was really a patchwork of additions. My father and his siblings—there were twelve of them—"

"*Twelve?*"

He smiled, giving her a look. "You have to remember, there was no television back then, and Canadian winters are long."

"I'm sure," she returned, rolling her eyes.

Checking for traffic, they crossed the street to a storefront that was nestled between a tattoo parlor and a dog-grooming shop. A handmade sign taped to the white-painted steel door stated, 'Second Hope' with a phone number. Posters covered plywood panels over what should have been a plate-glass window, and proclaimed that, "Paying for Sex is Against the Law!"

Jamie tried the door, but found it locked. She glanced at Lucas.

He rapped at the steel door. "Protection for their clients. There are some who do not appreciate the work Christine and her organization do here, especially when it comes to losing what they see as their property—their *assets*. The heavy door gives them pause."

"That's sick."

He paused and looked hard at her. "What you'll learn here is a lot worse than that. Better be ready for it."

"I'm not a child," she said, eyes glaring.

"That's not what I was implying, Jamie; but what is on the other side of this door is raw. Really raw."

Before she could answer, the door cracked open, a heavy security chain still in place. A pair of eyes blinked first at the daylight, then in recognition.

"Lucas."

The door closed and the scrape of the chain being unhooked announced their welcome. The woman practically threw herself at Lucas before the door was fully open again. He stumbled backwards with a laugh. As he extracted himself from the woman's embrace, he indicated Jamie.

"Christine. Meet Jamie. She and I are working together."

The two nodded towards each other, and Lucas felt sudden discomfort. It was almost as if he was watching two she-wolves circling each other. The feeling lasted for only a second and as smiles broke out between them, he questioned if he hadn't imagined the feeling.

"Welcome," Christine was saying, extending her hand. "Come on in. Join us. I've just put on a pot a coffee, as a matter of fact." She glanced up and down the street in what Lucas knew was survival instinct while closing and locking the door and ushering them inside. "Jamie, you might not know it, but only strong dark-roast coffee and very little else can motivate your partner. In fact, I can't remember him ever sitting down long enough to consume an entire meal."

As they moved into the room, Christine double-checked the door at their backs and slid the heavy security chain into place.

Christine's one-room office held a couple of computer stations along the back wall, but the center part of the area was set up with a coffee table that sat centrally, surrounded by two couches and a couple of used, but comfortable, high-backed chairs.

"Grab a seat," Christine said as she practically skipped past them towards a Keurig coffee machine. "I know Lucas' poison; how do you like your coffee, Jamie?"

"Just black, thank you." She settled herself in one of the single chairs while Lucas dropped onto the corner of the couch that faced the office window, which was boarded up outside.

"I love what you've done with the office," Lucas commented as he noted that the sheets of plywood he'd seen outside were reinforced with metal strapping bolted into the walls.

Christine laughed over her shoulder, her voice husky and low. "In this neighborhood, it is trending design. According to my landlord, boarding the window from the outside lowered the chances of selling the building. But after three smashed picture windows, we can't afford not to board it up, despite the landlord. And if the landlord won't allow the plywood outside, well ... The last thing I want to do is to keep spending fund-raising dollars replacing glass. There's little enough to go around as it is. And besides, with the windows boarded, there is no longer any glass to break."

After handing out steaming mugs of coffee, she practically jumped onto the couch across from Lucas and curled her legs under her.

Lucas wasted no time. "The reason for our visit, Christine, is we're hearing some unusual rumors on the street. With your contacts, we're hoping that you might have heard something."

"Can you be more specific? There's a rule in this area," she said with a smirk towards Jamie. "If you haven't heard a new rumor by ten in the morning, start one."

Jamie chuckled, but Lucas just smiled, having heard the joke before. "Word has it that there might be a couple of women putting the boots to some of the local handlers."

Christine's eyes crinkled in mirth. "And why is that a bad thing?"

Lucas gave a little laugh. "Not judging. Just looking for facts."

The humor left Christine's face, and she sighed deeply. "Lucas, you've always been up front and honest with me; and through your stories, you've supported the work we're doing here."

She stopped and stared at Lucas and then at Jamie, before returning her attention back to Lucas.

"If someone is actually going around and targeting these scumbags, why should anyone give a shit?" She stood up suddenly, her hands squeezing into fists. "You, of all people, know what they do to women. It's next to impossible to get the police off their asses to deal—really deal—with these assholes. And when they do, they forget the *girls* when they hold their press conferences and pat *themselves* on the back for doing society such a great service!"

She walked around the couch with pent-up anger. Placing her hands on the back of the couch, she leaned towards the two reporters. "If someone is doing this, and to answer your question, this is the first I've heard about it ... then we should give them a fucking *medal*!"

"Surely you don't condone this?" Jamie said.

Christine stared at her with wide eyes and open mouth. She looked over at Lucas incredulously. She straightened up and walked around the couch to drop onto the cushion near Jamie.

"You're new, so I'll cut you some slack." She leaned towards the younger woman. "If you spent some time dealing with the aftermath of what those animals do to these girls—and they *are* girls, some as young as thirteen—you might change your mind. But apparently, you do not know what it's like on the street. People like you—"

"What do you mean, *people like me*?"

"Honey, I know who you are and who your daddy is. In fact, he has supported our group. You may be Black, but I know that you've never wanted for anything. In your perfect world, there is no way you can understand what and why things happen in our part of town. You see, laws get written by rich, asshole lawyers and judges who have never known a day without an income, a job. They've never had to decide whether to pay for rent or for food. Yet they draft these laws as if everyone was living in their perfect little world. And then they act surprised when jails get filled. Then they look for ways of cutting down on numbers of incarcerations, so they pick which crimes are worse than others. They don't have the guts to hand out real penalties. And they always give the guilty more rights than the victims."

Lucas had never seen Christine this upset, and it shocked him; but before he could interject, she continued.

"Ninety-five percent of the girls would not *be* on the street if it weren't for the handlers. The other five percent leave home to avoid being abused, only to sell themselves just to get by. If the goddamn law actually *dealt* with the pimps and child abusers, it would take care of most of the problem. But men rather than woman wrote those laws. It's almost like they give themselves an out if ever, in a drunken haze they get, shall we say, the urge to try out the local cuisine."

"Christine," Lucas said, trying to calm her down. "Regardless of how you feel, the last thing you'd want is for any of this to escalate and have the women who did this go to jail for more than common assault. And I remind you as I say that, that you know that I *am* fully aware what happens to these girls."

For a minute, he thought she would lash out at him, too; but she seemed almost to collapse into herself. With elbows on knees, she tilted her head so that her long dark curls fell across her face. Lucas and Jamie exchanged a confused look.

When the silence extended uncomfortably, Lucas said in a low voice, "Christine?"

One hand reached to the top of her head, while the other she held up as if to give them pause. Throwing back her head so that her long hair fell back across her shoulders, she took a deep breath before looking directly at Jamie and said, "I'm sorry, Jamie. Shit, the first time I meet you, and here I am coming down on you for no other reason than I'm frustrated with this mad, fucking world."

With no warning, she got up, stepped over the coffee table, and dropped beside Jamie, hands clenched against her chest. "I'll understand if you tell me to get stuffed, but please forgive me. I was totally out of line."

Lucas watched the two women and found he was almost holding his breath. He might not know much about Jamie, but he knew Christine was always candid with her feelings. If Jamie didn't accept her apology, it would devastate Christine.

Jamie's nod was barely discernible, but Christine's heavy sigh released the heavy tension in the room. Christine put a hand over Jamie's. "Can we begin again?"

"Yes, I'd like that."

Chapter 6

"The first thing you have to do," Christine began, "Is to throw out everything you think you know about pimps." Her hands fluttered as she spoke. She stood and paced around the furniture.

Christine reminded Jamie of the Eveready Bunny and had to bite her lip, especially with what the woman was saying.

"Pimps are not the outlandish men in flamboyant outfits that you see in the movies. The real pimp is an animal who only is concerned with making as much money as he can. They do not see the women they deal with as anything more than commodities to be sold over and over. When the woman no longer produces, they discard them, the same way you toss out food that has passed its expiry date."

Jamie looked at Lucas, but he was zeroed in on what the social worker was saying. Even though Jamie realized she deserved some of the criticism that Christine had thrown at her, it still stung. At least Christine had apologized.

"Today's pimps live on social media, and they join every type of social group you can think of. They actively target girls who have low self-esteem or have been bullied at school or online. They offer friendship to lonely kids, teenagers who don't feel they fit, and start grooming them so that they feel accepted by the pimp. These girls—and a few boys—are eager to feel like they belong and matter. The pimp will give them the attention they desire; and as the relationship gains ground, he becomes the center of their existence. And it doesn't take long. I've seen it happen in as little as a few weeks."

"Weeks!" Jamie blurted, eyes widening.

Christine nodded. "They're desperate to feel wanted. He'll tell them they're special. That they're pretty. He'll tell them he needs them as much as they need him. Eventually they'll meet. He'll swoon over her. Buy her gifts. Take her places, and all the while, become indispensable to her. They'll become intimate. Then, he'll introduce her to drugs. Soft stuff at first, unless she has already experimented. But it'll always move to harder stuff until she's addicted. If she resists, he slips the stuff into a drink. Rohypnol or something similar. The minute she goes under, he will inject her with a hard drug, so she becomes an addict who'll do anything for the next fix. When she is really high, he'll start having one of his buddies or even paid clients to replace him so that she learns about multiple partners."

Christine bowed her head before looking directly at Jamie. "For her next fix and to please her *boyfriend*, she is desperate enough to do anything, including selling herself to please him."

"But aren't people out there looking for her? These girls must have friends and family."

Christine laughed ruefully. "Many of the girls don't, or, if they do, the family doesn't give a shit. But for the ones who do have family, they'll keep her hidden for up to a month in some cheap apartment or motel. Or he'll transport her to another city where no one knows her. There is a circuit of cities the girls travel. Clients are always looking for fresh faces. Absolutely no one she knows will put eyes on her until the transformation is complete."

Jamie glanced down at her hands and was surprised that her fists were white from clenching so tightly. Knowing prostitution was happening was one thing, but hearing how it happened was quite another. And seeing the raw injury in Christine's eyes was even more disturbing. The woman had been dealing with the fallout from this horrible social affliction for years, with limited success. Lucas had not been exaggerating when he called what she would hear as *raw*. It was more than raw; it was savagery.

When she looked up again, she saw that this suddenly beautiful, heroic woman waiting. Christine's smile turned sad, showing that she realized the weight of the words she'd spoken and couldn't be un-heard, like the contents of Pandora's box. Janie knew she could make a difference. This was not only a job. Lucas was right. The story is all that matters.

Jamie hadn't been feeding Lucas a line last night. His stories had moved her and made her want to make a similar difference in the world. But as a woman, what Christine had told her touched her in a deeper way than it ever could for a man. Comparably, very few men would ever experience the horrors that these women did.

"I can see why you got upset earlier," she said.

"You don't know the half of it. I could tell you stories that would rock your world," Christine said, looking over at Lucas and smiling. "This guy's done more than most getting the word out, and we love him for it."

Lucas squirmed at the attention. "So, I wrote a few stories. Any-one could have done that."

"But no one did." She returned her attention to Jamie. "Don't let his tough guy act fool you. Under all that, is someone who cares. The girls trust him and trip over themselves whenever he comes around. He's become like a big brother to all my girls."

Jamie looked at her fellow reporter. She wanted to do something, but it was his story. It's why Felix wanted him on it. He already has the contacts and trust of these women.

"Maybe we can—"

Lucas stood up. "Wait a minute. I don't want to rain on anyone's parade ..." He looked over at Jamie. "We're working together, but Fe-lix assigned this story to me, and I need to follow it up. I know there is much we both can do for Christine's girls and I have no problem doing that; but right now, we have our marching orders."

"But ..." Jamie tried to interrupt.

"If the explosion at the mine goes national, and it probably will, you do not know how much time that's going to eat up; and you, as the lead, well, it could swamp you."

Jamie's eyes went wide at the reminder.

"The human trafficking story may become involved," Lucas continued, "but at this point we have no idea where it's going, if anywhere. We're working on the word of two cons talking shit. We need to find out if there's anything to it."

Jamie nodded reluctantly.

He turned to Christine, who was watching the interaction with increasing impatience. "You know I'm in your corner, Christine, and," he said, waving at Jamie, "you have a new convert; but this might have to wait until there's more time."

"Some girls might not have that time, Lucas," Christine said, her back rigid.

Chapter 7

Leaving Christine, Lucas and Jamie drove up Pine Street. Lucas crossed the railway tracks and pointed out the laneway that hugged the embankment around the tracks. "The trafficker supposedly was beaten there, off of One Pine Road. Depending on what we learn at the press conference, we'll want to canvass the neighboring homes."

"Sounds good." She was silent for a moment, then turned to him. "Do you really think the government might revisit laws about soliciting sex?"

It was his turn to remain quiet as he maneuvered the vehicle. He let out an enormous sigh, then shook his head with obvious frustration. "I just don't know. Maybe. Hopefully. I just don't have any faith in any government doing what is right unless there's something in it for them. I mean, let's face it, look at the so-called sin taxes. They can say what they want about bootleg liquor or evil marijuana dealers, but it's all about the government getting its cut. We wouldn't have casinos, on-line gambling and lotteries if the government didn't get a piece of the action. Hell, provincial lottery and gaming is a just branch of *government*. And in the US, it is no different."

He sneaked a glance at her. "In the very first year after marijuana was legalized, Canadians spent 908 million dollars on it and the government collected almost 190 million of that!

"Rather than putting a stop to the prostitution, if anyone could actually do that—remember, it's claimed to be the oldest profession—if the government could figure a way to *profit* from the trade, they would. They pay lip service to curing addiction, both narcotic and gambling, yet profit from both, so why would they do anything less for prostitution?"

"That's pretty cynical, Lucas."

"I call it realistic."

He shrugged, not taking his eyes off the road. "Do this job for as long as I have, see the misery I have, and you view the world through a different lens. Everyone acknowledges that the system is broken, but no one will fix it. There's no actual justice in the legal system. Ask any lawyer. But few of them try to change it, because they're too busy grabbing every dollar they can."

"So, what can we do to change things?" she asked.

He stared ahead, deep in thought.

Jamie ventured. "Would it help if we concentrated on the female politicians? If we could open a dialogue that was gender-specific, we might find some powerful allies from all political parties."

Lucas's head snapped towards her before returning eyes to the road. His mind turned the idea over, and he nodded.

"You might be on to something. It would align with the prime minister's goal of gender parity for his cabinet. He's been pushing that for years. This issue would prove whether it's just a political move to influence female votes, or if he really believes that women should have a say that is worth hearing."

Jamie nodded with growing enthusiasm. "There are more women in the center of government than ever before. And with a minority government in Ottawa, if the political left supported the government, the issue would stand a chance of moving forward."

"I like it," Lucas said, smiling at her. *There's definitely more to her than I gave her credit for.* "But we have to see both stories finished first, or Felix will eat us for lunch."

As the car slowed for a traffic light, she said, "Are you ever sorry you became a journalist?"

He coughed an abrupt laugh. "No. I love my job. The need for a truthful dialog is more important today than ever. I might not be changing the world, but at least I am bringing an honest view of the world to our readers. And I think that's important. There's so much misinformation that people don't know what to think. And the looming AI revolution has already begun to make that worse. At least I can give them the truth. There will still be lots who ignore everything I write because there are people who love to feed off false information, especially from social media, like lemmings, until they run off the cliff. The argument about Covid vaccines proves my point."

She smiled evilly. "Everyone knows the government is using the vaccine to inject microchips into us so they can track us."

He laughed. "Yes. That one. And all the while, they grasp their cell phones like a lifeline." In a fair imitation of Forrest Gump, he said, "I don't know how Google and Amazon know I like Nike runners."

She laughed and slapped her thigh.

He sighed again and became serious. "I might be sardonic at times, but I think there needs to be people like you and me to bring things into the light. Asking hard questions. Now, more than ever. Our society has become so callous to the world's problems that, unless it affects them personally, people turn a blind eye to what is all around them."

"So, you haven't lost hope?"

"Not entirely. People still read our stories—and I'm not talking about the idiots who banter among themselves online at the bottom of a digital article—they're part of the problem, not a solution. No, I'm talking about a regular person who is still concerned with the safety of their community, and useful rules, and standards of our institutions. For me, holding our institutions accountable is part of our responsibility. City council has to be transparent. The police chief has to be made to take issues like human trafficking seriously and expose the guilty."

"That's one hell of a responsibility."

He looked directly at her and nodded. "You're damned right it is. That's why each story is all that matters to me."

Because of the strike at the smelter and the issue of crossing picket lines, as well as the police investigation into the explosion, the participants had agreed to move the press conference to the large central courtyard outside the city's municipal offices.

Lucas pulled his car into an underground parking lot near the square; and after finding a parking spot only two levels down, got out of the car with Jamie. Together, they made their way to a staircase that led to the courtyard. A provincial office building, city hall, and police headquarters surrounded a massive courtyard. The local cellphone provider's offices closed off the end of the courtyard. White concrete with darkened glass covered the municipal building attached to police headquarters. A large fountain was the focal point of the open area.

Several chairs were spread out facing the podium. Lucas recognized the other reporters who had already arrived, and he either nodded or waved a greeting. He noticed Jamie seemed to know most of them as she greeted them as well.

"You're the lead on this, so I'll hang back and watch," Lucas said in a low voice, so it didn't carry to others in the small crowd.

He moved away as individuals came through the revolving door of the municipal building. He recognized Police Chief Theo Dillard, and Fire Chief Terry Clement from their uniforms. The third uniformed man, Lucas didn't know, but his shoulder flashes held the provincial coat of arms. Lucas guessed the man was from the fire marshal's office and was the lead for fire investigation.

Behind the officials, a tall, dark-haired woman in a smart pant suit walked towards the podium side of the gathering. He recognized

Loretta Vincenta, the Ontario spokesperson for Nova. He had interviewed the woman more than once and even had gone out with her once for dinner, but the only thing on Loretta's mind was her career. She made that very clear before the meal arrived. In fact, the entire conversation, mainly one sided, was about the mining company. But they had stayed friendly; and even now, as their eyes met, she gave him a nod, her eyes sparkling.

Jamie noticed her look and glanced from Loretta to Lucas with a questioning tilt to her head. He shrugged.

The last man out of the building Lucas recognized as Mike Burgess, the president of the union. He did not approach the others, but stood at the back of the reporters, hands deep in his pockets, a bored expression on his face.

Loretta approached the podium. She carried no notes and began immediately. "Good morning. Thank you all for coming. My name is Loretta Vincenta, and I am here representing Nova. Yesterday evening, at approximately 10:12 PM, an incendiary device exploded at the North Shore Complex. There were no injuries, since we had shut down the plant because of ongoing labor issues between the company and its workforce. The explosion is currently under investigation."

"I call on the Chief Dillard to speak to his investigation."

The police chief moved to the microphone and nodded to the audience. "Good morning. The Fox Lake Police, in partnership with Fox Lake Fire Services, and the office of the Fire Marshall, are investigating the explosion that occurred at the North Shore Complex. We currently have no suspects. Preliminary inspection of the site showed an explosive was used to rupture the main feed from the sulfuric-acid plant. Had the plant been in production, the possibility of both massive casualties and an environmental event would have been a certainty. Because of the likelihood that this points to a domestic terrorist attack, both the Royal Canadian Mounted Police and Canadian Security Intelligence Service have joined our investigation."

As expected, every reporter had their hand raised to gain the police chief's attention. Lucas saw Jamie pull off her bright green scarf and shake it towards the podium to attract the attention of the spokesman. He had to bite his lip, because Chief Dillard took the bait immediately. *Nice tactic.*

"Yes, Ms. Coleman?"

She stood before asking, "Thank you, Chief Dillard. Have you identified the type of explosive?"

The chief turned and exchanged a look with one of his colleagues, and the man from the office of the fire marshal stepped forward to stand beside Dillard.

"Good morning, I'm Kyle Watson of the OFM—the office of the fire marshal, for any newbies out there. We've collected samples at the scene, but it will take some time before we get the results."

"Could the explosive be what they use at the mine?" Jamie asked before they could move on to another question.

"It is certainly a possibility, but as I said, we are waiting for results from the lab."

The chief stepped forward and pointed at another reporter.

"Len Taylor, CTV. Chief, you mentioned the risk of both mass casualties and an environmental hazard. Could you explain to our viewers what that might have entailed?"

"Had the acid plant been active, we would have had a massive sulfuric acid spill. Apart from the well-known corrosive effects, with this product, there is an inhalation hazard—and with the prevailing westerly winds, the city would have been at risk. Plant workers would have died horribly; and, of course, this kind of spill would be an environmental hazard to both the soil and air."

"Jillian Moreau, CBC. A direct question to Ms. Vincenta. Will this incident derail contract talks between Nova and the union?"

Lucas watched as a couple of reporters glanced at the union president for a reaction, but the man's expression was neutral. His attention zeroed in on Vincenta, as if waiting for her to make accusations.

"Although talks have stalled between the union and Nova, we are always ready to return to the table. The company has expressed willingness to meet with the provincial mediator any time the union wishes. This incident does not change that."

Burgess had a smirk on his face, and Lucas could feel the animosity coming from the union president. *There's no love lost between him and Loretta.* He had covered other labor disputes between the two adversaries and knew some violence had resulted. Although in the past, when the previous owner, a mining giant, owned the company, both sides knew the rules of engagement. From his sources when he was photographing the strike, Lucas also knew that it was the mining company that had broken off talks.

Nova, having done business in third world countries, was not used to dealing in an environment where labor laws were entrenched though legislation and enforced by both regulations and the court system. Their approach to negotiations had been heavy-handed and threatening. Nova had fired several union leaders for alleged wrongdoing, but it had fooled no one. The union might have to take the issues to court and would more than likely win. Firing someone today was a very complicated process, and the company no longer had the legal right to terminate without due cause.

As if he had been thinking aloud, a reporter from the *Sudbury Daily* asked a question. "Chief Dillard, we've seen improper actions by both the union and the company in past labor disputes. Is there any evidence that this explosion might be a tactic to hurt the bargaining talks?"

Lucas threw a glance at the union president. The man's mouth was open, but he held himself in place. He looked like he was ready to pounce on anyone who attacked his people.

Chief Dillard's normally calm demeanor changed instantly. His eyes became hard as he stepped forward, cutting off Loretta's retort.

"Look," he began. "I find that question highly inflammatory and a shameless attempt at sensationalism!" he said in a stern voice. He tore his eyes from the reporter in question, who now was recording the answer on his iPhone. "I already mentioned earlier that we had no suspect. If, through our investigation, we discover anything solid, we will do our due diligence and follow the evidence in whichever direction it takes. Anyone involved will be charged, regardless of alliances."

Burgess relaxed, but his eyes swung to Loretta. The two glared at each other.

Each believes the other is guilty. Lucas' eyes went back and forth between the two adversaries. *Which means neither is.*

Chapter 8

Cracking the door, Dragoljub Petkovic, Drago to his men, peered into the darkened room. His eyes were drawn to the candle glow surrounding a small, improvised shrine on the back wall. In front of the shrine dedicated to the Virgin Mary, the Brazilian, Jaren Pinheiro, knelt in prayer. Drago mentally translated Jaren's soft muttering of the Apostle's Creed.

"...the Holy Spirit; the holy catholic Church, the communion of saints; the forgiveness of sins; the resurrection of the body; and life ever-lasting. Amen."

Assured that the man was behaving, Drago closed the door with a smirk that pulled at the ragged scar on his cheek: an old gunshot wound from the time the Serbs attempted to tear their homeland from the Muslim thieves, a leftover from the Ottoman Empire. He had been lucky that day. The weapon had been small caliber. He had lost teeth, and it had hurt like a bitch for months, and he had spit blood every time he ate. But he had survived to take his revenge by raping the man's daughter and wife while he was made to watch. All resistance had fled the man before Drago slowly pulled his blade across the man's throat.

He had been twenty as the war ended with the interference of the United States and NATO. Had they had a few more months, he could only imagine how many more of the Muslim Bosniaks they would have killed or at least pushed out of the country that had been Serbia before the hated Russians had swallowed them up.

As soon as the Dayton Peace Agreement had been signed, NA-TO investigators swarmed the country, snapping up suspected war criminals. Drago had known that, for him, the writing was on the wall and had quickly fled his homeland.

Eventually, he arrived in Zaire as part of a mercenary corps attempting to shore up government forces. But as the rebels marched on Kisangani, and the president's own forces left their posts, Drago and his fellow mercenaries knew better than to make a stand. With a knack for survival and evading hunters, Drago escaped the country by hiding in a Fodineum equipment truck.

It was where Drago met a fellow ex-soldier turned mercenary, Felipe Vautour, and his running days ended. And it was Vautour who had brought Jaren here from Brazil.

Vautour was a troubleshooter for Fodineum, a commodity and trading company, which was also one of the largest mining companies in the world. Once the two realized their skill set, as well as moral compass, was aligned, the two became joined at the hip. *We could have been brothers.*

Over the next two decades, both men helped deal with any *sensitive* "wet" work for Fodineum. They bribed government officials to ignore environmental or industrial regulations. They also armed rebel forces, so they could distract the different governments while the company exploited the land of its resources. With Vautour, Drago had traveled and helped move minerals across rogue states like Iraq and Iran under the noses of inspectors for the US embargoes.

If a village was taking too long to move out of an area that held a rich deposit of oil or some other resource, an accident or shooting would usually speed things up. To silence environmentalists, they easily convinced police to search the interfering individual's belongings where they almost always found contraband—thanks to Drago or one of his men.

The work was exciting and different with each mission. And of course, the money was fantastic. Despite owning a Bavaria E40 Fly yacht and a vintage 1940 Indian Military Chief Model 340B motor-cycle, Drago had saved over two million dollars.

Eighteen months ago, when the big boss arrived to offer him this new job, he could not believe what they were offering him. His instincts had awoken and screamed a warning to run. It was the same instinctive warning that had saved him in Bosnia and in Zaire.

On the surface, the missions seemed simple. He had carried out sabotage in the past, but never on this scale, and never in North America. He spent a lot of time in underdeveloped countries where corruption was common and modern law-enforcement methods non-existent. But now he had to plan for a sophisticated response by multiple police forces using the latest technology. Of course, the price tag compensated for that. However, even if he managed to fulfill the tasks assigned to his select group, there would be a target on his back from then on. Nowhere would be safe, and he could never move in the open again.

Drago thought back to the pious man in the other room who prayed to a god who taught forgiveness, to give him the strength to exact his revenge. Did no one but him, Drago, realize the absurdity of that plea? Nothing changed. During the last war, the Croatians, with the blessings of Hitler, and the help of the Muslim Bosniaks, killed thousands of Serbians in the name of God. During the Bosnian War, the Serbs and Croats fought in the name of the same God, against those same Bosniaks, as if it were a Holy War.

There was no God.

God was just the excuse that men used to justify the beast within themselves. Drago understood that long ago. Money was God. Information was God. Power was God.

Nothing—nothing else mattered.

Drago knew where to strike. He had the data he needed to get the best bang for the buck. He had the tools—and the scapegoat. And he had an escape plan.

He pushed the little voice of worry to the back of his consciousness. His power stemmed from the fact that he processed one thing these civilized Canadians didn't: he didn't give a *fuck* about their rights, their laws, or their lives! He'd do his job without a thought.

THE MINUTE THE DOOR closed; Jaren's shoulders slumped. His eyes held an image of the Madonna, but he actually saw nothing as fear ran rampant through him. For so many nights after the funeral for Francesca and his mother-in-law, he had lain staring into the darkness as his stomach rolled at the injustice of their deaths.

So many people had died, yet the Novo mining company denied any wrongdoing. The villagers who had survived the flood were becoming sick. The government people said that the river water was no longer safe but filled with heavy metals from the tailings pond.

The river ran three hundred miles before emptying into the ocean. Countless villages drew water from the river for drinking, for livestock, for produce, but now they were being told the water was poison.

Still, the company refused to listen.

Each day, one or two of the surviving villagers left. *To where?* Jaren had heard many stories. To the city. To inland villages that did not rely on this river. But no one could answer the question: Is work available there?

Hot tears scalded his eyes night after night as he contemplated leaving the only home he'd known. Where he'd grown up, met, married—and become a widower. The birthplace of his children. And now, the graves of his family.

He would leave his house with nothing to show for all the years invested in it. No one was buying homes in what was quickly becoming a ghost town.

They had run the last government people out of their village in fear of the lives. The villagers who were left had demanded to know what *o presidente* was doing to force the mining conglomerate to help the people of the area. The government had shut down the mine while an investigation was being conducted, which made matters even worse because it meant there was no work for people like Jaren. No work meant no income.

In the end, he felt he had no choice but to turn to the stranger who had approached him that day outside the church.

If the government would not help the people bring the company to task, maybe this stranger could, with the help of others.

That had been months ago.

He remembered that brief conversation as if it were yesterday. It had felt so right. He would make Novo *pay*. With trembling fingers, he called the number on the business card. "I'm ready to make them pay," he said.

The voice on the other end didn't hesitate. "It would have surprised me if you hadn't called, *Senhor*. I have been monitoring the situation. We cannot allow Novo to walk away unscathed. We have a plan to teach them a lesson, and there is a role for you to play. I'll be there within a week."

The voice belonged to a Frenchman, Felipe Vautour. It was the same man who had attended his family's funeral. He arranged a passport for Jaren and together the two traveled three hundred miles in a small, private plane from Brumadinho in Minas Gerais state to Rio de Janeiro. It had been Jaren's first flight, and his fascination with the experience, mixed equally with terror, left him giddy. He marveled at the overhead view of the mining site and its visible destruction that the overhead view gave him. Once he had seen enough, Vautour had signaled the pilot, and they headed south. Nose pressed to the cool window-glass, Jaren watched light sparkling off lakes and rivers that crisscrossed the countryside. It all looked so clean and peaceful from this height.

But he was shocked as they approached the city. As he took in the size of a city he had only heard of, his mind could not wrap around the idea of so many people living together in one spot. Compared to the only home he had ever known, he realized how insignificant he was in the world's immensity. It was humbling.

But it was all a prelude to the next leg of their trip. After boarding an Air Canada flight to Toronto, he could not believe the power that thrust his thin frame into the seat's cushions as the massive jet took to the skies. Within minutes, they breached the clouds and Jaren witnessed sights he'd thought were only reserved for God.

Except for a brief stop in Miami, they arrived in Toronto in just over fourteen hours. He felt exhausted even though he had done little more than sit staring out the oval window.

His companion said little the entire trip; either dozing or exploring his phone. But while they were landing, Vautour advised Jaren just to say he was exploring Canada on vacation if anyone in Customs asked about his trip.

After a night in a hotel on the edge of Pearson Airport, the pair completed the last leg of the journey and landed at Sudbury Airport less than an hour after departure.

They were met by a white Dodge cargo van that took them to a big two-story house in a dense forest. A locked steel gate blocked the dirt road leading to the home.

It was here that Jaren met the Slovakian, Drago. He shuddered as he remembered extending a hand in greeting, only to have the man ignore the gesture as Drago's black eyes bored into him.

"You'll do as you're told, or I'll gut you," Drago said in a growl. "I will not allow our mission to be jeopardized by an amateur. Do you understand?"

Evidently, Vautour had briefed everyone on Jaren's adequate English.

They gave him his own room, but it soon became apparent that it was actually a cell. No one would explain what they planned or what Jaren's role would be. He could not understand how any of this would help him get revenge on Novo. He could not leave the building without one of the hard-eyed men who watched his every move as if waiting for him to bolt.

Jaren spent hours praying to the Madonna for strength. He feared he had made a deadly mistake in reaching out to these people.

Two nights ago, a group of the men left the property. When they returned, they brought several women back with them. In a gesture of welcome, he had offered each woman a small gift, hoping one of them would find his secret cry for help. He could hear drunken laughter and cries of sexual release throughout the night. Drago had even offered him a woman to bed for himself, but he had shrunk back in horror at the thought, and the big man had laughed at him.

Chapter 9

As the press conference broke up, the uniformed first responders marched back through the revolving door to the depths of City Hall. Lucas led Jamie to where the Novo spokesperson, Loretta Vincenta, was standing and talking on-camera to a TV reporter.

He leaned close to Jamie's ear and whispered, "I'll introduce you to Loretta, and maybe you could ask for a chance to get photos of the damaged equipment. I gave the photos of the explosion to Felix, but we have none of the damage that it did."

She nodded and together, they waited for their chance to speak with the woman.

Once the interview was over, Loretta shook hands with the reporter before striding over to where Lucas and Jamie stood. With no thought, she threw her arms around Lucas and pulled him in for a hug.

"Damn, Lucas," she said. "It's been far too long."

Jamie almost laughed at the surprised expression in his eyes. It was obvious he had been totally caught off guard by the woman's familiarity.

"Yes," he stammered. "A long time."

Loretta put out her hand to Jamie. "And are you the reason for Lucas's absenteeism from the social scene? I'm Loretta; and from your earlier questions, I'm guessing you're working with Lucas."

Jamie laughed at the insinuation and said, "No and yes in that order. We are working on a couple of different stories. I'm Jamie Coleman. It's nice to meet you, Ms. Vincenta."

The woman nodded at Jamie, but then tilted her head at Lucas. "That means you're still single. Interesting."

It surprised Jamie to see her partner so off his game. He seemed so sure of himself, but this woman's attention seemed to rattle him. *A past lover, maybe?*

"Listen, Loretta," Lucas said as he tried to find his footing. "Jamie is leading the story on the explosion, and we're wondering if there would be a chance to get some photos of the damage for the paper. With CISIS and the RCMP adding themselves to the investigation, the story will go national; and, as they say, 'a picture paints a thousand words.'"

She eyed him as she considered, and then looked at Jamie. "You're new to the paper, but from what I've read of yours, you're quite good; so, I don't mind helping you out. Lucas seems to be ignoring me, so the favor is just for you," she said, rolling her eyes towards Lucas. "And not him."

Jamie smiled and bowed her head. "Thank you. I appreciate the help."

"Of course," Loretta said. "Let's see ... There is the issue of the picket line. We can ask the union for permission—" She looked across the courtyard and spotted the union president still standing off to one side. "Wait one," she said to Jamie, and turned toward Mike Burgess.

"Mr. Burgess," Loretta said, raising her voice. The man's head snapped towards her, his eyes narrowing. "A moment of your time, please."

He looked around as if to see if anyone might be paying attention.

Strange. It's like he's worried about optics. Jamie studied the man as he approached. Rugged in a tough-guy kind of way. His hair was dark and neat, but his goatee carried a splattering of gray. He wore a casual sports jacket over a shirt that was tight across the chest, indicating the man was in good shape—maybe worked out regularly. He wasn't very tall, and that made Jamie wonder if suffered from 'short-man' syndrome since the aggression in his expression and obvious hostility to Loretta and the company she represented was clear.

"What's up?" he said in a voice that bordered on boredom.

He plays it as if he couldn't give a damn, but he's interested in what we're discussing.

"Mike, I'm sure you know Lucas, but I'm not sure if you've met Jamie Coleman. She's fairly new at the paper."

The unionist nodded at Lucas. "Yeah, Lucas and I have spoken a few occasions. I'm happy to meet you, Ms. Coleman. I'm Mike Burgess, union president of the USW."

"Please call me Jamie," she said, accepting his hand. It was dry, yet soft. That surprised her. She would have figured that as a miner, his hand would have been rough and covered with calluses from working underground.

"Jamie wondered if she could get some pictures of the damage in the plant. But we wouldn't presume making that decision without your consent to cross the picket line."

His eyes flickered from her to Lucas and then Jamie. She could almost see his mind whirling through different scenarios to see how they might hurt or help his cause.

"Would I be able to see the photos?"

"If you are interested, Mike, you could join us at the site and see for yourself."

His eyes narrowed as if trying to see if this might be some kind of trap Loretta had placed for him. The moment was fleeting as he nodded. "Yeah. Okay. I have no issue with going in there. When do you want to go?"

Jamie looked at Lucas, who nodded. "I'm ready when you are. I just have to pick up my car."

"No need," Burgess said. "I can drive and then get you to your car once we're done. The union office is just around the corner."

"Thank you. That would be helpful," Jamie said, and turned to Loretta. "Thank you for setting this up, Ms. Vincenta."

"No problem. I'm happy to help. And it's just Loretta, please." She pressed a business card into Jamie's hand. "If you need anything, call me. Anything at all.

Jamie nodded and turned to Lucas.

"I'll drop you a text when I'm back at the office. Are you going to canvass the neighborhood like we spoke about?"

He looked at his watch and nodded. "We'll meet up afterward and compare notes. Here, take my Canon. Use the automatic setting. The pictures will be a lot clearer than your phone's camera." Once she had the case secured over her shoulder, he nodded thanks at Burgess before turning to Loretta. "Nice seeing you, Loretta. Thanks for setting this up."

"I already told you, Lucas," she said with a stern look. "The favor was *not* for you, but for your delightful companion." With that, she turned on her heel and headed for the door that led into city hall.

Jamie had to bite back a laugh at the confused expression on Lucas's face. He had no idea what he had done wrong to offend the Novo spokesperson. Jamie couldn't be a hundred-percent sure either, but she could hazard a guess. No woman enjoyed being ignored.

LUCAS UNLOCKED HIS car, got in and started it, and exited the underground parking with little attention to his surroundings. His mind grappled with Loretta's words and her attitude. He couldn't understand her reaction. The one time they had gone out, she'd made it clear that she was not interested in a relationship. He respected that. So why open contempt that apparently wasn't just in fun? At first, it seemed like she was toying with him, but the last held a bite.

Lucas's phone buzzed inside his shirt pocket, and he shook himself out of the fog of confusion. He pulled it out and saw a text from his boss, Felix Cameron.

Call me when you get a chance.

He pulled over to the curb and hit the speed dial for Felix's private number. When the man answered, his voice was curt. "Where are you?"

"Heading toward One Pine Road, where the pimp was supposed to have been beaten."

"Then why did I see you at the Novo press conference? I told you that Jamie was the lead on that story."

"She didn't talk with you?"

"About what?"

"She came to me and asked to work together. She's still the lead on the strike and the explosion, but I'm helping her. In fact, I just helped arrange an inclusive trip inside the smelter for her to take photos of the bomb site."

"How the hell did you manage that?"

"Contacts, Felix."

The man paused, and Lucas knew that Felix understood that arranging for the photos was not only for Jamie, but for the paper. The move would go far to soothe his boss's bruised ego. Not too many openly opposed Felix.

"And what about your story?" Felix asked, and Lucas noticed a definite softening in his tone.

"Jamie is working with me on that, too. We met with your contact from the jail and then had a chat with Christine over at Second Chance. She'd heard nothing about the incident. So, while Jamie is out taking photos at the sulfuric-acid plant, I'm on my way to canvass the area where the attack allegedly took place."

"You sound like the story is a bust."

"Not sure yet. It could have been two jailbirds flapping their gums. That Christine hasn't heard about it makes me suspicious. Her ear is usually close to the ground when it comes to human trafficking, but I'll follow the trail as far as I can. Worst case is that just I write another story about human trafficking in the city and see if I can get the police chief on record about how he plans to deal with it."

"Okay," Felix finally said after a moment. "Keep digging. Just remember that you are assisting Jamie and not taking over from her. She needs to learn to stand her ground and fend for herself."

"I realize that, but you know as well I do that our biggest assets are our contacts. The more people I introduce her to, the better off she'll be. It'll take months, if not years, to build her own list of contacts otherwise."

"Keep me informed."

The phone went silent in Lucas's hand. It had been so tempting to add "Uncle Felix" into the conversation, but he didn't need to piss off his boss with no return.

Chapter 10

Watching for broken glass, Lucas pulled his old Honda into an empty lot that sat neglected between the lane and the railroad line that serviced the mines, now dormant because of the strike. The usual cargo on the rail was sulfuric acid, which they shipped to industries that needed it in the south and abroad. The sulfuric-acid plant at the smelter—where the explosion had ruptured the main line—captured its acid from the smelting process, and it was sold around the world. The fact that such dangerous freight traveled through multiple neighborhoods across the city to reach the main line validated the expression that ignorance was bliss. Not that the citizens of the city would have any recourse, Lucas knew. The mines and the rails were here before the people.

The old neighborhood was seeing a change as investors looked to exploit a growing real-estate market. Even these homes, some over a hundred years old, were being scooped up for surprising profits. Despite rental laws, the poor were being pushed out as property owners invested more money in property updates.

Where is it going to end? We're already seeing a rise in homelessness in the city's core. He'd definitely have to talk with Felix about doing a story on the real-estate market and how it impacted those on low income. It wasn't what they called hard news, but it deeply affected the community.

In search of details about the pimp attack, Lucas started knocking on doors in the apartment block next to the lane.

There was no answer at the first door. He could hear sounds of a television, its volume competing with a child crying; but no one came to his knock. After a third knock, he moved to the next apartment.

He figured he had struck out again and was turning to leave when the door was reefed open with force. A thin man of about thirty years stood squinting at the daylight. He wore only a blanket over his shoulders and Lucas had to avert his gaze because the covering did little to hide the man's nakedness.

"What the fuck do you want, man?" the skinny guy growled, his voice rough from sleep.

"Hi, I'm Lucas Kucher from the *Fox Lake Journal*. There was an attack in this lane a few nights ago, and I want to talk to anyone who saw something."

Even from this guy's apartment, Lucas could hear the blare of the television from the first apartment. So could the guy. He reached down and grabbed a tan workboot and threw it with force at the wall separating the units. It thumped hard against the surface with a hollow echo.

"Shut that shit off, bitch!" He screamed, face red with anger. "Some of us are trying to sleep."

Two responding bangs reverberated through the walls, but the volume on the television was lowered.

"Fucking welfare bitch. She knows I work all night and have to sleep during the day, but do you think she'd cut me some slack?" He shook his head, obviously frustrated.

He looked back at Lucas. "Look. I don't know nothing about no attack. I work steady graveyard, six days a week." Without waiting for Lucas to reply, the man swung the door closed.

At the next apartment, a young child of about three opened the door. The child's vacant eyes took him in, a pacifier rhythmically being pulled at. Lucas couldn't tell if it was a boy or girl. He crouched down. "Hi there. Is your mommy home?"

The child's little head swung slowly back and forth. He looked past the child and saw what might have been every dish, pot and pan, and glass the household owned covering a small counter and table. None were clean.

"How about your daddy? Is he home?"

The child once again shook its head and gently closed the door. Lucas stood there at a loss. Was there an adult in the apartment, maybe asleep, or had the child been left on its own? Should he call someone? The decision was made for him.

"Hey!" came an angry voice behind him. "Who are you? Whad'you want?"

Lucas turned to see a heavy-set woman lumbering through the empty lot where his car was parked. She wore leggings that disappeared under a low-cut, bruise-purple, floral dress and carried a blue Walmart shopping bag. Squinting through smoke that rose from a joint clamped in the corner of her mouth, she looked ready to kill. A sleeve of tattoos of demons, skulls and monsters that covered her thick left arm made her grimace even more menacing.

"I'm Lucas Kucher for the *Fox Lake Journal*. I'm looking for anyone who might have witnessed a fight or attack the other night, and I was told that it happened right here."

Her posture relaxed, and she pulled on the joint, holding the smoke in for a turn, before releasing it in a gush. "Shit, I thought you're a fucking cop."

"No," he reassured her. He pulled out a business card and handed it to her. "I'm just a reporter looking for information."

"I'm Tammy. Gimme a minute. Goddam kid ate up all the cereal, and I had to get more. Lemme feed her."

She entered the apartment, leaving the door fully open. She pulled a box of cereal out of the plastic grocery bag. The woman slid a finger under the cardboard opening of the box, and extracted the end of the bag of roasted, sugary oats. She tore open the bag and handed the box and its contents to the child that waited with hungry eyes on its meal. When the woman lowered the box to the toddler, needful hands pulled it to its chest. The little girl retreated to a couch in front of a television, where a cartoon flashed on the screen. The last Lucas saw was the child's eyes glued to the television while greedily stuffing her mouth with cereal from the box.

"That'll keep her quiet for a while," said the woman as she escorted Lucas outside, closing the door behind them.

"She eats that without milk?"

"I can't afford milk. We just get by as it is. Goddam ex don't pay no child support, and the government doesn't give enough to live on when you take away rent and hydro." She pulled a cigarette out of her purse and lit it. "We all have to make sacrifices, you know?"

She offered him a cigarette, and he shook his head.

"So, you saw something the other night?" he asked.

She nodded and blew out a long lungful of smoke. "Yeah, I saw it. Funniest shit I seen in a long while."

He gave her a confused look. "Funny?"

"It's the irony, man. When you know the players and know what they're about, it's fucking great to see the big old world bring on some good old payback."

"I'm sorry?" Lucas said, wondering what that joint had been laced with.

"I've watched Gabriel Kebede beat on five or six of his women over the past year. It felt so good to watch those two women beat the fuck out of that asshole. He deserved that and a helluva lot more!"

Lucas scribbled the name in his notebook before asking, "How did it go down?"

"I'd just put the brat down to bed and came out for a smoke. Gabriel was screaming at one of his girls—something about pocketing money—when these two broads pushed him off the street and into the shadows. There was a lot of cursing—mainly by

Gabriel—but then they started wailing on him. One had a baseball bat—one of them metal ones—and it made a hollow clunk when it connected with his skull. The other enjoyed stomping on him with workboots—y'know, the kind with steel toes."

She wiped her chin like she'd just had bitten into juicy melon. "It was the best karma I've seen." She said in a dreamy voice. "It's the first time I ever seen one of those assholes get some payback."

"Did you recognize either of the women who laid into this Gabriel?" Lucas asked.

"Even if I did, I'd never rat on them. What they did was right-eous!" she said, flicking away the cigarette stub to smolder in the tall grass of the empty lot.

"Tammy, I'm not a cop. I am not looking to have them charged. I just need to know why they did it."

"Well, even if what you say is true, I wouldn't know these women. Never seen them before." She narrowed her eyes at him. "Give me an extra card and I'll pass it along to them if I see them again. But no promises."

He passed her another card. "Were any others watching the fight?"

"Might have been. I was watching the action. Figured he was dead though, because he sure as hell wasn't moving. But he was gone by morning."

"You didn't check?"

She gave him a look that implied he had lost his mind.

Lucas knew if the police had found the pimp dead or injured, they would have been banging on doors, like he was doing now, looking for witnesses. The fact she hadn't mentioned it was obvious enough.

He thanked the woman and moved along the street. He was able to speak with three more individuals, but found nobody else who had witnessed the attack.

But he had the name of the victim—and the event itself—confirmed.

Chapter 11

Jamie sat uncomfortably in the passenger seat of Mike Burgess's car. Although excited about the opportunity to view the site of the explosion, being in a car with an aggressive man she knew very little about had her on edge. Because of their roles, she didn't think he'd try anything, but she'd had other encounters that had come close to being more than just uncomfortable.

What also added to her discomfort was that Burgess wasn't talkative. It might be because she was a reporter, and he feared she could use anything he said against him. But her few attempts at small talk had failed, so she sat quietly as he focused on the traffic.

She thought about Lucas and realized that although they had just begun to work together, she had felt no similar apprehension with him. She was comfortable with him from the start. Part of it might have been a little hero worship. After all, she'd been sort of stalking him since that first story of his she had read. But the passion in the stories he wrote was exactly who he was. He cared about the issues and the people he wrote about.

Most people were so self-absorbed today that it was nice to see someone like Lucas who gave more than he took. She didn't delude herself that he was perfect. He could be abrupt, but she couldn't detect any malice in his behavior.

Their car slowed for the turning lane that entered North Shore and the entrance to the complex. Burgess pulled up to the picket line and parked behind the makeshift shelter. Jamie found herself the center of attention as a newcomer. She felt the eyes of the strikers on her as Burgess strode into the small group with comfortable familiarity, clapping backs and shaking hands.

"Novo's allowing me in to see the damage," he said to the small crowd of strikers. "I'll have more to pass on, soon."

He turned back to Jamie, and with a wave of his hand said, "This is Jamie Coleman. She's from the *Fox Lake Journal,* so please answer any questions she might have." In a voice loud enough for everyone to hear, he continued. "The Union follows the rules, so we have nothing to hide. Our people will cooperate any way we can, Ms. Coleman. Don't hesitate to contact me if you're not getting answers to your questions."

She nodded, realizing that he could have said this on the ride over, but had waited to say it in front of the troops, where it would have more effect. *He's definitely a politician. I'll have to be on my toes.*

She smiled at him. "Would it be possible to get an interview with you about the concerns the Union has with Novo?"

"Most definitely. I'd be honored." His smile looked to Jamie like that of a crocodile waiting for his next meal.

He stepped away as a dark SUV pulled up to the picket line. Jamie recognized Loretta in the front seat, even though the sun's reflection blocked her features. Her window rolled down, and she and Burgess exchanged a few words before he strode back towards his own vehicle, waving for Jamie to join him.

As Loretta led the way, the union leader allowed some space to increase between the two vehicles, so he had time to swerve between rutted breaks in the pavement. "The shareholders are making massive dividends, but they can't even fix the freakin' roads that service the plant," Burgess muttered almost to himself. Jamie realized he had directed the comment towards her. Passing the security building, they crossed a set of tracks that led to the slag dump in the northwest.

As the vehicles made their way deeper into the plant, Jamie's eyes swept back and forth across the massive industrial site. Pipes and covered conveyor-belts ran overhead in what looked like a maze.

In between weary, cinder-block buildings, dried clumps of coarse grass were the only vegetation visible. The hard, baked soil was flecked with multicolored smears of previous fuel spills. Black, sulfur-stained rocks bordered puddles of brackish rainwater.

Since Jamie had only been inside the complex once before years ago during a school trip, the sight of the huge converter building and the menacing superstack towering over it left her breathless. Being this close, she had to lean forward, craning her neck along the dashboard to glimpse the stack's white tip. Shadows of clouds darkened patches of the concrete chimney.

"I've never been this close to the stack," she said, her voice barely a whisper.

Burgess grunted. "I'm so used to it, I don't even see it anymore."

Jamie cast her gaze at him in disbelief. *How could anyone get used to all that weight hovering above them?*

Ahead, the sun flashed across the only structure that wasn't covered with rust or dirt. A collection of white silos was being fed by a series of pipes of varying sizes. To Jamie, it looked like a mechanical multi-legged crab that squatted in wait for a meal. In the center of the maze of pipes rose a thin white chimney. It stood tall against the landscape, but a fraction of the size of its larger partner, both in diameter and height. Pipes ran into and out of the plant from the main converter building.

There was a similar, yet newer structure with its own stack behind this one. Pipes ran into and out of it from the massive converter building, where the metals were heated to liquid to separate the different minerals.

"Hard to believe," Burgess said, pointing at the structure, "but that is part of the billion-dollar Clean AER Project. AER stands for

Atmospheric Emissions Reduction. We simply call it the acid plant. Basically, it captures about eighty-five percent of the sulfur emissions that would otherwise be released into the atmosphere. We can now collect and sell pollution for a profit."

Jamie nodded. "I read about it, but this is the first time I've actually seen it." She turned to face him. "It's nice to know the company is putting this technology in place to help the environment."

"Oh, yeah!" he snorted.

"You disagree?" Jamie said, surprised.

"Listen, what you need to understand is that this company only does what's good for its bottom line. Does the acid plant help the environment? Definitely, but government regulations were forcing Novo's hand, anyway. And it was only a matter of time before the government got tougher on polluters. This place was one of the worst in the country. This project put them way ahead of the government, and left them years ahead of any tougher regulations, while also making a great profit."

"Isn't that good business?"

"Sure, but they did it because they had to. Do your homework," he snapped abruptly, his eyes tightened in anger. "Check out their other operations worldwide. Take a look at their environmental records in undeveloped countries. And while you're at it, check out how they treat their employees in those places. Canadian labor laws are a colossal pain in the ass for this company, which is the main reason we're on strike. They think they can bully us. If this was South America, they'd send in strike breakers—or worse."

He slapped the steering wheel to emphasize his point, startling Jamie. *From zero to sixty in the blink of an eye.* She wet her lips nervously. His change in demeanor was scary as shit. She wondered how he could hold himself under wraps in public. That he was acting this way with a member of the press was the most shocking.

He seemed to sense her unease. "Sorry," he said, taking a deep breath. "These people bring out the worst in me. They throw Novo money around funding different charities around town, but no one sees what they are truly like."

He looked at her as he turned off the road beside the acid plant. "Listen," he said in a calmer voice. "If you want to write a fair representation of the issues, do some research about the Novo tailings pond that ruptured in Brazil last year. It killed hundreds of people. It dumped into a river, which is three hundred miles long and supplies drinking and irrigation water for most of the area and is now toxic with heavy metals. Novo refuses to accept responsibility for that—and also refuses to pay for the cleanup. What they've done here," he said, pointing out the front window at the gleaming structure, "wasn't because they believe in the environment. They did it to keep the government and environmentalist groups off their back. No other reason."

Jamie nodded. "I will research the event and the fallout, Mr. Burgess." Deep down, she wondered what he'd say or do if she refused. But to be fair, she had to look at both sides with an unbiased eye.

His familiar and *public* smile almost cut his face in two. "That's all I can ask."

He opened the car door and stepped out into the heat. Hesitating, to gather her thoughts, Jamie followed, suddenly glad that Loretta and a couple of security people were there. The shift in his personality had unsettled her.

Yellow police tape stretched around the entire plant. As they walked towards the structure, Jamie's eyes scanned for any obvious damage, but nothing caught her eye. Bright shiny metal reflected the sun's glare, heat waves hovering over the plant.

When they reached Loretta, she turned on her heel and strode towards the side of the first unit. Over her shoulder, she said, "According to the police, the explosive was set to cut the output pipe from the acid manufacturing plant to the storage facility. If we were in production, it would have pumped raw sulfuric acid over the grounds. Because of the strike, we had shut everything down; so other than the equipment, there is no risk to the environment or the city."

Jamie recalled an article she'd read about a sulfuric leak in the 1980s that allowed a cloud of gas to pass over the western part of the city. Many people rushed to the hospital with breathing problems. This was prior to the Novo buy-out of the original company. Thinking about that, she realized just how lucky the city had been.

When they moved around the corner of the building, blast damage was clearly evident. Pipes and containment vessels had been torn apart, razor-sharp metal bent away from the origin of the blast, the gleam of steel and aluminum dulled by blast residue from the explosive heat and energy. The single overhead pipe that came from the converter building was severed from its mooring, its tip dug into the ground, while the other end hung from the next raised support-column leading towards the smelter.

"As you can see," Loretta said. "The police identify this as the origin of the explosion. It is definitely a case of sabotage. The investigators are going over all of our CCTV recordings and hope to identify the culprits." She looked directly at Burgess as she spoke, but he refused to rise to the bait.

Jamie kept quiet, hoping that either would say something that might be recorded as part of her story. When neither did, she raised Lucas's Canon EOS toward the company's spokesperson for permission to photograph the scene. Loretta nodded.

She walked away from the structure so she could get as much of the building in her lens-viewer as possible. With the union leader and his opponent in the foreground, it gave scale to what she was looking at. Moving closer and feeling more comfortable with Lucas's camera, she photographed the immediate blast area and then zoomed in on the stressed and contorted metal that bent away in all directions.

Finally, she snapped a couple shots of the feed-pipe where it hung haphazardly. She walked further back, between the two acid plants, to gain a larger view of the collapsed pipe with the converter building in the background. Even using the camera's zoom, the image was too big for the lens-viewer to show its scale because of the height of the raised pipe and the structure behind it. Scooting backwards, her shoes raising a fine acrid-scented dust from the industrial soil, she positioned herself even farther back. In her lens, she could capture the pipe and the building with sky peeking overhead. The base of the enormous stack poked out of the top-left corner of the photo.

All the time she was photographing the damage, her mind whirled with questions she needed answers for. And all of it fell into the familiar *Who, What, When, Where, and Why* that they drilled into her at school.

Who had done this?
What was the purpose?
When would the police have a lead?
Where is this leading?

And the most critical question: *Why damage the equipment? It hurts both the company and the workers.*

Satisfied with her shots, she began walking back to the others, when her eye caught sight of a flash of white against the stained dirt. Bending down, she saw it was a paper lizard or origami gecko made from a book of matches. She stared at the beautifully rendered figure in surprise. It was the last thing she would ever expect to see in the middle of an industrial complex. She snapped a photo of the small artwork before the reporter in her picked it up to examine it, despite this being a crime-scene under investigation. The underside revealed a paper matchstick, the red igniter acting like a tongue for the tiny reptile. It was less than an inch long, and she marveled at the intricacy of the folds. That someone could create such a small figurine from a matchbook was amazing.

Where had it come from? One of the employees? It wasn't even dirty. No industrial dust marred its white surface. She thought about showing it to Loretta and Burgess—or the cops, but some instinct warned her not to. Carefully, she placed it in one of the free pockets of her kit bag.

Jamie walked back to the others. "Did the police give you any idea of how long their study of the camera system will take?" she asked, looking at Loretta.

"The figured they might have something within a day or two. We just released the files this morning. They're checking multiple days because they're not sure when the charges were planted." She folded her arms across her chest, the body language telling Jamie that the woman felt they were done, and she wanted to wrap up the interview.

"Have the police determined what kind of explosive was used? Is it something the company uses?" Jamie asked.

The arms unfolded and her eyes narrowed as she considered her words. "The police didn't want to commit without an analysis of the samples they captured as evidence. We have given them a list of all the explosives that we use throughout our local locations."

"Well, I hope they move their asses," Burgess said, his voice stern. "The longer there are questions of who did this and why, the more unnecessary speculations will move through the community. I don't think it will benefit either side, do you, Loretta?"

Jamie watched the tense standoff. It was short, but ended with a nod.

"Of course. We are all anxious for definitive answers. The culprit or culprits need to be identified and brought to justice."

The two glared at each other, each believing the other involved, neither willing to cross the line with an outright accusation.

"Thank you both!" Jamie said brightly, hoping to defuse the tension. It was obvious that neither was aware of who might be involved, but they each wore distrust on their sleeves.

There's a lot of history between these two. That's a story in itself.

Chapter 12

Back at the newsroom, Lucas reread his notes of the morning's events while he waited for Jamie. They could both pay a visit to the pimp Gabriel Kebede, in the hospital. Lucas had contacted Health Sciences North, or HSN in Sudbury, as most referred to it, Fox Lake's closest hospital, to confirm that the pimp was still a patient and to see if visitors were allowed.

Felix eyed him when he'd entered the newsroom, but hadn't approached. So far, it seemed the editor was watching how this new partnership would work out. The man was fair, and always allowed his people the opportunity to rise to a challenge. However, he would be quick to pull the rug out from under Lucas if he felt the arrangement wasn't working—or if Lucas abused the partnership.

Lucas's cell phone vibrated on his desk, dancing a tiny jig on the imitation wood. Glancing at caller identification, his adrenalin rose a notch as he hoped the caller had news. He swiped his finger across the screen.

"Kucher," he said.

"Hi Lucas, Christine. Look, I just got some news that you're going to want to follow up on. I got a phone call from the hospital. One of my girls was brought in a couple of nights ago and someone fucked her up, big time."

"Shit," he said, closing his eyes as the realization of what she was telling him hit home. He felt his face flush with anger.

"She was so bad off, that it took three days before they could identify her. When they realized who she was, police contacted me because I had been working with her for the past couple of years."

Lucas could hear pain in Christine's voice as she tried to keep it together. "She was trying so hard to make a break. You might remember her. She was one of the girls you featured a couple of years ago."

"What was her name?" Lucas asked, a sinking feeling in his gut.

"Amber Thibodeaux."

With his head tilted down and eyes closed, Lucas tried to picture the girl. It only took a minute and then his eyes snapped open with her image sharp in his mind.

"Tall and skinny? Usually wore a pink feather in her hair?"

"When you talked to her, yeah. She's filled out some since then and did away with the feather. I'm afraid her best efforts weren't enough. She's fallen further since your interview." Christine's voice held such sorrow that Lucas wondered if she was crying. How much further could a young First Nations girl have fallen? She had been only fifteen at the time and already hooked on prescription drugs.

"What else can you tell me? Was there a police report?"

"No. Not yet. I'll help her with that; but whoever did this to her has to *pay*, Lucas. We can't just ignore it or sweep it aside."

"I'll try my best to sort this out. For you—and for Amber."

"You might start with her pimp. Calls himself Gabriel. Gabriel Kebede. He's a Black guy. He has a place at the old International Hotel—"

"Hey! That's the pimp who was beaten, Christine. The one we came by this morning to ask you about."

Lucas drew a line connecting Amber's name to Gabriel's name on his notepad and marked it with a capitalized 'P' in a circle to show their relationship. It was another line of inquiry he and Jamie could take up with the pimp when they visited him.

There was a pause on the line before she said, "Serves the bastard right."

"He's in the hospital, too, so he can't be the one who hurt her. I think someone else got to her first."

"Well, he has a history of hurting his girls. Even if he didn't do it this time, he's guilty for the other times."

"I won't argue with you with that. But it means someone else hurt Amber, and that person is still out there."

"Could the attacker be the same person who went after Gabriel himself?" Christine wondered.

"Could very well be." He said, his mind whirling at the implication. *Why both? Drugs? Territory?*

"You said she had fallen. Was it drugs? Was she using or pushing?"

"Using, yes. I was waiting for a call that she overdosed on fentanyl," she admitted, but then scoffed. "Pushing—no one in their right mind would trust her with an ounce of dope. It'd be long gone before it reached its destination."

"How about another group muscling in?" he said, reaching for any clue.

"Nothing I've heard, but that means nothing." Sadness had crept back into her voice, but then Lucas realized it was mixed with tiredness. It troubled him that his energetic crusader sounded so beaten down.

"I might get more concrete answers this afternoon," Lucas told her, but worried he was giving hope for something he might not deliver.

"Lucas, please keep me in the loop."

"Guaranteed."

He said goodbye and disconnected as Jamie pushed through the door of the newsroom.

With his two star-journalists in the same room, Felix strode out of his office, eying both Jamie and Lucas.

"Tell me what you have," he said without preamble.

Lucas filled in his editor about the interviews with the jail guard, and with Christine from Second Chance. He then gave a condensed version of the canvassing he had done. He described the confrontation between the human trafficker and the two unknown women as the neighbor had told it.

"I've already checked, and Gabriel Kebede is on the sixth floor at HSN," Lucas said, then filled them in on Christine's phone call and the information about Amber.

"I'm guessing we can speak with both of them this afternoon."

Jamie nodded enthusiastically while Felix grunted agreement.

"Try to nail down the timeline," Felix advised. "It may be critical." He shook his head before adding, "I can't believe the police aren't all over this."

"According to Christine," Lucas said, "the hospital was only just able to identify Amber now that the worst of the swelling has subsided. Once Christine files a report, they'll be paying Amber a visit. Which means we can get her story first. It might be the pressure we need to ensure a solid follow-up."

Felix pointed at Lucas with his pen. "I know your opinion of police priorities on these types of crimes, Lucas; but please go through me before trying to bull your way through the cops. A little finesse with the right person might get a more positive outcome."

Lucas and Felix stared at each other, reading each other's sentiments: not hostile, but firm. Lucas gave his boss a curt nod in assurance. He would play ball, but both knew if it didn't get the results they hoped for, Lucas would do it his way.

To hell with political niceties.

Jamie's turn, and both men listened attentively as Jamie filled them in on her visit to the acid plant and then had Felix download the photos that showed the damage caused by the explosion.

Felix nodded at the news that the union leader had agreed to a one-on-one interview concerning the negotiations. But he frowned at Jamie's recollections of Burgess's outburst about Novo's alleged unsavory dealings.

This hadn't been the first time that rumors had risen about third-world labor issues and the company's strong-arm tactics. Environmental groups and non-governmental organizations, the NGOs, had reported Novo's ecological practices over the years. Reports worldwide painted a dark picture of the company, but no different from most of Novo's competitive mining conglomerates. But without real proof of wrongdoing, all were just rumors.

The tailing pond collapse in Brazil was major news last year, but was pushed off the grid by other stories. It was the nature of the news business. As much as the Fourth Estate tried to bring truth and honesty to the stories it produced, news services were still businesses, and big stories sold papers.

Felix advised his team. "Do a full background on the dam and have Burgess fill in the blanks. Sounds like he could shed more light on Novo's past safety and environmental practices outside of Canada."

"Last I heard," Felix said, "Novo fired a couple of executives in retaliation for the burst dam; but apparently these were mere buyouts with stock options, at least according to rumors."

"That's disgusting," Jamie said, her eyes moving from Felix to Lucas and back again.

"No proper punishment was ever meted out. It was just a public-relations show to appease the Brazilian people, but it fooled no one."

Lucas could feel anger rise in him.

Almost as if sensing it, Felix turned to him, once again pointing his pen. "Find me proof, Lucas. Number one rule. You know that. And you know I'm good to my word."

A concerned look from his new partner—and Felix's warning—calmed Lucas; and, with lips pulled tight, he nodded.

"It wouldn't hurt to do some in-depth research of the Brazil event and any other international issues. It'll add some substance that might get a rise out of Novo. If we're lucky, they might drop the nice-guy act and reveal a true piece of themselves."

Lucas's smile almost hurt his face.

Chapter 13

They drove to the hospital in Jamie's Jeep. They agreed with Felix about speaking with Amber first. If Christine forced the police to move on the young girl's case, they might find access to her closed to their own inquiry. The police never like it when media gets involved in an open case. And their news releases only give out sterile information that the police service feels will not harm the prosecution of the case. But by getting there ahead of the police, they might gain enough raw information to draw a clearer picture of the events leading up to Amber's assault. Of course, solving a crime before the police was every reporter's dream. It made up for years of "No comment!"

Having called ahead about the room numbers for their visits, they easily avoided the nursing stations. No sense getting into it with a highly protective head nurse who might find their presence detrimental to the wellbeing of their patients.

There were four patients to a room, but two of the women were gray-haired. One was fast asleep, the sheet barely rising and falling. The other nodded from behind a bundle of wool that she attacked with a pair of long, bamboo needles. The third bed had the sheets thrown back, but the patient was nowhere to be seen.

A curtain surrounded the farthest bed, the hiss from an oxygen machine muted.

"Amber?" Lucas called out softly. "Amber, It's Lucas Kucher, from the *Fox Lake Journal*. Christine sent me."

From behind the curtain came a mewing that caused Lucas and Jamie to exchange a glance. Hoping the noise was some kind of invitation, Lucas pushed the curtain aside and slowly eased around the fabric, with Jamie following right behind him.

He did not know what he expected, but the wholescale damage caught him completely by surprise. Angry lines of blood crisscrossed the dressing covering most of Amber's face, as if a mad scientist had dissected it. More cuts appeared on her arms and neck but seemed superficial and had scabbed over. The face's white gauze was stretched tight because of swelling that closed one eye completely, while leaving the other only partially shut. *The poor kid knows the damage that has been done to her.* Amber held the one arm not encased in plaster, across her face to shield her visitors from her shattered features. Her chest shook with sobs and the mewing grew.

As Jamie stood back, horrified, Lucas eased onto the side of the bed and took the girl's hand that emerged from the plaster carefully in his. It was cold to the touch. The girl's sobs grew, tears absorbed by the layer of bandages. He said nothing and allowed her the release she needed. Nothing he could say would ease this pain. Although he had interviewed her and written about the trauma she lived under, he didn't know the shattered young woman that lay helplessly in front of him. Feeling her pain, he tried to contain his growing anger at the animal who could inflict such savagery. *She's little more than a child.* But his anger wouldn't help Amber.

Jamie moved beside him, silent.

While Amber cried, Lucas's eyes swept the enclosed area of the hospital bed. Heavy curtains covered the window to cut the light to allow the patient to sleep. The entire area, and there was not much of it to speak of, was sterile. There were no 'Get Well' cards, no flowers. She had no one close enough to call her friend—and no family. He remembered from her interview that she had escaped a toxic home life, only to fall into a worse one on the streets.

The only people concerned for Amber's well-being were those like Christine, while others had their own problems to deal with.

And there were few enough of them.

When her crying was spent, and Amber's breathing calmed to a shallow double-huffing. Her arm came down, but she refused to lift her gaze to meet Lucas's eyes.

"Christine called me," he said. "She's coming up here later on to help you out but asked me to look in on you. This is my new partner, Jamie. You can trust her. Do you want to talk about what happened?"

She moved the cast and pulled her hand from Lucas's to reach with her free hand to the table angled across the bed. From it, she picked up a pad of paper and a pencil. Leaning the pad onto her other arm's cast, she painfully scribbled a message. While she worked, Lucas was shocked to notice that although the bandages left a hole where her mouth was located, only swollen flesh protruded. *She can't even talk.* He swung his eyes to Jamie, who had stepped to the other side of the bed. Her damp eyes expressed the same haunted feeling that filled him.

The girl turned the pad towards him, her good eye pleading.

"Will you stop him!" she had written.

"I'll do everything I can to find the man who did this and make sure he never gets the chance to hurt anyone else. I promise, Amber."

He leaned forward. "Was it Gabriel?"

She began to shake her head violently, but groaned in pain with the movement. Tearing the paper from the notepad, she attacked the clean sheet with her pencil.

Foreigner. Dragon tattoo on chest.

"How did he find you? On the street?"

Turning back to her pad, she didn't seem to register the growling buzz from Jamie's cell phone but wrote with a vengeance; almost stabbing the paper.

Lucas looked over at Jamie, who, after checking the caller ID, signified to him she had to take the call. Lucas didn't watch her leave but swung back in time to accept the next note from the Amber.

Darcy and Rosie.

Lucas gawked at her. "The pimps?"

Her bandaged head managed a firm nod.

The two were notorious street workers who were known for their violent past after they beat a couple of customers for trying to run out without paying. Because of their treatment by men since their teens, the two were self-described man-haters. Ironically, they began running their own string of prostitutes. Lucas had heard an earful about the pair from Christine, who became damned-near rabid when their names came up. That they forced young girls into the brutality of the pay-for-sex profession made little sense. Did they not understand how sick they had become to commit the same abuse that they'd suffered, on others?

"So, they set it up?"

Again, the girl nodded.

"I have to ask you, Amber. They didn't do this themselves, did they?"

She shook her head cautiously. Awkwardly digging through the pile of notes with her good hand, she thrust the first one back to Lucas.

Foreigner. Dragon tattoo on chest.

The curtain pulled back and Jamie put her head close to Lucas and whispered, "Got to go. There's been another explosion at Novo. I need the Jeep, so you might have to call Felix to arrange a ride. I'll text you." Without waiting for a reply, she turned and slipped past the curtain, leaving her stunned partner to deal with this story on his own.

It took a minute for Lucas to re-focus, his mind racing across the implications of another attack on the mining giant. *Was it domestic or international? How long before someone gets killed?* He shook his head and turned his attention back to the wounded girl.

"Sorry, my partner had to run for another story."

If the girl heard, she didn't acknowledge it. She was too busy scribbling the next message.

Soldier types. A bunch of them. Way out of town in the bush.

Soldier types? His mind went immediately to the explosion—now a second one. *Could the two incidents be related?*

"Could you find your way back to where they took you, Amber?" Lucas had to struggle to keep the excitement out of his voice.

The girl shook her head and bent to the notepad. *Took us there in a white cargo van—no windows.*

"Do you remember anything about the ride? Which way did they drive? How about the place they brought you to? Do you remember the house? Were there any outbuildings? Anything that you remember might help find this guy and stop him from doing this to some other girl."

Amber looked down at her hands and was quiet for enough time that Lucas feared she had fallen asleep. He felt a tinge of guilt at pushing the injured girl, knowing that she needed her rest to heal, but then she raised her head and started writing. He watched as she wrote carefully on the pad, unlike the earlier frantic scrawl. Lucas had no choice but to wait as she put her thoughts together. While he waited, he made his own notes.

When he looked up, she was still bent over her pad.

Christine's voice echoed through the ward. "Here's the room. Amber! No worries. Your favorite Street Lady is here to help you. Amber, I hope you're decent. I have two cops here who are going to catch the idiot who hurt you, or I'll run them out of town myself."

Lucas heard Amber chuckle at the cheerful arrival of a beloved street crusader. When Christine was in the house, everyone knew it. Even if you were both blind and deaf, the energy she gave off touched you—and everyone nearby, pulling each person into the center of the tempest. But Lucas also knew that the reference to the police was a warning.

Someone ripped aside the privacy curtain with dramatic flair. Christine stood wide eyed, nostrils flaring at the sight of the beaten sex-worker. Behind her, Lucas saw two uniformed police officers; and from the expressions on their faces, they didn't care for Christine's dramatics.

Unlike her garb this morning, Christine was decked out in a business suit that could have been cut out of a *Forbes Woman* magazine. It screamed, "Don't fuck with me!" and Christine commandeered the room.

But her shoulders slumped as she took in the obvious injuries of her young ward's body before she stiffened in anger. She whirled to the two lawmen.

"So, when this hospital reported these injuries, why wasn't a full investigation initiated?" The tone in her voice dripped with both incredulous and suppressed fury, causing the younger officer to lower his eyes.

The older of the two, hands clenched on his service belt, showed no expression. "As you have been told, Ms. Satori, our people did respond, but because the victim was unidentified and unconscious, we had to wait until we at least knew who she was. And we began a file the night they brought her in."

Lucas could tell he was a seasoned officer and would not be intimidated by the social worker. "Our officers have also canvassed the neighborhood where the victim was located and found nobody who knew or recognized her. And because of the neighborhood itself, it was obvious that someone had dumped her there. There also has been no missing-persons report matching her."

"That's good," she said, rounding on him. "Because Lucas here," indicating him, "works for the *Fox Lake Journal*, and he'll make sure your investigation is carried out properly."

Lucas bit back an angry retort. He didn't like being used, especially by someone he considered a friend. He understood Christine's frustrations with previous investigations or the lack thereof, but she was doing what Felix had warned him *not* to do. Luca caught the lawman's surprised expression before the officer got control of himself. The look turned into a flash of annoyance. Most wouldn't have noticed it at all, but Lucas was trained to pick up on little things.

Not much different from cops.

Glaring at Christine, he stood and handed a card to the senior officer. "Lucas Kucher. It would mean a lot of if you could keep me informed of any progress you make on this case, Officer ... Sullivan," he said, reading the name tag on the man's uniform. "I'll be happy to pass on anything I learn to you as well."

Taking the card, the officer pulled out a notebook and opened it, sliding the business card under the heavy elastic band that held the pages in place. He nodded. "Happy to help."

"Thank you," Lucas returned in a professional tone. He knew that any information shared would first be cleared and sanitized by the public relations division of the department first. There was never any clear give and take with the media and police. He turned to Amber. "I can come back once you're done with the officers."

She nodded tiredly and slipped him a wad of papers, her small, printed script covering each page.

"I think I'll go downstairs and visit our friend," he told her with a wink. A barely noticeable nod told him she understood.

Lucas moved towards the door of the ward. He could feel the officer's eyes on the sheaf of papers he held tight against his leg. He was posed to argue hard if the cop ordered him to hand over the papers before he could read what Amber had confided to him. But he made it out the door and escaped towards the elevators. He heard Christine begin to badger the officer again and guessed that she was running interference for him.

To play it safe, he veered around the bank of elevators and pushed through the door that indicated the stairs. Taking the stairs two at a time, he climbed to the next floor and waited at the exit door, listening for any pursuit. Hearing none, he took a moment to read what the young sex-worker had written.

What he read shocked him, but raised more questions than it answered. *What the hell was going on?*

Chapter 14

Jamie was glad she had offered to drive into Sudbury. It saved her from begging for Lucas's car, especially during what had been an upsetting interview. The severity of the young girl's injuries shocked her. Who could be that cruel? Even animals only killed to survive, either to eat or to protect their own. But this violence was something she had never confronted before, and it shook her. She had been so glad Lucas had the lead and could do the talking. All she could do was stare. She didn't trust her voice at all.

The empathy that Lucas expressed in his writing was also clear in the way he spoke with Amber. Although he'd stayed professional, she had heard the suppressed anger and sympathy in his voice as he tried to find out what had happened to the young girl. How he could push through that, especially having known the girl previously, was a skill she knew she would have to learn. She had wanted to take the girl in her arms and hold her like a scared child.

It wasn't a motherly instinct, she knew. It was even more basic than that—a connection from one human being to another. She wanted to give comfort and assurance that she would allow no one else to hurt the poor girl again—not that she could really promise that.

Jamie had to force her thoughts back to the news story she was now chasing. It seemed incredible that another attack against the mining giant had occurred barely an hour since she last walked the property. A sudden shudder racked her as she thought of being caught in an explosion. It might have happened while she'd been inspecting the original blast scene with Burgess and Loretta.

She shook her head. The complex was massive. The new explosion might have been in a different area altogether. She had to deal with facts, not imagination. But as she crested Tower Hill, her fear returned.

Far off, she could see a massive column of black smoke rising over the plant like a second smokestack. It rose straight as an arrow until the winds higher up tore the solid pillar askew, bending it over the city, leaving a trail of soot that muddied the sky.

The horizon was cut off as her car descended the steep hillside toward the smelter site.

At a traffic light, she tapped the steering wheel with impatience, pushing back an urge to jump the curb and pass the line of cars. The story was happening while she sat there, immobile in traffic.

The only blessing from her point of view was that news of the attack could not have spread yet, considering how traffic wasn't moving with any urgency. People were totally oblivious to the major catastrophe unfolding a half-dozen miles away.

It was surreal. *I must try to get this feeling into my story!*

As the last car turned, leaving her free to move forward, she took a shortcut through a residential area with less traffic and no traffic lights to contend with. From there, it would be a straight run to the North Shore complex and the Novo property.

With squealing tires and roaring engine, she spotted the rail-crossing that led to her destination. She gave the car its head, only to have to brake and veer to the curb. An ambulance chasing a fire pumper using the same shortcut came up behind her, sirens competing with an air horn as they demanded the right of way.

As the two massive vehicles shot past her, Jamie swung the wheel and stomped on the gas pedal to follow in their wake.

Ahead, the two emergency vehicles bounced across the rail crossing and swung westward towards the entrance to the complex.

Jamie took advantage of the forced stoppage of the traffic and sped after them, her bumper mere feet from theirs. If stopped, no police officer would accept the excuse that she was driving like a lunatic to chase a breaking story. Hell, Felix might fire her on the spot. That last thought sobered her, and she eased off the gas, allowing the two first responders to pull ahead. She was still over the speed limit, but not running blindly behind them.

Astonishingly, she beat all the odds and caught every green light until the city street turned onto the highway that led out of town. The straight stretch of pavement allowed her to push the Jeep to its max.

At the entrance to North Shore, traffic had bunched up again, this time with rubberneckers trying to glimpse what had attracted first responders. And when drivers saw smoke rising over the smelter, more vehicles pulled over haphazardly, causing more blockage and near-accidents. Indignant blasts of car horns competed with skidding tires.

Leaving their vehicles parked in the roadway, occupants threw open car doors to walk towards a vantage spot. Most had open-mouthed expressions and cellphones held at arm's-length. The obsessiveness of their attention reminded Jamie of a horde of walking dead.

Jamie drove between two pickup trucks and parked on the grass that surrounded a garden centered on an enormous sign: "Welcome to North Shore. Est. 1892."

Ignoring the sign, she grabbed her kit bag and joined the growing crowd, snapping a series of pictures with her phone. These she uploaded immediately to the *Journal*. It would give the paper first-hand photos and let Felix know she had arrived.

The scene before her held the crowd immobile with its immensity. She too was frozen, and for a moment could do nothing other than view the sight on the screen of her iPhone.

Central to the massive industrial complex was the converter aisle. She knew from a past tour of the mine complex with her high school years ago that it was where the ore was super-heated into molten metal to extract specific minerals from the base rock. Nickel, gold, copper, and other precious materials were worried loose from the crushed ores extracted from the area mines. The process was an alchemist's wet dream, as modern science separated the precious metals to leave only coarse, black slag, empty of all worth other than as fill. Yet the company even profited by selling this dross as backfill seen as preferable to more expensive gravel because it would allow water to run away from house foundations without the higher price. And the company had a hundred years of waste to sell!

Not a cent of profit was lost.

Jamie knew some steelworkers spent their careers sweeping up mineral dust from the smelting process, never going into a mine. Dust that itself was processed.

But now, half of the massive building's roof was swallowed in rolling fireballs, smothered in dense, black, billowing smoke. When the metals refinery originally had been built in the early twentieth century, no one had thought it a problem to use square timber for the roof. After all, the area was littered with old-growth forests. But years of being subjected to intense heat from the furnaces had dried the once sturdy material to nothing less than kindling.

How much precious metal in the form of dust rose over the smelter in that conflagration, to escape the company's clutches? She imagined the dust settling over the city, becoming one with the neighborhoods.

The base of the structure was a sea of emergency vehicles, their rotating red and white lights turning impotently. More and more trucks arrived, brought in from the further reaches of a municipal area that could have swallowed Toronto.

Two pumper trucks flung streams of water uselessly at the burning building. Too much was burning; so even though the trucks pumped out thousands of gallons of water, it did little to cool the massive structure's fire. Even fully extended, the hundred-foot ladders of the rescue trucks only reached the lower edges of the roof. Smaller water cannons reached ineffectively, barely dampening the base of the roof.

Jamie wished Lucas was with her for the better reach of his camera. Her photos were taken from too far, and even with the digital zoom, details of the struggle would, she knew would be blurred and barely distinguishable.

Felix must have come to the same conclusion after seeing her pictures, because her phone buzzed to alert her to watch for a camera crew he had just dispatched.

She acknowledged the text and then moved towards the picket line and the hastily erected wooden barriers. The camera crew would be a while as all traffic on the highway had come to a complete stop.

She aimed her phone to catch a shot of a small cluster of gawkers standing on top of a shipping container on a transport truck that had parked along the roadway.

If any vehicle hit their truck ... She shuddered and turned back to the smelter. *I have enough to report without worrying about something that might never happen. Still ...*

The front entrance to the mining company was a parking lot of emergency vehicles, mainly police and ambulances, as the fire apparatus surrounded the burning converter aisle. Between them, looking lost and lonely, were the strikers, although their attention was on the colossal inferno now consuming their jobs.

A uniformed police officer held up his hand as she approached, and she presented her press credentials.

Shaking his head with a bored expression, he said, "Sorry, Miss. This is private property, there's a fire, and unless I get a confirmation from Novo administration that you are allowed inside, this is as far as you go."

Her shoulders slumped, and she allowed her eyes to scan the crowd. She definitely wanted to record some reactions from the strikers. Across from the union's makeshift shelter, she spied several company security vehicles, the Novo logo pasted on the side panels. They were parked in a long line on the pavement's shoulder, keeping the blacktop free for responding emergency vehicles. Parked at the rear was a familiar silver BMW convertible.

Loretta leaned against the wheel-well, a phone glued to her ear. Even from this distance, Jamie could tell she was giving someone a full report on the situation in front of her. Her hands flew towards the burning building as if the caller could see what she was describing. The woman's eyes never left the developing disaster before her.

Jamie snapped a few more photos while she waited for the spokeswoman to complete her call. She made a snap decision, pulled out Loretta's business card, and sent the photos to the woman's cell phone. The action interrupted Loretta's dialog. She checked the text message and her head turned until she caught sight of Jamie, and then bent back over her phone. With a few more words, she ended her call and turned to the blockade. She walked to the hastily raised wooden barrier.

"Maybe you and I should just travel together," Loretta said to Jamie, sarcasm dripping from her smile.

"Was it only a couple of hours ago?"

The cop who had stopped Jamie had walked over and was taking in the conversation.

"It's fine, my dear," she told the officer. "She's with me."

The man said nothing and turned away as if he didn't give a damn either way.

To Jamie, Loretta said, "Thank you for interrupting. I was so wrapped up talking to the board members that I didn't even think to send them a picture. The picture you sent me showed them the scope of the damage instantly."

"Glad I could be of help," Jamie said.

Loretta spun on the spot and began striding towards her car. Jamie had to rush to keep up with the woman. "Listen," said Loretta, "I have to make a couple of calls; but if you are interested, I'm going to get closer to the fire. The board wants a more detailed briefing, and your photos would help, if your editor doesn't mind releasing a few."

"I'll clear it with him, but I can't see it as an issue, especially as you're allowing me access to the property." She pointed to the union members milling about. "I'll talk with the strikers while you make your phone calls."

Loretta nodded as she placed the phone to her ear. Jamie walked over to the cluster of men and women gawking at the seemingly useless efforts of the fire crews. The structure and the fire dwarfed the tiny streams of water, pointed almost vertically, that attempted to reach the seat of the fire. Sections of timber, most over a hundred years old, were falling inside the older building as the roof burned through. *I guess the abundance of wood seemed like a good idea at the time, but rebuilding this place won't be done with flammable materials.*

Jamie moved among the striking men and women, who, as she spoke to them, expressed a fear that this blow might cripple the mining giant. Would they have to cut their losses and move out of the country? To rebuild the furnaces under today's standards and costs would take an astronomical investment. To say nothing of the continuing supply-chain issues that still held the world captive, even after the recent pandemic.

In the meantime, a massive job loss would cripple both the union workers and the city's economy. The trickle-down effect would be felt right across the country.

There was a story a few years ago that she recalled. There was some speculation about shipping ore to Voisey's Bay, which had its own smelter. The article predicted the cost of moving ore from Ontario to Labrador would decimate the company's profit. It would also do nothing for the jobs here in Ontario.

"If they lose the converter building," one striker was asking his colleague, "do you think they'll build a smelter in Mexico? Wouldn't have to worry about the union or environmentalists,"

Jamie could hear the man's fear and could see his apprehension spread through the group.

Jamie began to record a video of the workers on her phone, going through the group, asking what everyone was feeling.

"What the hell do you think I'm feeling? That's my *living* going up in smoke! It's bad enough having to live on strike pay. How long are we going to wait to get back to work after this?"

"My old man worked here for forty years. I'm into my fifteenth year. I don't know nothing else but hard-rock mining."

"What will happen to the company? Will they sell, do you think? Rebuild? Or maybe just cut their losses?"

She could tell that no matter how much these workers bitched about the job and the company, they carried a tremendous sense of pride in what they did for a living.

For her, Jamie knew that for all the money in the world, she'd never be able to descend into the bowels of the earth to toil in Stygian blackness.

She walked back across the road after some last photos that seemed to catch some of the worry and desperation these people were feeling. Loretta was still on the phone, her back to Jamie. It was obvious she was in a heated conversation with someone. One hand was stiffly at her ear, the other tight around her chest. She looked ready to take on the world.

"Julio Silva says that there's been a run on the company's shares. The entire board is shitting themselves. They're scared. They're sure Fischer is behind all this. It's definitely his MO to cripple a company before snatching it up once the market—." With no warning, as if she had a sixth sense and knew someone was within earshot, her tone changed, and her posture straightened. "... So, we hope you would drop anything you're currently working on and get up here ASAP. The sooner we start the cleanup, the sooner we can assess the damage to the furnaces. I need you here to go in the minute the fire department leaves the scene."

Jamie was only half a car's length from the woman. She turned her back to Loretta and began uploading her photos to the cloud service. She tried to look as if she had not been eavesdropping and was uninterested in the one-sided conversation.

On her phone, she watched the bar indicating upload progress scroll slowly across the screen. She jumped as a hand clamped down on her shoulder.

"Sorry," Loretta said, surprised at Jamie's edginess. "I didn't mean to startle you."

"Didn't hear you approach," she said with a laugh, but felt her cheeks heat. "I was uploading my photographs to the paper." She laughed again. "Now you know why I steer away from slasher movies."

Loretta gave her a tight smile, as if the act hadn't taken her in. "Are you ready?"

They climbed into Loretta's BMW, and neither woman bothered with seatbelts. They weren't going far. As the sleek convertible sped up, there was an icy atmosphere in the vehicle that had nothing to do with the high-speed fan pumping A/C through the car.

Might as well get it out into the open. "So, who is Fischer, and is he behind the explosion yesterday—and this?" Jamie asked, pointing at the raging inferno.

Loretta's head turned to her, and the woman's eyes drilled into Jamie's. She held the glare before returning her gaze to the windshield. She laughed loudly.

"And that's what I like about you," Loretta said. "You don't miss a thing and you're not afraid to ask tough questions." She threw a smile at Jamie. "You remind me a lot of me when I was your age. Fearless."

Her eyes went back to the road as she maneuvered around a group of security vehicles parked on the side of the road.

When Jamie looked over, the spokeswoman was more composed, but her brows were tight as her mind turned things over. Finally, she turned back to Jamie.

"Off the record?"

Chapter 15

Folding the batch of Amber's notes, Lucas carefully inserted them into a concealed pocket that he'd added to the rear of his media windbreaker. The *Journal's* logo on the back of the nylon garment camouflaged the slim pouch in the thin material. He rarely used it, except to carry sensitive material that might be confiscated. Usually, it was a memory stick or flash drive with sensational photos or governmental documents leaked by a bitter or outraged employee. The pack of Amber's notes were bulkier, and he couldn't afford to lose her statement before Felix saw it. If he were in a more secure place than a stairwell, he could have photographed each of the pages and uploaded them to the paper's cloud service. But he couldn't take the risk that the police officer might demand to see them.

Not that the cop had any legal right to them, but the time taken to deal with the seizure through the courts could effectively render the information useless.

Amber's notes were vague and incomplete. He would definitely have to follow up to draw out the details he'd need to paint a complete picture. But the central facts that flowed through the quickly written pages scared the hell out of him.

He needed time. Both with the girl, and the story she outlined.

Descending to the floor where the pimp was recuperating, Lucas eased open the stairwell door and allowed himself a quick glance down the hallway. Seeing no police, he pushed through and walked unhurriedly to the far end, his eyes tracking room numbers.

He found the sex-handler strung to the bed. Literally.

Both of the man's legs hung over the bed, as did one arm. The doctors had skewered his three appendages with a variety of gold or brass pins that protruded on either side of his knees and one ankle. The arm boasted two rows of three pins, holding his forearm together. Dried blood stained the gauze covering the wounded areas.

Damn, hurts just looking at it!

When he caught sight of what they'd left of the pimp's face, he had to brace himself not to gasp out loud. Swollen, the skin on the ebony face was fading from a dark purplish black and blue to a sickly pale yellow that reminded Lucas of dead fish that had sat out too long in the sun.

Two dark pig-eyes glared at him through eye sockets that were still swollen to slits.

"Who the fuck are you?" growled the immobilized flesh peddler.

His voice garbled and wet, Lucas realized the man's jaw was wired shut.

"Lucas Kucher. *Fox Lake Journal.*"

"Fuck off!" said the guy, trying a tough, I'm-going-to-kick-your-ass-if-you-don't-listen-to-me routine, even while hanging suspended like a rotisserie chicken over a bed of coals.

Lucas pulled a chair beside the bed and sat as if he had not heard. He pulled out his notepad and filled in the date and location of the interview. With no expression on his face, he stared at the sorry-looking criminal, letting tension build.

When Lucas finally spoke, he said, "I have an eyewitness that says Darcy and Rose were the ones who put the boots to you. You know they've taken over your girls and are moving on your area, right?"

The man's face tightened as his swollen eyes went wide with rage. But he was impotent from the very wounds those two particular women had inflicted on him.

"The reason I'm here is that one of your girls, Amber, was set up with a client by Darcy and Rose. The guy did some real damage to her. I'm hoping you might know something about that. You get any inquiries before your minor mishap?"

"Why should I give a damn?"

"Well, I can write this story a couple of ways. For example, I could talk about how you got beat up by a pair of girls. As funny as the story might sound, others might see it as a sign of weakness. Others might figure that while you're out of commission, your territory is open-season for new operators. Only a couple of women to deal with. Know what I mean?"

The man's legs jerked in their straps and swung painfully, the man's anger turning to pain instantly, his eyes squeezed tight from the agony.

Lucas ignored his discomfort. "On the other hand, if I get the information I think is out there, that story would be much more important, and your *accident* is not newsworthy.

"And before you ask, I'm going to be talking to Darcy and Rose next, so I would be more inclined to write a story that would be beneficial to whoever helped me out the most."

The sharp inhalations and exhalations of the pimp's breath sounded like the breathing of an athlete running a race. But in this case, it was the only expression of anger he could display that would not cause him more pain. *I'd hate being around if he wasn't hog-tied.*

His breathing slowed as he considered Lucas's offer. The dark eyes flicked towards Lucas when he came to a decision. He lifted his head in a quick jerk for Lucas to continue.

"Was there anyone looking to hire out a bunch of your girls? Not one or two, but *all* the girls you run?"

The eyes bored into his, but eventually Gabriel nodded. "Two guys in a van. Wanted ten to twelve girls. Flashed a wad of bills, but I don't have that many girls, y'know?"

Lucas had to lean forward to make out what the pimp was saying. Between a heavy gangsta accent and words slurred by the jaw being wired, it came out a garbled mess.

"Any idea why they needed so many girls? Isn't that unusual?"

"Maybe they was having a party. Who gives a shit? They pay, they play."

A thought occurred to Lucas. "Was that why Darcy and her sidekick went after you? To add your girls to theirs?"

"That'd be my guess. But they'd gotta know I'd be back in their business."

"From the sight of you, Gabriel, I don't think they'd expect you to be *coming* back." The man stared at him as if he hadn't considered just how badly off he was.

"Getting back to the men in the van. Anything you can tell me about them?"

"Big. Both of them was huge. Only the driver talked. The other guy just listened. But he was in charge. No doubt about it. Big ugly son-of-a-bitch. Big scar on his face as if someone had shot him point-blank."

"Seen either of them before?"

"No," he said, shaking his head. "Oh, and the dude talked funny—like maybe he's Russian or something. Maybe he didn't grow up speaking English."

Lucas kept his expression neutral but made a note about the accent. It seemed to corroborate what Amber said—wrote, that is. He tried another question.

"Any other identifying features?"

"The driver had some ink on his arm, a skull with sharp teeth. Kinda like what a dead vampire would look. Didn't see any on the other guy."

"Anything else you can remember?"

He shook his head, then winced at the pain.

Lucas pulled out a business card. "Drop me a line if you think of anything else." He dropped the card on the serving table that stood beside the bed.

"Why you interested in these guys?"

"Because they cut Amber up pretty bad and dumped her like yesterday's trash. I'd like to see them pay."

The pimp stared at him in disbelief and, for a second, Lucas thought he might have seen regret in his expression. But the man's features hardened again before he shrugged. *She's only a commodity to buy and sell. To this asshole, she's not even human.*

Lucas left before he did something he might regret later. He didn't think there'd be any repercussions, but he left, just to play it safe.

Chapter 16

Loretta and Jamie sat against the hood of the BMW watching the fire service tackling the massive roof fire. From their position, it looked like the fire was finally being contained on the south side of the roof. The shrill whine of chainsaws reached them, and Jamie pointed at a line of firefighters cutting into the ancient wooden roof. Three groups of two cut parallel lines down the roof's slope ahead of the creeping fire. The only blessing was that the wind was driving the smoke and flames away from the crews and the unburned section. As the cut lines progressed down the slope, other men began ripping at the roofing material and planks to form a trench in the roof.

"A fire-break," Loretta muttered almost to herself and nodded her appreciation of the tactic. "With luck," she said to Jamie, "that might save the rest of the roof. Maybe we'll still be able to use one furnace."

Jamie waited patiently, knowing there was no pushing Novo's spokesperson. If the woman wanted to talk, Jamie would be happy to listen and hopefully gain some insight into the events over the past two days. *Damn, it's hard.* The last thing she wanted to do was spook the woman. It was obvious Loretta had something on her mind, but sharing it had to be on her own terms.

Loretta finally spoke and said, "You must give me your word that you will not mention or even imply my name or position in anything you write. There can be no reference to my telling you anything."

"I wouldn't do anything that might endanger your job," Jamie promised, noting apprehension and paleness in the woman's face.

Loretta stared at Jamie with an expression that suggested there were much worse consequences than losing her job, and Jamie felt her stomach drop.

Loretta turned back to the fire. "Novo is under attack." She made the announcement with no more emotion than a doctor handing out a poor diagnosis.

"By whom?" Jamie said. Her surprise immediately gave way to anger. "You're not going to try to feed me some line about the union being behind this. I'm new to this job, but I'm no idiot."

But Loretta was shaking her head. "No, no. Mike Burgess and his merry men might be a royal pain-in-the-ass, but this is way beyond their reach. Not that there haven't been violent protests and attacks during past strikes. But neither the company nor the union gain by destroying part of the plant."

Loretta turned back to look at Jamie. "Have you heard of Fodineum?"

Jamie shook her head.

"I'm not surprised. They have no holdings in North America but operate in third-world countries. Over the past couple of decades, they've taken over smaller operations that larger corporations like Novo ignore. But collectively and quietly, they've become huge. Felipe Vautour is the company's front man, but he takes his orders from higher up. He has a private army, made up of ex-soldiers from several international conflicts. From Indonesia to Africa, they've grown their assets to rival some of their larger competitors. They've infiltrated South America in both Peru and Brazil in the past year."

"Where are they based?"

Loretta paused as if summoning the will to continue. She looked at the billowing smoke rising over the converter aisle.

"China."

Jamie stared at the spokeswoman in shock. "You think *China* is behind the attacks? I know they're aggressive, but this," she pointed at the inferno, "surely would be an act of terror, if not war."

Loretta nodded.

"It's no secret that China has been making record purchases of iron and copper ore. Their economy has grown to where they can't keep up with its demand for resources. Most of Novo's profit margin is reliant on that demand. But now, Beijing has turned to taking what they can't purchase—and they are playing a long game. They've become capitalists in every way but at home. And they play by their own rules."

"But *this* ..."

"I suggest you do some research, Jamie. This kind of attack might shock us in the West, but in Africa and other areas of the world, this is standard operating procedure. What they can't buy, they take."

Loretta pushed away from the BMW hood and turned to Jamie.

"Have you heard of the Belt and Road Initiative, or just BRI?"

Jamie shook her head.

"China has been financing countries worldwide. New or improved roads in Africa, infrastructure in Sri Lanka and Pakistan. There are all kinds of papers and articles on the internet about it. Long story short, they are dumping tons of money into third-world countries that will never have a hope in hell of paying off the loans. Of course, when they do default, China is more than willing to refinance, but with strings attached."

"Like what?"

"Well, that depends on what China needs and what the specific country has to offer. In Sri Lanka, the Chinese loaned money to build a massive international seaport that moves products and resources worldwide. When the loan was not paid, a new deal was penned, and China took possession of the entire port for a ninety-nine-year lease."

"How did that not make international news?"

"It's not like the government in Sri Lanka is going to advertise that they were beholden to China."

Jamie suddenly felt like she was in way over her head. This was all new to her, and it had moved well beyond an explosion at the smelter.

Not that it would stop her. This was huge, and she was going to run it for all it's worth.

"And get this, all the projects that are being built are done with Chinese labor and expertise. Locals need not apply, so there is little incentive to the local economy." Novo's public-relations woman let out a harsh laugh that startled Jamie. "You think Novo's environmental record is poor? The companies that do China's bidding opened over three hundred coal mines in countries like Turkey, Vietnam, Indonesia, Bangladesh, Egypt, and the Philippines in the last few years. All the while, the Chinese government boasted that they were going green in China by converting from coal to gas—for the public image.

"Half the rag-tag rebels and dictators in Africa are armed with Chinese weaponry. They arm both sides so they can use one against the other to ensure they get exactly what they want."

"Okay," Jamie said. "If what you're telling me is true and China is taking over the world through debt consolidation, why would they even bother to attack Novo?"

Loretta crouched down on her haunches and grabbed a handful of bits of slag and absently threw them one at a time at a traffic sign, the metal vibrating loudly.

"It's because China needs more basic resources, particularly iron and copper. They want in on the EV battery game. For years they've screamed that the world's biggest suppliers, Novo among them, have been inflating the prices because of China's demands." She looked up. "They're not wrong."

"Supply and demand?"

"Right. Now what would happen if China, through Fodineum, could gain ownership of one of the larger mining companies?"

"They'd have some say in the price."

Loretta nodded. "With the strike and now these recent attacks, our stocks have taken a tumble. Keep an eye on Novo's stock after today. The price is dropping because investors are scared and are selling short. We're seeing any loose shares being gobbled up by smaller entities at a reduced price. More than a few we've identified as subsidiaries of Fodineum."

"So why hasn't Novo just gone to the authorities? I would think that Canada and its allies could put some pretty good pressure on China, especially if these attacks can be linked back to them."

"For two reasons. First, we've seen this behavior in past Fodineum acquisitions where the Belt and Roads strategy were unsuccessful. But we've only seen the results, not the actual perpetrators. Novo is not an intelligence agency. We have people on the ground; but other than rumors, we've got no proof."

Loretta's gaze went back to the converter aisle, where the firefighters had cut a good section of roof to form a fire-stop trench. They were directing their fire streams on the trench to keep the fire from jumping the gap.

"And secondly ..." she said, and Jamie could sense the hesitation, or was it fear of admitting the rest?

"Novo is guilty of the same kind of heavy-handed tactics." Jamie said out loud as the thought came to her.

Loretta only nodded without looking back.

Both were silent for a while as the information settled. The only sounds were the low rumble of the fire pumps in the distance and the garbled transmissions from the truck speakers.

"It's why I need you to keep my identity anonymous. I'm just a talking head. The actions of these companies towards people in third world countries and locals are unacceptable to me. It's one thing to bribe corrupt government officials. That's the price of doing business in that part of the world, but this ..."

"So," Janice said, "Everything Mike Burgess said earlier was spot-on." It was a statement.

Loretta nodded, and a tear slid down her cheek unnoticed, like a lost memory.

Or was it lost?

"Mike has been crying foul ever since Novo bought the company. He has made it his life's mission to bring their business practices to light. Problem is," she wiped at her eyes, "he's been bad-mouthing the company for so long, no one listens anymore. Every time he goes on a rant, the company shells out money to the local food bank or hospital. Their donations drown out the truth."

In the silence that followed, Jamie's mind raced over all she had heard. The fundamental problem was that she now had to prove what she had been told before she could go public with it. And do it in a way that protected Loretta. She needed to talk with Uncle Felix. He'd be able to guide her.

And Lucas.

She suddenly could not wait to share this information with him. She was sure he'd give her valuable advice as well. But it was more than that.

She loved how confident he was. His passion for truth and for justice for those forgotten by society was contagious. She was certain he'd want to hunt down the international corporate thieves and help those hurt by their greed and total disregard for common decency. This had become so much bigger than an individual or company.

This foreshadowed a fundamental change in international relationships.

"We used to be a thing, you know?" Loretta said in a whisper, breaking into Jamie's thoughts. She looked up.

"What?"

"Mike. Mike Burgess and me. We used to be together. We had a house and both of us were part of the union."

"What happened?"

"The company offered me a manager's position. I've worked hard to get where I am today, and it hasn't been easy. But when I made the switch, I didn't know it then, but it was the beginning of the end. We were on opposite sides of an ever-growing chasm."

Loretta looked at Jamie, confidence and energy drained from her face.

"Be careful what you wish for ..."

Thank God, I would never have to deal with that kind of choice. With Jamie's job, just facts were important. Felix, Lucas and the slimmed-down staff of other reporters all just strove to find the truth. Politics be damned.

LORETTA EASED HER VEHICLE behind a row of company trucks set back and out of the way of the firefighting efforts. Before leaving the car, she said, "Stay here while I try to get an update." She left the car running and the air conditioning on high, for Jamie's sake. She clamped a white hard hat over her dark hair and marched, all business, to an island of white hardhats.

Feeling useless, Jamie tried to capture the closer images of the gigantic roof fire, but the dust on the car's windshield interfered with a clear picture. Getting out of the BMW, she aimed her smartphone and captured a number of shots that caught the immensity of the blaze.

She noticed a cluster of activity near the back of the last fire truck; and, after checking to see that Loretta was still occupied, headed towards the trucks.

As she closed on the scene, she saw that an area in between the trucks had been covered with a couple of vinyl tarps to create a shaded area for the firefighters. A crew crouched or slumped in the dirt having shed their heavy turnout coats; navy blue t-shirts darkened with sweat clung to them like second skins.

Two Novo vans filled with cases of bottled water were being unloaded into ice-filled coolers for the rescuers. A pair of men handed out bottles to the worn-out men and women.

After a few photos of the resting rescuers, Jamie approached and introduced herself, flashing her credentials. Wordlessly, one man pointed to a fire officer who stood in front of a folding table and a large command board.

"I don't know how you got this far, lady, but I can't have you getting any closer. If that thing comes down, we're going to need everyone out of the collapse zone," said the officer.

Jamie could see by his pointed hand how all the fire apparatus was positioned to one side of the burning converter aisle. She would never have noticed it otherwise.

"I won't get any closer. Promise."

He grinned appreciation.

"Any idea how the fire started?" she asked.

"You've got to wait for the police for that. There'll be a press conference later today. We've handed the investigation over to them and the OFM—the office of the fire marshal," he said without looking at her.

Although she heard him, what she saw over his shoulder had caught her attention.

Only sixty feet away, she spied standard yellow police ribbon to ward off the curious. It was off to one side, nowhere near the collapse zone he had warned her away from.

"Thank you. I'll be at the press conference. Good luck to you and your crews."

He had turned to do something else as she side-stepped between two of the Novo vans and approached the barrier tape, which formed a rough rectangle. Checking to see that no one was watching, she moved closer.

Two police officers stood on the other side of the protected area, but both had their backs to her as they watched the drama playing out on the converter aisle.

On the ground within the closed-off area were several large canvas tarps and several rolls of rope. The folded material seemed to be wet, but she couldn't fathom why they'd have to be guarded until the breeze shifted and brought a familiar scent to her.

Gasoline.

The fumes coming off the canvas were strong enough to cause her eyes to burn. But she forgot the discomfort as she saw what lay beyond the pile of tarps.

Covered in a white sheet, the kind used by the hospital or paramedics, was what could only be a body. Bright red had bled through the sheet's fabric.

Someone had died in this attack!

Chapter 17

Hoping the police had finished interviewing Amber, Lucas visited Amber's room, only to find the girl asleep. Rather than wake her, Lucas left the hospital, having seen no sign of either Christine or the police. He was thankful Felix had made arrangements to have his car dropped off after Jamie had left. He made a beeline to Fox Lake and the paper's office, crossing the John Creek that promised speckled trout to outdoorsmen. The openness of the main road allowed Lucas to catch sight of a large plume of dirty smoke rising from the west and dragging low across the city.

Turning on his car radio, an all-news channel confirmed where Jamie had been called to. He hoped she was safe as he shot another look at the smoke column and thought of her at risk. Although they'd worked in the same office for a while, they had really only just met. His concern felt ridiculous. *I must be tired.* From what he had learned so far with his dealings with her, she was earnest in her desire to learn the trade and was obviously dedicated. He liked the fact that she felt confident enough to look him in the eye when she spoke and wasn't afraid to defend her ideas. Today, it seemed that younger people *didn't* look you in the eye, and fewer still seemed able to hold a conversation. Of course, he reminded himself, she wasn't all that young, and the job demanded conversation.

There was no denying he found her attractive. *Especially those eyes.* He'd have to be a blind hermit locked away in a dark cave not to recognize a beautiful woman. But he especially liked the way she held herself. She was strong and self-reliant, and those were traits that he found especially attractive. He didn't know her well enough, but he didn't think she was the type to take and post selfies of herself continuously. She didn't seem to need the world's opinion of herself. She seemed to know what she was capable of and didn't seem to give a damn who liked it or not.

He appreciated that attitude.

At the entrance to the newsroom, he stopped, remembering the bustling activity that was part of his own early days as a reporter. Almost every computer terminal had been occupied. The volume of different conversations was enough to wake the dead. People rushed between the desks while others held phones to their ears trying to hear over the roar. Now, the room was almost deserted.

Felix waved at him from his office door. Lucas moved between empty desks to reach his boss. Ducking gratefully into the office, he didn't bother closing the glass door that once cut the noise to a dull hum. Lucas and his boss stood watching the empty newsroom for a moment before Lucas broke the spell.

"Miss the old days."

The older man nodded. "I miss the excitement, but I don't miss the noise."

Lucas laughed. "Yeah, but years ago, we'd hit every concert that came to town and stand next to the amplifiers. Today, we download the same music but listen at a fraction of the volume. Well, except for 'We will Rock You' by Freddy Mercury and the boys. You just have to crank *that* up!"

Felix laughed and waved him to a seat. "What did you find out?"

"Read Amber's notes," Lucas said, handing Felix the notes he'd taken from his secret pocket. "She mentioned these guys looked military and that the others at the farmhouse openly carried weapons."

Felix bent over the pages that Amber had written and read through them twice, his eyes narrowing and widening at different sections. Finally, he pushed the loose papers into a neat pile and sat mulling over what he had read.

Lucas had no choice but to sit there with his mouth shut while his boss absorbed the incredible statements.

The older man pushed the papers back towards Lucas. "That's disturbing, to say the least. And I'm not talking about what that poor girl went through. This place sounds like an armed camp. That they carried their weapons in the open definitely sounds like something illicit, but that she saw no uniforms is equally troubling." He curled his fingers around his chin, his eyes on the papers, before looking at Lucas. "The police took her statement, but you don't know if she shared the same information?"

"I'll let you deal with the police, Felix. I know it might be far-fetched ... but what if these Russians or whatever they are—Gabriel thought they might be military—what if they had something to do with the explosion and fire at the Novo property?"

Felix shook his head. "I think you might be right. There's not a lot to link them to what's happening at Novo, but it's all a little too coincidental, isn't it. This has to go to the police. If Amber told them the same thing, then there's no harm done. But if she didn't ... the last thing we want is for a cop to get killed because we sat on a story." He stared at Lucas. "On the other hand, if this is a Canadian anti-terrorist team that brought in some local talent, you might have a very different story to write."

"Anti-terrorist—?"

"We know that CSIS, our own Canadian CIA, is part of the investigation at the plant. If they think for a minute that the incident at Novo is a terrorist attack, I don't think it's that far-fetched that they'd have resources close by. This is Canada." And with a semi-grin, he added, "Canadian criminals would never walk around with weapons in sight. This sounds military to me."

Lucas snorted. "But this was a week before anything happened at Novo. I could understand if they moved into the area after today's incident. But any earlier would mean they're not our people, or that someone up the food chain hasn't clued the local cops to what might really be happening at the smelter." He shook his head. "This feels totally wrong, Felix. Like you said, this is Canada. With our gun laws, the idea of an armed camp is totally off the wall."

"Okay," Felix said, sitting up in his chair, back in charge. "We've worked together too long for me to ignore your instincts. What else?"

Lucas explained what he had learned from both Amber and Gabriel.

"I went back to Amber to go over some details that the police visit interrupted, but she was out of it when I got to her room. I'll try again tomorrow."

"And the pimp?"

"Well, we know that the two who put him in the hospital were the two female sex-traders, Darcy and Rosie. And that it was to fill an order for a bunch of girls to service the two strange men in the van.

"What do we know about them?"

"Two white males, both huge. One with a tattoo of a vampire skull on his arm. The other, 'a scary-looking dude.' He said that the guy doing the talking had a heavy accent, maybe Russian or eastern Europe. I'm hoping I can get more from Darcy and her shadow. They are the ones who ended up filling the order."

Felix nodded, deep in thought. After a moment, the editor looked up.

"Follow up with those two, but be careful. If word gets back to these guys that you're on their trail, there's no telling what they might do. From what happened to Amber, we know at least one of them is unhinged."

Lucas shrugged and smiled. "People on the street know better than to go after a reporter. It only brings more attention to them. Al Capone warned them a century ago."

Felix didn't return the smile. He stared hard at Lucas. "These guys aren't Italian. There are enough true stories about Russian mobsters and their violence. And if the pimp is right about the accent, these guys sound Russian."

Lucas almost dismissed the warning, but an image of Amber's wounds flashed before him. His boss might be right.

"Check out the two tough women and get back to me," Felix said. "In the meantime, I'll set up a meeting with the police chief. You find anything—I don't care how minute, call me."

The two men stared at each other for a second before Lucas nodded.

Lucas left the office, grateful he worked for someone like Felix. The man trusted his people and let them run with their ideas, as long as the facts bore scrutiny. The old newspaperman didn't mince words and forced people to meet his high standards, but he had never tried to micro-manage any of Lucas's stories.

That relationship had strengthened Lucas's work, both as an investigator and as a writer.

Before he left the newsroom, he took photos of Amber's notes—the originals he would leave with Felix. He added his own notes for both interviews to his online folder. This way, if anything happened to him, it was all safely recorded and could not be lost. For added insurance, he emailed a copy of everything to his home computer, which was backed up every night to a cloud service different from the newspaper's. He had learned the hard way to protect his work in different, redundant ways. Between computer crashes and ransomware viruses, you could never be too safe.

Grabbing his windbreaker, he headed for the door. It was time to talk with Darcy and Rosie. He felt the acid from his last coffee rise and burn his throat. Any confrontation with Rosie was like walking in a minefield.

Chapter 18

Lucas drove slowly through the older neighborhood. Newly renovated homes stood out among older, dilapidated houses and rentals, squeezed tightly between the rail line and steep mountain cliffs that backed the homes.

Denver street was the transition between the Terrace and Maleberry neighborhoods. The major problem, other than its age, was the high volume of cheap rentals in the area, which brought with them the desperate—but also the most depraved.

To renew the area would take many agencies and government initiatives, that is, if they could orchestrate the political will to work together for a change. Most rebuilds came because of the many fires attributed to careless smoking, cooking and drunkenness. The old, dry, wooden structures, insulated with wood chips or newsprint instead of proper insulation, did not help.

Police, ambulance, and fire services were regular visitors to the area.

As was he, Lucas reminded himself. A lot of stories came from this street.

Halfway to the corner, Lucas pulled his car to the curb and shut off the engine. He had an unobstructed view of the street. Yet he hoped he was far enough from it not to be spotted.

Even in mid-day, a girl stood on either side of the street, watching for clients. On the closest corner, there was a confectionery that did brisk business because of its location between two neighborhoods. A side door to the store allowed Johns to pay for a different kind of confectionery—a quick sexual release without the cops witnessing the exchange of cash. They could make arrangements without approaching either of the girls.

Lucas knew the door led to an apartment above the store that housed Darcy and Rosie. They watched their girls from an upstairs window and were quick to charge out to deal with anyone hassling the merchandise.

He'd prefer talking with Darcy alone, but the two women were never apart. Not only business partners, the two were lovers. Of the two, Darcy was the more intelligent and approachable. Rosie, Lucas knew from experience, hated men, especially cops and journalists. Lucas in particular. With an almost legendary violent side, the woman could turn in a heartbeat. Her preferred tools of persuasion were either a butterfly knife or a baseball bat that she carried in the open. She had long ago begun wearing a Blue Jays jersey to serve as an excuse for carrying the bat, if only for the benefit of the police.

It fooled no one.

Lucas had filed a story about the two women a couple of years ago. To Darcy, it meant nothing. But to Rosie, it was as if he had physically attacked her. On more than one occasion since that story, the woman had tried to take his head off with that bat of hers.

Taking a deep breath to reinforce his resolve, Lucas left the security of his car and approached the corner on foot. The last thing he wanted was to give Rosie an easy target to demonstrate her disdain on his old Honda. His car wasn't much, but it was all he had.

From the upstairs window, he heard a female's voice hiss a curse and knew he'd been spotted. A minute later, the screen door beside the storefront burst open and a hundred and eighty pounds of man-hating meanness hurled herself at Lucas.

He raised his hands to show he was unarmed, but that didn't slow the she-devil in the least. Her fist bowled him over, and felt the tear of skin as his hands stopped him from doing a face-plant on the sidewalk. He rolled instinctively, and Rosie's foot carried through where his stomach had just been. With nothing to hit, her foot flew by, momentum causing her to fall, her head slamming into the unforgiving concrete with a thud.

Lucas scrambled to his feet, only to find his assailant rolling from side to side, her hands cradling her head.

"I'm going to fucking kill you, Kucher!" groaned the enforcer.

Before he could answer, another woman pushed through the screen door. Although not as large as Rosie, Darcy was not what anyone would describe as petite. At five foot eight inches, rolls at her waist did nothing to distract from her large bosom held haphazardly in a black 'Metallica' muscle-shirt. Her skull was shaved tight on one side, while on the other side, her hair hung to her shoulder in a bright green fountain. A sleeve of mismatched ink covered her right arm.

"Lucas, what in hell did you do to her?" Darcy asked, her voice a mixture of surprise and anger.

"Nothing. She came at me," he said, indicating his bleeding palm. "That, she did to herself."

Shaking her head, she bent down to help her partner to her feet. Over her shoulder, she asked, "What do you want, Lucas?"

"I've come to talk to you. It's about Amber." The woman threw him an incredulous look before aiming Rosie towards the door to the apartment.

"Come on up, then. I've got to look at her head."

He held the door open as Darcy led her lover into the building. Following behind, he was careful to keep away from Rosie. Even hurt, she could be dangerous.

Darcy lowered Rosie onto a couch and told her to sit still. She crossed to a fridge and pulled a tray of ice from its upper freezer. Cracking the tray, she dumped the pile of cubes into a tea towel.

"Hold this against your noggin. There's no blood, but you've got one hell of a goose egg coming."

Lucas looked around the room. His gaze caught movement from a dark bedroom off the kitchen. In the shadows, he saw what looked to him like a child, a girl, staring back at him. Her eyes were wide, and her mouth gaped open as her head bobbed from side to side in a stupor. Ropes pulled at both her arms, and he realized they tied her to the bed. *Oh my God!* Before he could move towards her, Darcy stepped past him and closed the door with a click.

"What—?"

"None of your goddamn business, Lucas." She was in his face, and he could smell the sour smell of sweat under her cheap perfume. Eyes narrowed, she brought up a blade and pressed it against his throat.

He froze as he felt the cold steel.

"Forget anything you think you saw, Lucas, or I swear I'll cut off your balls and feed them to you," she said, spittle warming his cheek.

He swallowed hard, keenly aware of the weapon biting into his skin.

She pulled back slowly, her eyes never leaving his. She pointed to a chair beside a kitchen table. Without asking, she pulled three beers from the fridge, twisting the caps off, handed one to Lucas, kept one and set the other down in front of Rosie. She took a seat across the table and pulled a slug from the bottle as if she had not just threatened his life—or his balls.

"So, what do you want?"

Cradling the ice-cold beer to his bleeding hand took away the sting. He used the moment to think. Seeing the young girl had thrown him. He had to figure a way to get the girl free. He looked at her. "You set up a party a week ago for some foreign guys. You needed more girls, so you jumped Gabriel and took over his crib."

She opened her mouth to dispute, but he raised his hand.

"Eyewitness confirmed the beating you and Rosie put on Gabriel. Amber confirmed the deal with the guys in the white van.

Frankly, I don't give a shit about all that. What I want to know is where I can find these two guys and their friends?"

"The hell you say. Where's Amber? No one's seen her since she left to party with those guys."

"Police picked her up in the south-end of the city. Someone cut her up pretty bad, Darcy. She's been in the hospital since last Thursday. Unconscious the whole time. They ID'd her yesterday when she finally came out of it."

Darcy stared at him intensely before looking towards the couch where her partner sat. "You know anything about this, Rosie?"

Still holding the ice-filled cloth to her skull, Rosie shook her head, the movement causing her obvious pain.

Lucas felt little pity for the hostile pimp. She was overweight, with greasy, black hair flecked with strands of gray. Usually, a loose-fitting jersey covered any hint of her being a woman. Rosie had a reputation for meanness and violence, and had hurt many people on the street.

"I don't know these guys, except they had a ton of cash. My girls made three times their normal rate. They said Amber ran off. None of the other girls saw her after they arrived at the place these guys were staying at."

"Any idea where?"

Rosie shook her head before tipping her bottle. "The girls were in the back of the van. They said that there was a curtain between the driver and the rear compartment. They mentioned they drove for a while before turning onto a gravel road. The place was a farm, set back in the bush."

"Did any of the other girls talk about any rough play?"

"No."

"Any chance I could speak with a few of the girls, myself?"

The woman gave him a tight grin. "Time is money, Lucas. You pay the fee, I don't care what you do with them. Your loss, if all you want to do is talk."

Rosie let out a snort at that thought, even though it hurt her.

"I'll have to work something out with my boss. You have a phone number I can reach you at?"

She recited a number, and he wrote it in his notebook.

"Darcy, it's in the interest of everyone if we can stop these people from hurting anyone else. Both for the girls and your business."

"As if you give a shit about my business."

He stared at her flatly. "You're right. I'd love nothing more than to see this kind of exploitation end, but I'm not naïve enough to think it will stop." He leaned forward to emphasize his point. "But if I can make it safer for these women, then I'll figure it a win."

Chapter 19

Flashing police lights lit the growing crowd in a kaleidoscope of color. Three cruisers jammed the street in front of the storefront. The door to Darcy's apartment hung askew from rough treatment by invading police.

Lucas focused his camera on the scene and snapped off a couple of shots. He should have felt some guilt for creating his own story, but the two pimps deserved to be arrested. There was no way in hell he was going to walk away while they tied a young girl to a bed, evidently being force-fed drugs to make her pliable to the traffickers. He would have made the call to the police, even if Felix had paid the women for the interviews. Now that the police were involved, the girl would be safe for now, and the two pimps would be safely out of the way for what should be a long time. Two birds with one phone call.

Even from his position across the street, he could hear the angry screaming of the two sex traffickers as they struggled with the police. Through the open door, he saw a black covered figure crash down the stairs in a heap. His camera caught a uniformed officer stepping over the figure to drag her to her feet. It was Rosie, and her fall down the stairs seemed to have aggravated her head injury. Even with the officer's help, she staggered her way to the cruiser, no longer fighting.

Behind them, an officer on either side, Darcy pulled ineffectively at her captors, her arms pinned behind her back. Red faced and spitting mad, she screamed at the top of her lungs.

Lucas captured the scene in a series of shots, his camera set for continuous shots. The effect of multiple flashes lit the street like a strobe.

It also attracted Darcy's attention.

With a raw scream, the woman pulled at the cop on her right. As he swung near her, she head butted him, causing him to let go of her arm to grab at his face. Her left foot stamped on the other officer's instep, and he let out a howl. She pulled loose and ran towards Lucas.

He watched through the camera lens in amazement as she charged towards him, teeth bared. She was mere steps from him when his mind recognized the danger she posed, and he dropped the camera to hang from its strap and raised his hands to protect himself.

"I'm going to kill you, you motherfucker!" she spat as she kicked out at him. He jumped back, but her foot still caught him in the thigh, and he staggered back against the wooden picket fence behind him.

"I warned you! *No* one screws with me!"

He sensed more than saw her come at him again and rolled away as she launched herself towards him. Behind him, he heard her gasp and turned to see that she hung from the picket fence, three slats jammed into the loose flesh of her stomach, her hands still handcuffed behind her back. She screamed in pain as the fence collapsed under her weight. In agony, she rolled back and forth over broken slates and grass, the tips of the pickets coming away covered in blood as her knees tucked into her gut. Lucas could see how badly hurt she was.

Before he could do anything, two burly cops pushed through the broken fence and regained custody of the injured trafficker. Behind them ran two paramedics with a stretcher.

"Now you've done it, Darcy," said the first officer. "Resisting a police officer, assault of a police officer—times two, uttering death threats, and the assault on Mr. Kucher, here, is all going on your tab. That's over and above the other charges. We won't be seeing you for a good long time.

"Now, be nice and let these paramedics look at that cut before you bleed out." He stood by as the paramedics applied a pressure bandage, loaded Darcy onto their stretcher, and rolled her towards an ambulance that idled at the curb.

To Lucas, the other officer asked, "You, okay?"

"Yeah. I might have a bruise tomorrow, but I'll be all right."

"You'll have to come down to the station and fill out a statement about what you saw in the apartment and then the assault. Okay?"

Lucas nodded. "No problem. The longer that one is off the street, the better. Hey," he said to the cop's back. "How's the girl?"

The cop turned and gave him a broad smile. "You did good tonight, Lucas. She'll be fine."

Chapter 20

"I can't give you that information," Jamie said, her face heating up as everyone in the room focused on her.

She, Felix, and Lucas were sitting in a huge briefing room at police headquarters. Around the table sat officers from different services; local, provincial, and federal. It was an intimidating crowd. She was replying to a portly officer in a dark suit. His name-card, propped up on the table, informed the others that he was Francois Sauvion of the Royal Canadian Mounted Police.

"Can't or won't?" he said, his face red with indignation.

"I will not stand by," Felix said, drawing all eyes to him, even though he had spoken in a calm and quiet tone, "and allow you, or anyone else, to bully my reporter."

He reached over and poured water from a pitcher into a glass he took from the pitcher's tray. Quietly, over a rattle of ice cubes, he said, "The law is quite clear about the confidentiality of a reporter's source."

"You're absolutely right, Mr. Cameron, and the source is not as important as the information that has made its way to us through Miss Coleman." This came from another suit at the table, a suit of even finer quality.

Jamie read his name, Darren Forbes, a member of CSIS, Canadian security. She was impressed by how he had taken control of the conversation without even raising his voice. He obviously had gone to the same school as Felix. He sat back in his chair, his demeanor relaxed, or possibly even bored.

"I'm sure if one were to use a little imagination, the identity of this source would be clear, but I think that's irrelevant. It's the information itself that is key to our interests here today." He flicked a piece of lint from his tie and gave off an impression that he had no other care in the world.

Totally amused by the man, she almost jumped when Lucas leaned into her. "Careful of that one," he said in a whisper.

The RCMP officer rolled his eyes, not wanting to acknowledge having been subtly reprimanded, but kept quiet.

"Please continue, Ms. Coleman."

Jamie filled the group in on the information that Loretta had given her. She was careful not to give away any clue that might identify the mining spokesperson. She kept only to the facts, and kept her eyes on her notes to help steady her nerves. It was one thing to interview strangers, but quite another to be the center of attention, especially with these high-ranking officials. *Now I know how I make others feel when I interview them.* She made a mental note about that.

She closed her report by describing the body that had been at the scene and the large pile of tarps that had smelled of gasoline.

"What do you feel scares your source so that they would only talk with an assurance of confidentiality?" Forbes asked, studying her eyes as if any falsehood would be reflected there. "Are they afraid they'd lose their job?"

Jamie shook her head. "No, I don't believe so. I think it's because of plain and simple fear. If the information is correct, this organization, whether or not sponsored by the Chinese, seems to have the skills and knowledge to do whatever they want—and hurt whoever crosses them. I think my informant is scared for their safety."

"Has there been any interaction between the informant and this shadow group?" he asked.

"Not that I am aware of. As I mentioned, the tactics used to appropriate both resources and companies, if not governments, have been identified by Novo as a tremendous risk to their business. It was not said, but my informant suggested Novo has its own military assets in third-world countries."

"Any on Canadian soil?" This came from Sauvion, and he leaned forward, his gut pressed against the massive table.

Jaime sat further back in her chair to keep away from the officer. "It wasn't mentioned," she said.

The man's eyes flicked to Forbes. "This is why we can't work with the press. If we had access to the source, we could put pressure on them to give us the answers we need."

Forbes closed his eyes and gave a sigh, like a parent who was losing patience with a misbehaving child. He rubbed his forehead before looking up. Ignoring his federal counterpart, he looked at Felix.

"Forgive my colleague. We are all a little under the gun, so to speak," Forbes said. He looked directly at Jamie, but his eyes were kind, and she felt no apprehension. "Do you think your source might answer a list of questions from this panel? It could fill in the gaps and eliminate the need to identify the individual."

She looked over at Felix before nodding. "I could inquire."

"However," Felix said, his eyes on Forbes. "I think we have been very forthcoming with our information and cooperation."

Forbes nodded. "Very much so."

"Then, for us to continue, I need assurances that the cooperation will be a two-way street. My reporters work for the *Journal*. To continue to help you, I need some guarantees that they'll get a full exclusive and will continue to be *part* of this investigation until its completion. That means sharing any information that you come upon."

"Just who in the hell do you think you're talking to?" Sauvion said, his face flushed with indignation. "Any interference with a police investigation will end up with your people—"

"In this matter, I am authorized on behalf of the Canadian government," Forbes said, his voice stern, cutting off the RCMP officer, "and I can give you that assurance and promise in writing by the end of the day."

Sauvion's head cut to the master spy in disbelief, but something in Forbes' expression silenced the man.

Forbes nodded towards the journalists. "Will that be sufficient?"

"Thank you." Felix said.

"But I will need assurances from you as well, Felix," Forbes said.

"What kind?"

"That as you tell the story, you allow me to preview the articles prior to publication."

"So, you can censor us?"

"That is an ugly word.," Forbes said. "I'm betting that you would never intentionally want to hurt the country."

"No, of course not."

"Well, my only concern would be that you do not release information that might hurt Canada's best interests, both here and abroad. I will never demand a fabrication, but I think that between the two of us—and your reporters, of course—I think we can negotiate on end results. Rest assured, if the Chinese are responsible for these attacks, I will not try to stop you from reporting that. But if I am to share confidential and case-related material, so that we can trust each other, there will be some things that must be left unsaid."

Felix and the CSIS representative stared at each other for a minute, before the newsman nodded. "I look forward to the negotiations."

Forbes smiled and nodded.

Lucas glanced at Jamie, carefully hiding any sign of smugness, so as not to provoke the federal police officer.

Fox Lake Police Chief Dillard, hosting the meeting, but who had said nothing until now, looked around the room to ensure there was no other discussion on the subject. Then he looked over to the fire chief on his left. "How about you, Terry? Can you summarize your findings?"

The chief was blinding in a white shirt with five gold strips on the shoulders and golden bugles on the collar over his black tie. But his shirt sleeves were rolled halfway up his forearms and signalled that he was ready to pitch in. His uniform coat hung on the back of his seat, almost forgotten.

With a nod, he glanced at his notebook. "As we expected, the fire was deliberately set. The perpetrators lifted canvas tarps soaked in gasoline to the roof by a series of ropes and pulleys. Quite ingenious, considering they probably did the work under cover of darkness. Even with the plant closed, the strikers would have seen movement on the roof in the daytime." He looked up from the pad and scanned the others at the table. "They left eight five-gallon fuel cans, so they were not attempting to hide their actions—and when you do the math, you'll note that that is almost an entire barrel of gasoline. However, the perpetrators might have been caught off guard by a roving security guard. The company has confirmed the identity of the lone male guard found dead at the scene as Batte Carneiro. His throat had been cut."

"Sounds like he was the one surprised," said Sauvion with a stupid smirk on his face.

Jamie felt disgusted at the lack of sympathy from the federal officer. She was aware of the dark sense of humor many first responders used to normalize death in their jobs, but it didn't reflect well with his high rank.

The chief continued as if the other hadn't even spoken. The RCMP representative's irritation was evident through his expression, as the others at the table looked at him as Jamie had done.

"He had been one of the Brazilian workers the company brought in to help with security," the chief continued. "My people also found a flare gun at the scene. That was more than likely how the whole thing was lit up. The tarps and the gasoline explain how such a huge area could be ignited at the same time and allow the fire to grow so quickly." He laid his pen across his notepad to show he was done.

"Thanks, Chief," Dillard said. "To follow up on what we found on the scene, there were no fingerprints on the flare gun, or on any of the jerry cans. The fact that they bothered to wear gloves speaks to a higher criminal element than we would normally deal with. The cameras in the area picked up no movement, so I would suggest their locations were known and avoided."

"Do we know what the company plans for future security?" Sauvion asked.

Dillard nodded. "Novo is bringing in two different, private-security companies. They will implement roving patrols throughout the plant in pairs after this morning's murder. I've suggested they stagger the patrols to keep those who are doing this, guessing. No sense in making it easy for them."

"And how did the perpetrators gain access to the property?"

Dillard sighed. "There are only a few ways in that are accessible by vehicle, but none of the gates have been cut. The rest of the property is practically wide open. Anyone who wanted to hoof it could walk right in."

"Carrying all that gasoline?"

"Difficult, but doable. A number of roads can get you near enough and many of the fences are really old and in poor condition. Heck, in North Shore on the northwest corner of the plant, you're only a few hundred yards from the smokestack. The town was originally a company town, so everything is close to the plant. They built it at the turn of the *last* century, long before modern transportation. Most of the miners walked to work or rode a streetcar from Fox Lake."

The chief leaned forward, his eyes on Forbes and Sauvion. "With foreign involvement and a terrorist declaration, can we get military assistance to stop any potential attacks?"

Sauvion took a huge breath and raised his hands wide. Jamie read it that he did not know.

Forbes was quiet for a moment, and Jamie wondered if he was just as uncertain about federal reaction. But he slid his hands forward on the table before looking up.

"I will definitely brief the PM on the situation. I will also ask Foreign Affairs to look into the Chinese question. Right now, we have only this one source's say-so, and the information has to be confirmed. I have seen nothing come across my desk concerning this."

Jamie opened her mouth, but he lifted his finger.

"I am not disputing your information, Ms. Coleman. I just need to confirm it. The Chinese government has been following a program called the Road and Belt. It is no secret, and there have been many reports, both negative and positive, written on the subject, many of them online. I am also already aware of most of the underhanded tactics used by certain international companies to force their agendas on third-world countries. But again, I need proof. No different from what your editor would expect of you."

He looked at the others at the table, including Sauvion, before saying, "I think we all have to do some digging to refute or confirm these allegations. The government would appreciate the support of the media if any foreign influence is uncovered."

Felix nodded, and Jamie exchanged an excited look with Lucas. The twinkle in his eye must have mirrored her own. He was both curious and excited about following this story. She ran her hand over her arm to hide the fact that she had goosebumps.

Felix gave Lucas a nod. Lucas gave him back a wink and held up copies of Amber's notes. "I'm working a totally different story that might have ties to the group that's behind the attacks. This is just a guess, so hear me out."

He recounted the events that led up to his interview with Amber, including the solicitation of numerous girls for the night spent at the farmhouse. "The woman they left for dead handwrote these notes. She actually mentions that the men at this property were all armed with what she described here as machine guns. Others in the house wore shoulder-holstered weapons, and she said that most spoke with a foreign accent. I'm interviewing some of the other girls who worked that night. I'm hoping to find the location of the farmhouse and possibly the identity of the man who attacked her."

"My people can round up those women and question them in a couple of hours," said Chief Dillard.

Lucas sighed as his shoulders fell. "You don't get it. The people on the street don't trust the police. And they certainly will not offer you any information. These girls know me and more than a few trusts that I have their best interests at heart. Please. Let me do it my way."

Dillard stared at Lucas, and Jamie was sure he would shut him down cold; but then Felix leaned forward.

"Theo, Lucas got this information before your people could interview the girl. You and I both know that she did not pass this on to the officers who took her statement. Give Lucas a chance. We came to you with the information, not the other way around."

Dillard nodded. "Make it fast. This feels like a ticking time bomb. We have to get ahead of it."

Chapter 21

Lucas sat in the dark, waiting. His eyelids were sliding down; and part of him told himself to surrender, have a nap, that Christine would wake him once she returned. His three-hour nap this afternoon in anticipation of this late-night rendezvous was barely a memory. *What the hell was the old saying? You can't store sleep? Or was it that you can't make up sleep?* Either way, if this wasn't so important, he'd have crashed hours ago.

He regretted accepting Christine's invitation to wait inside her store, as the couch was lumpy, but awfully comfortable. If he had waited in the car, the hard seat and being able to lower a window for cooler evening air would have made staying awake so much easier.

A low murmur of voices made him sit up. A jangle of keys followed it, and the front door opened. Harsh lights blinded Lucas and he raised his hand to shield his eyes. "Give a guy some warning."

Christine looked at her two companions and shook her head. "Did we wake you, sweetheart?" she said as she locked the door behind her.

The two women—at least physically—they were still in their teens—stood hesitantly, although one was grinning at Christine's treatment of Lucas. Both were of Indigenous background, something Christine and Lucas had discussed earlier, and she had given him some reminders of how to approach. Lucas knew one of the women, but the younger of the two, was new to him. Christine had assured him that the two were almost inseparable, and that it might be easier to talk to the pair together.

"Lucas, this is Gabby and Jewel."

Then, to the girls, Christine said, "Just so you know, Lucas gets my seal of approval. Earlier, he helped save another lost one and made sure Darcy and Rosie will never hurt any of you again. They'll both be in jail for a long time, thanks to him."

Both stared at Lucas with wide eyes.

He nodded and then grabbed the bag he had brought. He pulled two linen pouches of tobacco and offered the first one with his left hand to Gabby, who he knew. "*Aaniin,*" he said in Ojibwa. The word meant 'Hello or Greetings.' "I come for your help." He repeated the same ceremony with the other woman, Jewel. Neither woman said anything, and he could see fear on both their faces. He knew that the abuse and callousness that they had come to expect came both from the men who bought their services, and from their traffickers, Darcy and Rosie. And he couldn't blame these young women. He wouldn't trust anyone if he had lived a similar life.

Christine finally broke the awkward silence. "Please, have a seat," she said, indicating the two chairs opposite the couch.

Only Gabby sat. Jewel stood behind her friend, her hand tapping against her leg as if ready to run. Lucas was sure she would bolt if he made any sudden move. Most of the street workers knew him and trusted him—to a point. With this girl, he knew it would take time to gain her trust, if he could at all. Then again, depending on her own story, it might never happen.

"The reason I asked Christine to set up this meeting is that I'm investigating an attack on Amber."

Both girls looked at each other, surprise evident in their expressions.

"You hadn't heard?"

Gabby shook her head. Jewel just stared wide-eyed.

"Amber is in the hospital and is in rough shape. I promised to do my best to find the guy who hurt her and make sure he pays for what he did. But I need your help."

Now, confusion lined their faces.

"The special event you girls were at a week ago, the one that was held out at a farm, was the last time anyone remembers Amber. Someone there cut her up, then left her to die on the side of the road."

Both gave a collective gasp. Jewel's fingers dug into Gabby's shoulder, causing her to wince. Wordlessly, Gabby pulled Jewel's rigid fingers loose and intertwined her own in reassurance. It was all that stopped the young girl from leaving.

"I saw Amber yesterday, and although she's badly injured, she will get better. It's just going to take a long time." Lucas leaned forward; his hands clasped together. "If you have any information that might help to identify these men or where they took you, we might be able to stop them from hurting anyone else."

The two women exchanged a nervous look, and Lucas was sure they would both leave without another word. People on the street who talked, paid for it, often with their lives.

"Listen," Christine said, her voice loud in the silence, yet gentle in its tone. "I've worked with Lucas for a long time and can tell you that you can trust him. No one will know that you've spoken to him. That's why I brought you here. It's only among the four of us."

Her shoulders slumped, and she bit her lip. "What's happened has to stop, and the only way to do that is to work together. I can't afford to lose another one of you. I've been to *too many funerals!*"

Lucas could hear the raw emotion in the social worker's voice and wondered how close she was to breaking. In her job, she saw more losses than wins. It would be hard for anyone doing that work to stay upbeat and positive.

As a tear slid down Christine's cheek, Lucas felt his throat close up. He pulled his gaze away from her to gauge how the two street women, so hardened by their nightmare called life, had reacted to Christine's appeal. The younger girl was crying silently, looking like the lost child she actually was, while the other, although stunned, was dry-eyed.

"What do you want?"

"Christine will meet you at the same time tomorrow night." He handed Gabby two notebooks and a pair of pens. "In the meantime, could you write down anything you think is important about that night? Description of the men you saw. Anything about the trip to the farmhouse. What do you remember of the buildings and the area? Who else did you meet? Did the men have accents? Any scars or tattoos? Anything and everything you can remember. And if you do this separately, one of you might remember something the other doesn't. You, Jewel, might have heard or seen something Gabby didn't. By writing separate statements, it gives a wider and clearer picture of that night."

Chapter 22

Jamie rubbed her eyes and stifled a yawn. Between her online searches and leafing through mining journals that spoke of wrongdoing by Chinese mining companies worldwide, it felt like her eyes were filled with sand.

Felix had provided her with a high-school-student intern to assist her with the paperwork and learn about journalism firsthand.

There was a treasure trove of information in the J.N. Desmarais Library at Laurentian University's School of Mines in nearby Sudbury. With students studying every aspect of mining worldwide, their collection was substantial.

After they arrived there, the intern, Tianna Dagastino, a senior from Lockerby Composite High School, disappeared somewhere in the stacks of books. She was looking for textbooks or articles that spoke of the expansion of Chinese mining companies.

Of course, with the sheer volume of material, it was an issue of too much information. Jamie sighed as she set up her laptop, knowing it would be a long and tedious day.

Because her helper was a volunteer, Jamie felt guilty enough to buy her hunch: an excellent vegan pizza and coffee. The girl's shoulder-length hair was bright pink with flashes of purple. She wore thick-rimmed oversized glasses that framed her face. Her Five Fingered Death Punch t-shirt hung loosely over a pair of jeans that must have cost a fortune from the number of shredded holes in each leg. *She would have covered more skin if she had chosen to wear shorts.*

But where her wardrobe was questionable, her energy and enthusiasm made up for it. She knew her way around a library, and her computer skills were a wonder.

After their quick lunch, it was not long before Tianna came racing from the stacks with several periodicals folded over her arm. "I just found these that have a bunch of complaints about Fodineum, that accuse the company of both bribery and violence."

Jamie looked up from her laptop where she was making notes on the articles that Tianna had found before lunch. A growing pile of documents stood waiting for her review.

"Who made the complaints?"

"Wives, whose husbands and sons who were apparently murdered by security people sent in by the company to clear a village. The complaint fell against deaf ears in Sudan. The United Nations filed an official complaint against the Sudanese government for corruption and inaction with the humanitarian charges. According to a follow-up article, the company paid the women one thousand U.S. dollars per family member as compensation."

"That's a pittance."

"To the people the company paid, that's probably a fortune."

Jamie eyed her helper, surprised at her perceptiveness.

"In another case," Tianna said, laying another report on the table. "The company is suspected of poisoning the local water source after the tribespeople refused to move to make way for a planned rare-earth mine. They had no choice but to move after that. In this case, no one died, but a number of older villagers did get sick."

"Any idea what was used to poison the water?"

"There's nothing mentioned in the report. Why?"

"It would be interesting if they used the same chemical in other areas. It might even point to the actual culprit."

"OMG! I never thought about that."

"It might also have long-term health effects for those who were exposed."

The girl nodded excitedly. "I can check that. And by the way, so far, two companies have shown up repeatedly in the reports I've found."

"Which ones?" Jamie sat up, giving her full attention to the student.

"Lhasa Ore and Xi Tu."

From her handbag, Jamie fished out her phone and checked her notes of her interview with the MSR spokesperson. Her fingers slid the screen upward until she found the information she knew was there. One company Loretta had mentioned matched what Tianna had found.

"Bingo! Xi Tu is definitely a name to watch for. We know Lhasa Ore is a subsidiary of Fodineum. I'll check on the other one."

Switching to her text app, she pulled up Loretta's contact number, typed in the name of the second company, and hit send. She placed the phone on the desk.

"Hopefully, we'll get confirmation on the other name. Keep digging!" she said, smiling her enthusiasm at the young student. *She's going to take over my job one day if she sticks with it.*

The phone danced across the desk as it vibrated. Snatching it up, Jamie refreshed the screen and then looked at Tianna. "Second name is a subsidiary of the first. So, Fodineum owns Lhasa Ore, and it owns Xi Tu. You're onto something."

With no hesitation, the seventeen-year-old spun in-place and dashed back to the stacks, her vibrant hair swinging like a flag.

Chapter 23

Forbes sauntered into the boardroom carrying a manila envelope that he spun across the table towards Jamie, Lucas, and Felix. "Congratulations, Ms. Coleman. Your information bore out." Undoing the bottom button on his suitcoat, he eased himself down and crossed his legs at the knee.

"Before I begin, I have to reiterate that we cannot release any of this information just yet. As promised, you'll get the exclusive once we bring the perpetrators to justice. But we can't take the chance of them going to ground. Also, Chief Dillard and Inspector Sauvion have already been briefed on the information I am sharing with you."

Felix nodded for the group.

"The photo of the gentleman in the envelope is of a rather nasty individual named, Dragoljub Petkovic, alias Drago."

Jamie had caught the envelope and undid the red string that held it closed before sliding out the eight-by-ten photo. She moved it so that her two colleagues could see it.

The individual in the picture was hard looking, even without the ragged scar on his cheek. Olive skin was darkened by years in the sun, and crows' feet that didn't seem to come from smiling edged dark-brown eyes. If this man smiled, it would make him look even more evil. Lifting her eyes, Jamie returned her gaze to the Canadian spy master.

"Our information came from several sources. Seems that over the past couple of decades, this guy's been one of the main trouble-shooters for Fodineum, the parent company of Xi Tu Mining. The CEO of Fodineum is a mid-ranking party official by the name of Bao

Daoming. Although he seems to have been given total autonomy, we assume he takes his marching orders directly from the Standing Committee of the Politburo, the actual power in China."

"So, if this Drago is behind the attacks, it's pretty safe to say that the Chinese government has approved of the operation," Jamie said.

"Easy to say, but totally another thing to prove. Especially on the world stage. Even if we caught Bao Daoming, himself in the very act of sabotage, there would be very little that Canada could do about it. You all saw what had happened with the Two Michaels."

Forbes was referring to the Chinese detainment of two Canadians after the arrest of the CEO of China's electronic company, Huawei. The men spent three years in brutal conditions, cut off from the world, in retaliation for Canada's insult to the Chinese government.

"So how do we fight this?" Felix asked.

"By shutting down the group responsible. It's not like Bao Daoming is going to stick his own neck out. He's almost certainly living in China, but equally certainly he pulls the strings."

Forbes pointed at the photo. "Drago is another story. He's a mercenary. A paid goon. If we can find him and shut him down, this threat will be over for the time being."

"Unless they move their base of operations to another Novo facility like Indonesia or Brazil," Jamie said. "According to my source, this attack is to force a hostile takeover."

Forbes nodded. "We can only fight what's in front of us."

Felix looked at both of his reporters, before turning back to Forbes. Before he could say anything, his phone vibrated. Checking the number, he said, "I have to take this." He stood up and left the room.

"Have you identified any of the others traveling with this Drago fellow?" asked Lucas.

"We have some known associates, but nothing has been confirmed. I have Customs looking into the names we have on file to see if they entered legally. His partner, this Philip Vautour, entered the country weeks ago, but left a few days later. We have seen no sign of him since. If he or any others are traveling under false identification ..." He lifted his hands to show the futility of the situation.

Jamie felt rather than saw the door behind her open and half turned to see Felix enter, a tight smile on his face. Without preamble he said, "Good news. Novo and the union have a tentative deal. The destruction seems to have given them a common cause. They have a news release set for ten o'clock tomorrow morning. I'm assigning both of you to this. This is monumental news for the company, the union, and the community."

"Sounds like they're actually wanting to work together for a change," Lucas said. "Might be the best idea, considering the rebuilding that they have to do."

"At least with workers back in the plant, there'll be less opportunity for a group sneaking around at night."

Forbes had listened as the trio spoke with a pensive expression.

"What?" asked Jamie. "Do you see this as a problem?"

"It puts those workers more at risk if the enemy is really determined."

Chapter 24

Lucas rushed through the entrance of the Second Chance office as Christine was still unlocking the door.

"Did they do it?" he asked.

"I think you'll be pleased."

"Let me see."

She laughed at his excitement, handing him the notebooks. "You're like a kid at Christmas."

He didn't answer, but opened the first notebook with "Gabby" etched in blue ink on its cover as he sat down on the couch.

As his eyes scanned the small, neat letters, he felt his excitement grow. Although the vehicle had been windowless and the rear compartment separated from the cab, Gabby had described the trip in the van to the farmhouse as someone who had grown up in the area. Judging by the time of travel and the speed of the vehicle, she was able to tell that they had traveled out of the city until turning south on Old Cartier Road. They had slowed down to turn south again on a gravel road before crossing two Baily bridges that she recognized from the clatter of wooden planks that make up the bridges' decks. They had traveled for five to ten more minutes before turning left onto a gravel drive.

Lucas traced the route in his own mind's eye and realized it could only be somewhere off Chicago Mine Road.

The van eventually turned left, and the roadway became gravel. They had finally turned left again onto the property.

Being night, there wasn't much to be seen but the house and barn. All the men were armed with pistols or rifles and spoke accented English. She mentioned meeting a smaller man, who had offered her a small paper figure of a horse. She couldn't remember much about the guy except that he was short and had darker skin.

She had written a detailed description of the two men she had serviced that night and explained she had made more money that one night than she usually earned in a week.

Lucas chuckled as she explained how the women had all agreed to a similar story, so they wouldn't have to give too much to Darcy or Rosie. Darcy had told him that the night had been a profitable venture, but she did not know just how much. Lucas' respect for Gabby rose. She was as smart as she was tough. If she could escape the streets, there would be nothing she couldn't do.

Jewel's recollection, while similar, did not hold the detail that Gabby had offered. She had described the man she had been with but couldn't tell where they had been. There had been no mention of the smaller man or his offering of a paper animal.

Closing the second notebook, he saw Christine staring intensely at him.

"What?"

She rolled her eyes. "Well, what do you think? Does it help?"

He nodded, smiling at her impatience. "Definitely. Gabby's attention to detail is amazing. I'm sure I could drive to the place right now."

"Good. Because we have to find that son-of-a-bitch that hurt Amber and put him away."

"Thanks to you and the help you've given me, I'm one step closer."

He couldn't tell her that the men they were trying to identify were possibly involved with the incidents at Novo. If that news got out prematurely, the saboteurs would fade away and might never be caught. But then again, maybe these people had nothing to do with the smelter. He didn't have enough information.

Changing the topic, he said, "Are you able to help these two?"

She smiled. "Gabby has already reached out to me. She's trying to convince Jewel to trust me enough to help her, but she's pretty heavily addicted, so we'll have to see. Jewel has to *want* to get clean. Only she can do it. She's relatively new in this life, so isn't jaded enough. Right now, it's like a party. She might have to spread her legs, but all the drugs are free for the taking. But at least Gabby is ready."

He shook his head, not able to understand how the lure of drugs could be that strong, even though he'd seen it himself many times.

Lucas had never been a big drinker, and he'd only experimented with weed back in high school. He hadn't liked the feeling, so never bothered with anything stronger.

He got his fixes by cracking open a new story or exposing the dark secrets of someone who took advantage of others.

That satisfaction of finding the truth was intoxicating and always motivated him to keep digging.

"Not a bad week, Lucas," Christine said, bringing him back to the present. "You're halfway to catching that animal; and thanks to you, there's a girl rescued, and two major sex traffickers are out of business. And at least one girl might be off the street for good."

"Now I just need to write it all up, and that'll take the rest of the night. So, I'd better get going. Thanks so much for your help, Christine."

She opened her mouth to say something, but reconsidered and nodded.

He hauled himself from the couch cushions, feeling the day's fatigue dragging him down.

"Don't be a stranger, Lucas. You're always welcome here," she said to his back as he pulled his camera case over his shoulder.

He heard the unspoken question in her tone, but refused to rise to the bait. In the past, there had been suggestive offers to explore a relationship with her, but he cared too much for her friendship to risk it on a maybe. Besides, lately all his thoughts centered on a certain young reporter who may have stolen his story, but had also allowed him a chance to be part of it.

Instead, he turned at the door. "I'll let you know what I find at the farmhouse."

She nodded but said nothing and he eased himself out into the night.

Chapter 25

Lucas leaned against the fender of his Honda parked outside his apartment and spoke into his phone. "Jamie, interested in going for a ride?" he asked. He'd been about to leave without her, but remembered that this was her story, too.

"Where to?"

"I have a lead to where Amber and the other women might have been taken. It's about a half-hour drive."

"Why don't you share that with Forbes?"

"Call it old-fashioned, but I want to confirm the information first. If I cry wolf, he'll second-guess anything else I bring him."

"But if these are the same people who are behind the attacks, they're trained killers, Lucas. We're not equipped for that."

"I don't plan on asking for an interview. I just want to follow up on the information Gabby gave me to confirm the farmhouse is really there. A drive-by. That's it."

"Fine. I'll be there in a few minutes. You're at home? Yeah? Meet me outside—we can take my ride."

Fifteen minutes later, Jamie pulled up to the curb outside Lucas's apartment. She lowered her window.

"I'm driving, or else I call Felix and fill him in on your lead. I want to make sure you behave. Get in," she said, pointing with her thumb to the far side of her black Wrangler.

He laughed. "Okay, but what's that going to accomplish?"

"This way, I can make sure it's just a drive-by." The expression of a schoolteacher making sure her student behaved, made him laugh again. Her laughter joined his, and they settled into the rugged, yet modern, full-sized jeep.

As they drove west, he summarized the route Gabby had passed on through her notes.

"That's pretty impressive."

He nodded. "She's grown up here in Fox Lake. Of course, unlike bigger cities in the south, there are only three routes in and out of this area. But you're right, the detail she gave us tells me she's very shrewd."

"Just the idea of her wanting to leave that kind of life speaks to that."

"I think with Darcy and Rosie no longer in the picture, she knows it's a perfect opportunity. If she's game, I'll do a follow-up story of her journey."

"That would be an interesting read. Unfortunately, the women who would really benefit from it more than likely will never see it."

"No, but Christine will make sure that they at least know about it. She's always out there spreading the news."

They were silent for a while before, Jamie asked, "Are you two involved?" She glanced at him, but he kept his eyes on the road.

"No. I've been tempted in the past. And she has hinted at it." He considered his actual feelings. "I love her enthusiasm and her cause, but she's always been more like a best friend—someone who is always there to help. She's like family—like a little sister, but nothing more."

"So, you're a lifetime bachelor?"

He smiled at her. "Why would you think that?"

"Well, in the past couple days, I've met two women who would love to latch onto you, but you don't seem interested."

"Two?" He turned to her in confusion.

"Christine, who I can understand from what you've just said. And Loretta."

"Loretta?" he blurted with a snort. "Loretta is nothing more than ambition. Her job and climbing the corporate ladder are all Loretta cares about. No way I could compete. Hell, she even gave up her relationship with Mike Burgess for Novo."

Her head turned to him. "The union leader? You knew about that?"

He pointed to the road. "Chicago Mine Road is on the left. And yes, I knew about them, but that happened years ago. I think it still plays a major role in their never-ending animosity."

She was quiet for a few miles as she considered his words.

"Why all the interest in my love life? You're not one of these compulsive matchmakers, are you?"

She barked out a laugh. "Oh my God, no. I'm just ... interested. That's all."

"Interested." It was a statement, not a question. How much? He felt his pulse rise, but it was subdued when the logical part of him reminded him of her relationship not only to Felix, as in "Uncle Felix" but also to her very rich and powerful father. What would they have to say about Jamie and Lucas together? He was a semi-employed journalist living from paycheck to paycheck. No benefits. No house. Even his car was held together with bailing wire and luck.

He glanced over at her and realized he didn't really care about her uncle or her father. He and Jamie might never work out, and he always tried to live in the moment. But if it happened, he would definitely be interested.

She gave him a shy smile, and his heart lurched.

It took a lot for him to pull his mind back to the real reason they were out here. Pulling out his phone, he called up Google Maps and searched Chicago Mine Road. "Ah, there are only a few roads that turn left off the main road once we cross the two bridges. Tusk Road or Jerico Road. The others are driveways or access roads to different lakes in the area."

"That should make it easier."

He shook his head with a rueful grin. "Never seems to work like that. Maybe my luck will change."

When they bumped across the wooden planks on the bridge and he caught the dull, white flash of rapids below, he said, "The first road to the left is Tusk. Should be just around the curve."

She slowed the vehicle down; and as her headlights caught sight of the street sign, she signaled and turned, leaving the relatively smooth gravel surface. They instantly hit a section of washboard and the jeep stuttered across the rough gravel as Jamie geared down.

"Damn, don't they grade these roads?" she said under her breath.

"The joys of rural living."

She gave him a look, and he laughed. "I heard your eyes roll that time."

She shook her head and kept the vehicle from fishtailing. Bringing the vehicle to a more reasonable speed for gravel, Jamie eased forward into a narrow, tree-lined lane rather than a normal city road. "I hope we don't meet any other traffic."

In the darkness, headlights showed that the road ended sixty feet ahead at what looked like a residence. Before that, a driveway cut off at an angle on the left. A bungalow with an attached garage was lit up by both interior and exterior lights. She stopped the vehicle.

"Wrong place," she said.

He leaned towards her to see from her vantage. The earthy, warm smell of her filled his nostrils, and he wanted to reach out to touch her hair and bury his face in it. *For Christ's sake, Kucher. You're acting like a horny seventeen-year-old who's never been with a girl.* "I can't see anything," he said, flopping back in his seat.

"Through a window, I'm watching two kids chasing each other in a family-room."

"I'll trust your instincts," he said in an impatient tone.

"Hey, it's the first place we looked at."

Moments later, they were back on the main road, heading south. Lucas consulted his phone. "Okay, there should be a gravel pit next on your left and Jerico Road is right after."

The night hid the extensive gravel pit, its presence acknowledged by a 'No Trespassing' sign. They could make out the shape of a heavy chain hanging between two posts, blocking off its access.

Jamie slowed considerably, having learned from her last encounter with gravel roads. She eased off the main roadway and turned onto Jerico road, which, surprisingly, was smooth gravel before it transitioned into packed soil.

"This doesn't seem right. Gabby's notes said that the road they turned left off the highway was gravel, not soil and then gravel. And her notes are explicit in their detail."

The road branched off to the right in two different places before a sign warned them that the road was private. Jamie turned the vehicle back towards the highway. "Must be another road further on."

"Nothing, according to this satellite map."

"Depends what year it was taken. They don't update them regularly."

She drove while he played with the app, hoping to get some idea where the road could be. "Except for the roads around Ministic Lake and the access road to Mosquito Lake, there are no other roads marked.

"We're down here now, so we might as well keep going until Worthington Road. If all else fails, maybe Gabby can come for a ride tomorrow after the press conference."

He sighed in frustration, but didn't disagree.

Because of the condition of the roadway and the darkness, Jamie kept the vehicle at a decent speed. Neither complained as both knew that frost-heaving made northern roads treacherous, and maintenance was always an issue. Even driving slowly, they passed a road on their left before they had actually registered it. With a three-point-turn, Jamie faced the Jeep back the way they had come and slowly made her way to the road they had glimpsed.

The light caught the reflection of a stack of three green address signs, which indicated three different properties. Jamie turned into the roadway, acknowledging the gravel surface with a look at Lucas. He was staring intently through the windshield as he tried to see past the beams of the headlights.

"Take it slow. We don't know what we'll find here."

"Now you want to be cautious?"

His eyes swung back and forth, watching for any driveway that forked off this main road. On the right side of the roadway there was a large pad of gravel that pushed right up into the trees. "Either a future road or maybe a place for graders to put snow," he said, thinking aloud.

Jamie nodded.

The grade of the road increased; and as they crested the hill, they saw a lone light on top of an electrical pole. It marked the entrance to a driveway that cut through the trees to their left. Jamie cut the headlights, following the line of the road against the darker grass edging the ditch. As they came even with the roadway, without touching the brakes, she allowed the vehicle to coast to a stop.

They both peered down the dark tunnel that cut through the trees before exchanging a look.

"Might be what we're looking for," Jamie said.

"Look, you keep going and find a place to turn around. I'll walk down the drive to see if I can spot a barn. That'll confirm it."

"No bloody way, Lucas. What happened to, 'Just a drive-by?'"

"Just think how the cops with treat us if we send them to the wrong property. By the time you turn around, I'll be back, and we can get out of here."

Before she could argue further, he opened the passenger door and ducked out, cursing when the vehicle's dome light flashed on.

Even though he eased the door shut, it sounded like the crack of a rifle in the quiet of the night.

Skirting the Jeep, he moved down the dark driveway. With the makeshift streetlamp behind him, it took only minutes for his eyes to adjust.

The property opened up to an area of a couple of acres. The house was a vast building with windows that stretched along a large wooden deck. Behind, and to the right of the structure, he could see the tip of a barn above the nearby trees, although the structure itself lay hidden in the deep shadows of the surrounding forest.

The whole place had an empty look to it. He knew it was fairly early, but there was no vehicle in sight. Looking back towards the road, he could not see Jamie's car and figured she hadn't yet turned around.

He ran for the house, his head on a swivel for any threat. *Doesn't everyone out here have big dogs?* The thought added a burst of speed, and he climbed onto the deck as if being chased. After a quick glance behind him, he cupped his hands around his face and peered through the large window. He could make out shadows of furniture and doorways in the dim light. The flashing of a security panel on the far wall drew his eyes.

Alarmed!

He moved across the deck and peered around the structure. The barn was there just as Amber had described it. It was huge and built of logs. Its silver-colored, metal roof reflected dully against the night sky. He was tempted to look in the barn in case they had parked the cargo van inside, but he heard the crunch of tires and knew Jamie had returned.

Looks like everyone is out for the evening. Better let Forbes and the cops deal with the owners, if this is really the place they had brought Gabby and Amber to.

He ran back to the road and slipped back into the Jeep to find one very annoyed Jamie.

"Damn it, Lucas!" she said as she shifted the vehicle into gear.

"No problem! No one was home."

"That's not the point and you know it!" Turning onto the main road, she hit the gas despite the washboard gravel, which pushed him into his seat. It would be a long ride home.

THE RED TAILLIGHTS turned off the gravel road, and the Wrangler shot ahead, its engine roaring.

From the shadows of the trees, a figure eased himself up on his knees. He pulled his camouflaged face-covering away, enjoying night's coolness on his skin. Opening up a side compartment in his jacket, he powered up a cellular phone, ensuring the bright screen was pressed against his chest so no light disturbed the night.

Then he speed-dialed a number. Through his earpiece, he heard two clicks that told him the recipient was listening. In a whisper, he said, "We had some visitors. A man and a woman in a black Jeep Wrangler. The woman driving. The man looked at the house but didn't enter. Not sure why. He got back into the Jeep, and they took off."

The man listened to new orders. He wouldn't be sitting in the dark waiting for nothing to happen for the rest of the night. Time to pack up, bug out—but not before he left a welcome package for the next visitors.

Chapter 26

Brilliant, clear-blue skies made the late morning almost too bright, except through tinted lenses or from under deep-brimmed hats. The colossal smokestack cut the sky in two. Rising over the plant, it seemed to pull all eyes, as if it were the main attraction. It reared over the converter-aisle building, making the immense building look small in comparison. It was an engineering marvel, taking the heat and the toxic by-products of the smelting process and dispersing them over a vast area, thereby lessening the immediate environmental damage.

Despite the previous two disasters at the smelter, the atmosphere at the press conference was festive with the expected announcement. A vast group of picketers gathered in groups, sharing the brotherly camaraderie common in unions and the anticipation of overtime wages during rebuilding.

Lucas was happy to see that Jamie seemed to have gotten over his risking himself and the story the night before. They would be calling Forbes right after this announcement, and hopefully be able to put the threat of more attacks to rest.

Lucas and Jamie originally stood at the back of the crowd so they could capture the whole picture; but Jamie soon left to move instinctively through the gathering, greeting strikers and asking open questions, to get a better sense of the atmosphere.

Lucas, on the other hand, captured the anticipation through the lens of his camera. Casual shots of men and women laughing and joking confirmed spirits were up, and that the proposed announcement was just a formality. Finally, after the strike, an explosion and a major fire, there was good news coming. He felt, rather than saw, the change in the assembly. Looking towards the makeshift stage, he saw the union president Mike Burgess literally dance up the steps. His body language belied his usual somber demeanor. There was no hiding the nature of the announcement.

Behind him, Loretta, the company spokesperson, followed in a much more reserved manner that signified her position as much as the company's.

The crowd of strikers moved towards the platform without encouragement. Lucas moved to a position where he could take shots towards the speakers, and also toward the crowd for their reactions, making sure the plant with its enormous stack was in the background. He caught a flash of Jamie's green scarf closer to the platform, obviously positioned so that she could record the announcement. She was also close enough to catch the tone and response of the strikers. He was impressed that she had the instinct to know where to stake a position to accomplish more than just one goal. She would hear the mutterings of the strikers, and they wouldn't even notice her being there.

Fly on the wall.

The shuffling and muttering began to slow to a stop until the only noise at the strike line was the passing traffic on the highway. Even the wind seemed to hold its breath.

Burgess grabbed the moment.

Raising a megaphone, he said, "Brothers and Sisters. We have a tentative agreement! It is a three-year, three-and-a-half percent deal, and we have left no concessions on the table. Both sides agreed that the time to work together against the recent attacks is now. Both sides need each other. We will hand summaries out as you leave, but your negotiation team is recommending full, one-hundred-percent acceptance."

Burgess smiled at the crowd before turning to Loretta, who moved forward, taking the bullhorn from the union president. "In these troubled times, both the company and its employees need to come together for our greater good. We need you as much as you need us, and I hope this agreement can signal a new era of cooperation between both sides, as we rebuild and grow together."

A staccato of blasts ripped the silent sky apart.

It sounded like a string of firecrackers, let off in a continuous line of snaps, only deeper and more powerful. The sound drew Lucas's eyes upward towards the super-stack, and he was aware that heads and eyes of the crowd followed the same line of sight.

He went cold.

Puffs of dust or concrete were coming from holes being blown out the base of the chimney, almost ten stories up. The blasts moved horizontally across the top edge of the massive base of the smoke-stack. Above the blasts, the tower seemed to shiver against the sky.

Lucas' camera snapped photos non-stop as a new string of duller-sounding pops ripped around the backside of the stack. Spalling debris showed it was coming from fifty feet higher.

Holy fuck! Someone is cutting down the stack like it was a fuck'ng tree. Except with explosives instead of a chainsaw.

He watched as a ripple rose up the massive 1,250-foot chimney before the unthinkable began to happen.

It began to tilt.

Beginning at its midway point, the enormous stack leaned towards the north end of the town of North Shore. As the lean pulled the stack from the base, thousands of tons of concrete and reinforcement steel broke off and slid forward. Lucas shuddered as sounds of cracking and crushing concrete became a roar that resembled the snapping of breaking bones. Shrill squeals of tearing metal hurt the ears and drowned the screams of the crowd below.

In terror of being crushed by the toppling of one of the world's highest structures, Lucas went cold as the crowd began to run. But there was nowhere to run. And no time.

He flicked his camera setting to video and kept his finger on the zoom button, trying to get the full picture. He tried to follow the fall of the colossal concrete funnel, but as it fell, the faster it went. It was like taking photos of a volcano with lava falling around you.

As the sheared-off base of the stack met the ground, nothing stood in its way—nothing could. Buildings ceased to exist as the gigantic weight settled across the complex and—

God, no!

—towards the Alta Italia section of the town of North Shore.

A collective gasp ripped through the strikers as they stopped in their panic to see where it was falling.

To Lucas's horror, he saw there was no way to warn anyone. *They wouldn't feel a thing.*

The stack rolled as it fell, creating its own steerage because of its base dragging behind and its massive weight still hovering over the community.

The falling concrete tube crushed straight through the old section of Alta Italia. It flattened buildings on both sides of Venice Street entirely or severed them like a laser through balsa.

The old-fashioned narrow streets seemed to guide the stack's fall, but Lucas knew that no force on earth except gravity could do that. To his eye, laws of physics blurred as the stack bent skyward like a falling tree in a forest as the stack's middle flexed downward as it hurtled towards the earth. The rough terrain solved the puzzle, as the roadway dipped naturally, following the curve of the rock and gave the middle part of the chimney a place to call its own—and crush the remaining buildings that refused to give way.

The heavy tip of the stack, which had swayed back and forth during the fall, gave up its post. With a crack like a whip, the tip broke off to follow the angle of the stack's last twist. The sudden jerk of the twist shifted it away from the main column of the chimney. With a life of its own, the tip snapped higher in the air, clearing the train trestle that separated North Shore from the downtown core of the Fox Lake.

Lucas watched, mouth open, and dry as sand, as the stack's tip crashed behind a cluster of buildings he knew were near Main Street. Rocky terrain prevented him seeing further damage or exactly where the tip fell. Even from this distance and angle, he could see a huge wave of dust rising from the collapsed stack. The dust billowed outward, hiding utter devastation.

JAMIE, LIKE THOSE SURROUNDING her, could do little but witness the unthinkable. Like everyone, she knew the company had plans to dismantle the superstack, as it no longer served any function. But not like this—it couldn't be.

This is madness.

She felt herself move with the crowd as people ran away or leaned forward, to watch what was happening hundreds of feet above them. *What the ...*

As Jamie felt the shocks of the ripple of explosions undulate along her spine, she thought she was being torn in two.

She pushed towards Lucas, but he kept darting back and forth, his camera leading the way.

Record. Remember. So, she could recall it all later. The story is all that matters.

She pivoted in place to watch the stack, rushed by weight and gravity, slam into the hilltop of North Shore. The tube twisted on itself as it fell, like a trunk of a tree felled by a hurricane. It left clouds of concrete dust and chimney ash to billow over the scene, blotting out the entire community. The dust trail followed an ear-splitting crash down the back slope, and she glimpsed the familiar smokestack tip, its aerial lights still flashing—

Must be battery fed—At a time like this, who cares!

—as it broke away and was flung forward, deeper towards the downtown core of North Shore.

The sight continued to hold every eye, and now there were no screams—just expletives of disbelief or confusion. Turning to the stage, Jamie saw Mike Burgess and Loretta holding hands in combined horror, their expressions mirroring the utter shock of the others. Jamie raised her phone and snapped a couple of shots of the two former antagonists, showing their human side in the face of disaster. She allowed her camera to scan the miners in the crowd, recording a microsecond of expressions frozen in time, before realization hit home.

As the last of the stack disappeared into the rough Northern Ontario terrain, the crowd collectively found its voice. Cries, curses, and calls to God shattered the stunned silence. Reality seemed to burst the bubble that had held the group in stasis.

Jamie was in time to see Loretta and Burgess shake their hands free of each other as if expecting to be burned by the other. She bit back a maniacal laugh. To hide their discomfort, both opponents stalked to the farthest corner of the raised platform, each with a phone clamped to their head.

Burgess, with one finger to his ear to block the rising voices of the strikers, was yelling into the device. Then, looking at it in frustration, he put it away and picked up the megaphone from the table.

The strikers were becoming animated, milling around, wiping long, calloused hands across numb faces. Others tugged at their hair, a reminder of the ability to feel—that they were alive.

Chapter 27

"Listen up!" Burgess barked through the megaphone, stopping the crowd, who were close to bolting towards the main road and the line of cars and trucks.

When all eyes were on the union president, he announced loudly, "Emergency Services are on their way! Before you think about heading home, remember this." He pointed at the dust still hovering over the community. "Those people are our neighbors, and they need our help." He looked over the crowd. "Decklin! Make a list of those who can help and those who need to get home." To another, "Tommy, contact the other picket lines. Have everyone assemble as close to Queen's Park as they can, by the townhouses, and to wait for deployment orders."

Jamie watched as Novo's spokesperson and the union president put their heads together for a minute. They pulled back quickly, nodding in agreement. Loretta's phone was to her ear, and she was barking orders. Two of the security cars that had been parked on the company side of the picket line roared to life and took off towards the interior of the complex. *My God, there must be hundreds dead.* She thought she might be sick.

Jamie jumped as a hand closed over her shoulder, and she turned to see Lucas.

"You, okay?" he asked, his eyes searching deep into hers.

She wrapped her arms around him and sobbed, "Oh, Lucas! Those poor people."

He held her close. It felt so right. After a minute, she said, "I need to text Felix and give him a heads-up."

Separating, he nodded. "Good. Did you get any photos on your phone? Well, send them to Felix. No chance of losing them if they're in the cloud." He held up his Canon. "I'm uploading mine with my phone's hotspot as we speak. I'm guessing I'll need the space for more moving forward. While your photos are sending, start putting everything you can recall in your notes. It'll help you recall hours from now. Try to wrap memories around photos as the day progresses because you'll be overwhelmed fairly fast with an event this size."

She nodded, feeling her numbness retreat, and felt more confident now that she had a plan. "What's going to happen? Are we reporters, or do we help with rescue efforts?"

He placed a hand on her arm. "If you're up to it—both. Helping is human and people will remember. You'll remember. But take a breather when you can, and record what's happening around you."

"Right."

"I heard Loretta calling for safety equipment. When it gets here, don't be shy. Grab whatever you can. Gloves, safety glasses—and especially water. Rescue efforts won't happen immediately. Emergency Management will need to figure out a clear picture before they set up a plan, so you have a lot of time to prepare. I'll be adding to my own notes while I'm waiting."

"Thank you, Lucas!" She said, genuine emotion in her voice.

"I've been involved in a few big events before, although none of the other stories were anywhere this big," he said, flashing her a smile. "You'll be all right. Just watch your step—and be careful! We're not the heroes. We *report* on the heroes. Your experiences will be your story. Make it a good one."

A long, low wail of approaching sirens reached their ears, and they gave each other a warm hug. For a moment, their eyes held. He stepped back as if he felt he had over-stepped a line. *He's blushing. That's sweet.* She stepped forward and placed a hand on his cheek, then kissed him lightly on the lips.

The first fire truck's arrival broke the moment.

Burgess and Loretta spoke with the responders, taking away an opportunity for Jamie to get closer to them. Lucas showed the emergency workers his video of the smokestack falling, to give them an idea of what they were up against.

With the chimney having been close to a quarter of a mile high, with it down, the immediate scene was at least that long. With movement of the debris on impact—rolling, crushing, and continuous expansion as the stack shattered—the scene would extend and widen as well.

Hindering everything was the thick canopy of gray-white dust that hovered over the community.

Emergency Management quickly made the nearest community sports arena the base camp for survivors. It was only a few streets away from where the smokestack had fallen, but central to the town. Jamie quickly offered to help with the intake center, clipboard in one hand and a never-ending supply of bottled water near the other for survivors. As shell-shocked citizens staggered out of the dust, responders guided them to the community center. There, they received medical checks and had their identification logged.

As Lucas had suggested, Jamie listened closely to the stories, muttering comments into her phone's recorder app for future reference. It soon became an endless line of faces in shock, tearstains trailing through caked dust.

Two hours after the stack's collapse, the first word of casualties made its way to the intake center. Jamie recorded every word.

LUCAS FOLLOWED THE street slowly on foot with a team of three of the strikers. They wore N95 masks, safety gloves, and hardhats, although Lucas' helmet refused to sit securely on his head, even after the others had tried to adjust it.

A pumper truck led the group slowly up the street, its rotating emergency lights creating a kaleidoscope of shapes through the thick dust. As they entered a thicker cloud of dust and dirt, it soon dulled the familiar red of the emergency vehicle with a layer of drab gray-white. Lucas saw that their clothes carried the same coating. He was glad he had the mask and safety goggles.

They were still four blocks from the business center, let alone the Alta Italia area. He was aware of another group taking a different route to reach Alta Italia through an underpass. From a news point of view, he had wanted to be with that group; however, they'd assigned him to this one. The goal was for both teams to meet up before attempting to enter the devastated suburb, and he was worried about what he might find. It was one thing to report a story, but he didn't need the residual nightmares that came from mass casualties.

As they moved forward, they approached homes in twos, banging on front doors, searching for people at home. They were to register all names of anyone sheltered in the homes. Lucas and his team were advising people to stay indoors unless they were having difficulty breathing, in which case they were to go to the community center.

"This is my home and I ain't leaving it. I know my rights!" said one homeowner, his angry eyes defiant. He was in his mid to late sixties.

"Nobody is asking you to leave, sir," Lucas's partner said. "This dust is making it hard to breathe. So, if you have trouble breathing, just make your way to the arena. We have people and supplies to assist you."

"I don't need any help. I just want to be left alone."

Lucas lifted gloved hands in a submissive gesture. "No problem. But make sure you shut any intakes, like your air conditioner. This dust will clog it up in no time."

The man grunted and slammed his door shut.

Lucas and his partner, a miner named Tim, looked at each other and shrugged. Tim tied off a length of florescent ribbon to the front doorknob to show someone was inside and might need checking on later. As if the owner could see through the door, he yanked the door open viciously and tore the tape off as if they had marked his home with a sign of the devil.

"I know my rights!" he yelled.

Lucas and Tim stepped back quickly, apprehensive about potential violence. Only when the door slammed shut did either of them exchange a surprised look.

"For a moment there," Tim said, "I thought he was going to attack us."

Lucas swallowed hard, his mouth as dry as the dust around him, and nodded.

The street ended at a huge community park. Lucas could see the dust cloud was thinning as it settled. A slight breeze sent swirls of dust back towards the smelter complex. His tension lifted a bit as cleaner air graced his sweaty, dust-covered skin.

At the far end of the park, near the elementary school, he spied a group of kids playing pickup baseball on the dusty field, as if nothing out of the ordinary had happened. *In denial?* Lucas wondered. He pulled out his camera and took a few shots. Laughter and the crack of the bat reached them as Lucas packed his camera; and for a moment, the horror he knew was around the next corner left him.

He turned to his partner. "The blessing of youth."

"Be nice to join them for a while. We ought to warn them to get out of the dust. They're breathing it."

"Aw. Let them play while they can. They're going to have to face ugly reality soon enough. Besides, look, the dust isn't as bad here, and it's settling."

Lucas nodded, and turned, and trudged back into the dust.

The street bent towards the business section, and the group encountered the first signs of damage. Concrete, masonry, and building material blocked the roadway. Through slow-shifting clouds of grit and dust, they could see that the entire end of a three-story commercial building was missing. It was if someone had chopped a diagonal line through the structure with a massive axe, severing a chunk of building.

From the hole in the building, Lucas could see that the upper floors were apartments. A porcelain toilet hung precariously over the building's edge, it's mooring just a sewage pipe—all that held it from falling to the street.

Among the scattered furnishings and building materials, they encountered their first casualties. A man and a woman, still wrapped in their bedsheets, lay crumpled on the pavement, the mattress of their bed lying beside them.

The pumper had already stopped, and firefighters were stepping out, air packs already mounted to fend against the powdery air. Without any orders, two of the first responders covered the two bodies with a canvas tarp. The fire captain radioed in the information and location for body recovery.

An alley ran behind the building, but more debris blocked it, making the area impassable for the truck.

Following the lead of the professional rescuers, Lucas and the small band of miners slowly rounded the decapitated structure. They found what had destroyed the older building. Lucas recorded the sight through the lens of his camera.

Nestled tight to the building across the street, an old hospital that had been converted to a senior's complex known as The Brookside, was the gigantic, shattered tip of the smokestack. Incredibly, most of the section of chimney was intact, towering over the three-story building. The massive, smoke-stained chunk of cement sat in a crater, dug into the front lawn by its own impact.

Having only ever seen it from a distance, the immensity of just the top end was mind-numbing, leaving the entire group to gape in shock and disbelief. For all its size and weight, it seemed to lean casually against the old hospital, its energy obviously bled out after it struck the apartment building. The only actual damage Lucas could make out was the broken glass of nearly every window facing the street. The building seemed stable, but they all had to jump back as shards of concrete suddenly broke off the stack's tip to scatter dangerously across the yard.

The captain radioed what they had encountered and announced that they would search for survivors. He called for a city transit bus and ambulances to stand by. The entire group made their way to the rear entrance and found the back parking lot was full of seniors sitting on walkers, wheelchairs, or on the lawn. All wore a layer of dust like a second skin, and a few were choking and coughing. Hands and canes rose as they spotted the first responders, and a ragged cheer met the team. The entire group of seniors had masks on and, for once, Lucas found one positive thing that had come from the Covid pandemic: People were used to wearing masks.

A man and a woman in nurse's uniforms ran to the firefighters with obvious relief. The woman held a large binder to her chest.

"Thank God you're here," said the woman, whose nametag read *Carol*. "We need to evacuate these people to a safer site. I don't know how safe the building is with that thing leaning on it."

"We have transportation standing by," said the captain. "Anyone injured?"

She shook her head and Lucas noticed her hands shook as from a palsy.

"No, but we lost three to heart attacks," she said. "The shock of the building being hit was too much for them. We found them after we accounted for everyone else. The telephone lines went down when that thing hit us, so we could not even contact 911."

"No one had a mobile phone?" Lucas asked before his brain told him that the captain was in charge. He just couldn't shut off his reporter's inquisitiveness. He nodded apology to the officer.

She shook her head. "We tried. No service. Maybe the cell tower was taken out as well."

The captain turned to the male nurse, checking his name tag. "Ben, can to you guide my men to the rooms where the deceased are? I'm not questioning your expertise, but we have to do our own checks." He turned to his crew, "Grab the med equipment, and do a thorough check for vitals and radio back."

The three quickly shadowed the nurse to the building entrance while the driver grabbed the equipment.

The captain raised his microphone to his mouth. "Brookside Command to dispatch."

"Go ahead, Command," came a calm, almost bored, female voice.

"We have three Vital Signs Absent on site. Advise EMS."

"Roger, Command. Three VSA." The woman's voice didn't change at the terrible news.

It's like she's doing a crossword puzzle.

The captain turned to Carol. "We'll let EMS do their thing with the three inside, and then we'll arrange transportation. Can I see your emergency action plan? I need to know what your plans for evacuation are."

She nodded, opened the binder to the table of contents, found the information, and turned to the tab before handing the binder to the fire officer. Lucas tried reading over the man's shoulder, but couldn't see anything. Rather than crowd the officer, he stepped away and pulled out his camera and began framing a shot.

The nurse stepped forward. "We have stiff rules about picture taking in our home."

"I'm press." Lucas said. "I need to document this!"

"You're not a reporter today, Lucas," the captain said without looking up from the binder. "You're just here as a volunteer rescuer, so put the camera away, please."

Lucas lowered his camera but held it against his leg. He would not antagonize the officer, but he knew perfectly well he was within his rights. He couldn't afford to be escorted out of the response area, though. Keeping his camera tight against his thigh, from memory, he pressed what he hoped was the video selector and slowly turned, so that the camera panned the parking lot, recording the group of seniors who waited patiently. He had used this technique in the past. After he had thirty seconds of video, he put the camera away.

Three ambulances arrived and backed towards the rear entrance. Lucas and the group of miners moved forward to help carry equipment while they paramedics set up stretchers. Then, as a group, they all entered the building. Lucas followed the medic he was assisting, a duffle bag in one hand and a heavy defibrillator machine in the other. He looked around, wondering if the building could come down on them all. His hands were sweating heavily under the safety gloves.

Inside, Ben, the nurse, met them. "The fire guys are saying we can't use the elevator, because it might have been damaged and there's no power anyway. Two of our residents are on the second floor, and the last one is on the third." Leaving the stretchers in the hall, the group began stomping up the stairs.

Ben directed Lucas's medic to the left when they reached the second floor. "Room 207." He pointed the other direction. "Room 202. Both found with vital signs absent a little over two and a half hours ago." As they moved down the hallway, they could hear the hollow steps of the third team moving upward.

They entered the open door of the apartment and were waved towards the bedroom by one firefighter. Broken glass crunched underfoot, and Lucas saw the windows had been blown inward. The shadow of the stack's tip blocked most of the light. *SHIT! It could crash into the apartment at any time!*

"VSA. Signs of lividity," said the firefighter.

The medic nodded. He checked the lone figure, an elderly man who lay in the bed. His eyes and mouth were wide open, as if something had scared him to death. He was thin as a rail. The medic checked for a pulse. Finding none, he pulled back the covers to expose the man's lower body. Lucas almost gagged on the smell that rose from the bed, and he had to swallow hard. *The poor guy soiled himself.* The medic lifted one leg and a dark-looking bruise was visible under the calf.

Noticing Lucas' expression, the firefighter said, "Lividity. After a couple of hours, gravity pulls the blood and it pools, so that it's visible."

The medic pulled out a cell, hit speed dial and spoke into the phone. "Morning Doctor. We're at the Brookside Retirement home. We have an elderly male, approximately eighty-five. VSA with obvious, lividity. Debris from the stack struck the building. They found him after he did not appear for a head count. Nurse on site said that was two and half hours ago."

He listened, then nodded. "Called. Time of Death, 12:44. Thank you, sir."

Hearing someone entering the apartment, Lucas turned to see a police officer. He moved aside to allow the constable into the room. The other rescuers looked up at the newcomer.

"You have two more in other areas of the building. Question is, with the instability of the building, do you want us to remove them?"

"I would," said the constable. "But let me check with the coroner."

He stepped into the other room and pulled out his phone. A minute later, he poked his head back inside. "I'll take a photo of the room and then you can transport them."

Everyone cleared the room to allow the officer to take his photos.

"Where are the others?" asked the constable.

"Apartment 202 and 306," said the medic.

"Thanks," he said and left the room.

"Do you want the stair-chair?" one firefighter asked the medic.

"No, it'll be easier if we use a sheet to carry him to the stretcher. It's only one set of stairs and there are enough of us."

They passed the medical bags back to Lucas while the medic spread the blanket from the bed onto the floor. With one fire fighter at the head and the medic at the man's feet, they lifted the corpse and gently laid him onto the sheet.

"Because of the doors, you and I will have to carry him. Once we reach the hallway, we'll spread the weight around."

The fire fighter nodded. They took the blanket in both hands and lifted the body. Moving in a shuffle, they left the bedroom. Lucas followed, laden with their equipment.

Reaching the hallway, they laid the body down so that they each could grab a corner of the blanket. The medic took the duffle bag from Lucas and slung the strap over his neck, so his hands were free. Even with the four of them carrying the man, it surprised Lucas how heavy the thin man was. He clenched the blanket as tightly as he could, his hands clammy. *Don't let me drop him!*

Moments later, the man's body was loaded and secured to a stretcher. The medic covered the man with a sheet, including the head. It impressed Lucas how the responders took every effort to allow the dead man every dignity they could in their handling of his body.

Once the last ambulance left the parking lot, a city transit bus pulled in. Lucas and the others helped the elder occupants of the retirement home onto the vehicle that would transport them to a safer location. Lucas made a mental note to speak with his editor, Felix.

What happened to the seniors would be a good follow-up to the disaster.

Chapter 28

Jamie passed a handout to the thirteen-year-old girl who had come to that refuge center with her mother and baby brother, but then reconsidered. The girl, whose name was Mandie—with an 'ie' and not a y—wore a baseball cap turned backwards, which fit with her dirty jeans and black-and-white runners. A mud-streaked t-shirt finished the ensemble and screamed, tomboy. The fact that this kid had her shit together was not lost on anyone who could hear her comforting her mother.

"Mom," she said in an annoyed voice, "You can stop with the waterworks. You're fine, baby Ryan is fine, and I'm cool. Dad's at work and the house is intact, so there's nothing to cry about."

The woman's lip quivered at the scolding, and Jamie had to fight not to laugh out loud.

Waving her clipboard, she motioned to the girl, "Grab some water for your mom and brother. Someone will call you when a phone opens up so you can get hold of your father to let him know everyone is okay. I'm sure he's worried."

All business-like, the girl nodded, as if taking care of adults was nothing new to her. She swept up three plastic bottles with one arm clamped to her side and grabbed her bother's diaper bag with the other. Flicking her head from her mother to the arena's floor, where chairs had been set up, she led the way like a general on a forced march.

The interchange with the feisty girl was a welcome break from the worried and shell-shocked citizens arriving out of the dust clouds. Other groups arriving were those searching for family members, only to find their way home blocked by authorities and debris. The arena, which had first felt cool, after spending most of the morning in the sun had become warm and breathless as more and more people joined the ranks of refugees.

Tears, pale expressions, and shaking hands had become the normal reactions. In between different encounters, Jamie recorded snippets of facts and opinion on her phone's recorder. She captured photos after receiving permission, usually via vacant nod from a numb individual, like the mother of Ryan and 'Mandie with an ie.'

When time allowed, she made her way back to the young family and sat down beside Mandie's mother. Checking her clipboard, she reminded herself that the woman's name was Clair.

"Clair," she asked. "Are you feeling better?"

The woman said nothing for a moment, as if Jamie hadn't spoken, but then her face crumbled. "I saw it—the stack. I watched it fall." She shuddered and rubbed her arms as if she was freezing. "I was washing dishes—the window over the sink faces the smelter. I watched it *fall*, and it came right towards the house. There was nothing I could do. I thought it would kill us all." Tears were falling silently down her cheeks, and she bit her lip.

Jamie and Mandie exchanged a look of horror.

"All I could think of was that my babies and I would be dead ... and Teddy would be alone." At this admission, the woman's sobs intensified.

"Teddy's my dad," Mandie said as she took a chair beside her mother and held her as she cried.

Feeling like an intruder, Jamie left them to themselves. It was all she could do to keep from losing it, herself. *There's too much misery. It's overwhelming.* She made a quick trip to the washroom and splashed cold water on her scarf, then used it to wipe her face and neck to help cool down. She took a swig from her water bottle, stared into the mirror, and said out loud, "This is what you wanted to do for a living, so put your big-girl pants on and get to work."

Returning to the floor, one of the Emergency management workers approached her.

"Jamie, we have a group of university students willing to help here. Would you be interested in setting up an advanced induction center closer to where the stack hit Alta Italia? The responders are getting ready to enter the impact area and are bound to find casualties. I don't want to send these young students there in case they start bringing in the wounded or ..."

Jamie's heart jumped, knowing that this might put her in the center of the story. She had captured a ton of material and individual stories so far, but the main story was going to be the collapse of the super stack.

"Tell me what you want."

Jamie walked the students through the process of collecting the information on new arrivals. Afterwards, Jamie, the students and an older emergency worker, named Curtis, loaded cases of water and energy bars into an SUV. There were pads of input forms for taking down personal and contact information. Curtis gave Jamie a quick lesson on using a satellite phone, which was to be her point of contact with Emergency Management Operations or EMO.

"You need anything," Curtis explained as he and Jamie drove out of the arena parking lot and turned to the right. "You contact EMO. Ambulances, Police, more water, all requests go through EMO, and they make it happen. I'll be back and forth, moving equipment and those people who don't require an ambulance, so you'll never be alone for long. There will also be at least one or two ambulances waiting for victims."

They passed the mine's parking lot, empty because of the strike.

Jamie nodded, feeling the excitement growing. "I'll be okay."

On their right, a fire truck was slowly crossing the rail tracks, and Curtis said, "The bigger trucks can't fit under the train trestle. They have to cross here and then drop down to the neighborhood."

It was a minor fact, but something she would never have thought to ask about. She whispered the fact into her phone, which earned her a raised eyebrow from her chauffeur. She lifted her phone. "Recording what I see for later, when I write the story."

"You going to write about me?"

"Yeah. I'd like to find a spot, if you are interested. Do you want to give me your full name and occupation?" she asked, holding out her phone towards him.

"Curtis Greer, Emergency Management volunteer and short-wave radio operator."

"Radio operator?"

"A ham. VE3, et cetera. They use us in case all the infrastructure goes down. Old School Rules!" he said with a smile.

On the corner of Main Street, beside a firetruck and two empty ambulances, and overlooking the underpass for the train line, Curtis pulled over. When the mine was working, the train carried molten waste from the smelter to dumping areas or slag dumps. Curtis and Jamie set up a tent that reminded her of a farmer's market. A folding table and a couple of chairs finished the setup. A large box held blankets, a first aid kit, and boxes of energy bars.

As Curtis drove away, back towards the reception center, Jamie turned to study the far neighborhood. The sight almost dropped her to her knees. The stack had fallen and was hemmed in by the buildings and the bald rock-structure of the topography. The stack had crushed houses and other buildings on either side of Venice Street under its massive weight, the stack itself now looking like a gigantic, fossilized prehistoric snake. The chimney, although deflated as it had mostly collapsed on its inner cavity, still rose over the neighboring buildings that stood intact, if not broken by the impact. From her vantage spot, she could not see the reflection of even one window in the neighborhood.

Earlier, she had googled the stack and knew that even at its tapered tip it was sixteen meters or fifty-two feet in diameter—almost five stories wide. Now the debris field was almost twice that, having flattened on impact.

The devastation reminded Jamie of the unpredictability of tornados that flatten one home, while leaving the next totally unmarked. She could see that the Cultural Club, the heart of the neighborhood, had been untouched.

The dust was settling, and she could see people moving on the streets north of the devastation, their movements staggering and hesitant in shock. Covered in dust, they looked like extras in a zombie movie. But they were alive. She bit her lip. The realization of the loss of life hit her like a hammer and she had to grab a tent pole to keep from falling. Grabbing a water bottle, she splashed semi-warm fluid across her brow, the sudden change in temperature helping her center.

With shaking hands, she lifted her phone and began recording a video of the scene. Her voice, sounding like a stranger, even to her. "The stack has... fallen across parts of Alta Italia. I can ... I can see firefighters moving through the area south of the impact area, herding people out of the danger zone to safety. Another crew is working on the north side of the neighborhood, which is mostly intact." She zoomed the camera into the area where pieces of crushed homes poked from under the massive weight of the broken stack. "It will take days—maybe weeks before emergency crews can account for all the victims of this horrible event." In her mind, she saw and heard the staccato of explosions that had cut across the base of the stack. From the sequence of explosions, she knew with certainty the superstack had been cut down purposely with no regard for human life. She also knew that Lucas had filmed the string of explosions and the toppling of the monumental structure.

"After the previous sabotages at the Novo's Fox Lake smelter and the systematic destruction of the superstack, one thing is for certain." She paused allowing her camera to reach out to where the base of the stack stood in the distance, at the far end of the serpentine cement rubble like a gigantic tree stump. "This was definitely a terrorist attack. Jamie Coleman, Fox Lake Journal." She uploaded the video and texted Felix that she would be busy for the next while, helping the people streaming out of the neighborhood.

The shock and immensity of the devastation had temporarily distracted her. It suddenly occurred to her that the people approaching would make their way to her. It was her job to gather their identification and family contact information before they were shuttled to the reception center. She tore the plastic cover off a case of water and readied her paperwork and pens while she waited for the refugees to stagger to her position. Using the sat phone, she requested a transit bus to move the people from her portable induction table to the reception center.

As the first group trudged to her table, she held out bottled water and greeted them with a sympathetic smile.

For hours, Jamie was inundated with refugees fleeing the nearest thing to a war zone that any of them had ever encountered. She heard various versions of how people were knocked off their feet as the floorboards of their homes seemed to ripple with the impact of the stack.

"The whole house was pushed off its foundation and rolled over onto its roof," one man told her, holding a bloodied cloth to his forehead. "When I came to, I was lying on the ceiling. I climbed out of a window and stepped right onto the street. It used to be a third-floor apartment."

Plaster walls splintered and cracked, threatening to collapse. Ceilings had rained down on homeowners as they fled the previously perceived safety of their own homes with friends and neighbors whose homes no longer existed. Had they been home? Were they at work? With school out for the summer, were the kids home?

The lineup of crying, shell-shocked individuals and clusters of families seemed endless to Jamie. She had openly wept with these strangers as they came together and shared their horrors with her.

During a lull, three hours into her stint, she rose and splashed more water onto her face, both to cool herself and to wash away the evidence of her own grief. She wondered if she would have to get help, herself, from someone. She had read too much about PTSD not to think she'd be untouched by the horror and pain surrounding her.

In the distance, she could see a line of covered bodies being laid out by the firefighters. There was no vehicle access to that part of the neighborhood because of the debris blocking the only road leading inward. The dead would have to be carried over the rail line by the rescuers, an arduous climb up an embankment of shifting slag.

Movement caught her eye, and she turned to see a man stumble from out of the underside of the trestle. He staggered, bent over, clutching his stomach in obvious pain. As the sun hit him, she could see a crimson smear that spread down his pant legs.

She dropped the bottle and raced forward to help him.

With a hand on the retaining wall leading into the underpass, he slid to the pavement, leaving a red streak of blood on the gray concrete. His body curled into a ball of pain.

Jamie slid to a halt beside the moaning man. "What happened?"

"Por favor," he gasped. "Me ajude!"

Por favor? Spanish? She didn't know the language, but it was clear he was asking for help. She patted the man's arm in what she prayed he realized was hope and ran back to her station.

Grabbing up the phone, she hit the speed dial and without pre-amble said, "This is the induction tent at Main, near the underpass. I need an ambulance here. There's a man—he's covered in blood."

Without waiting for a reply, she dropped the phone onto the table, grabbed the first aid kit, and ran back to the injured man. The man was struggling to stand. Jamie threw her arm around the man and guided him to the tent, so he was out of the sun. He whimpered as she helped him to the ground. It was time to put to use the skills she had learned years ago during a weekend course that combined CPR and First Aid. She had never had to practice them before but felt confident she could do it.

She dropped the large first aid kit on the ground and tore open the zippered opening. Recognizing a collection of compresses, she pulled them out and, using her teeth, tore the paper packaging. Bundling three together, she reached in and pulled the man's hand away from the wound. His startled expression registered him seeing her for the first time. Trying to be gentle, she pulled his shirt away to reveal a small hole in his stomach. Blood oozed from the wound. *Oh my God, has he been shot?* Checking, she saw that blood had saturated the rear of his shirt, indicating an exit wound. Placing one compress over the stomach injury, she placed the man's hands over the bandage. Reaching over him, she pulled his shirt back to reveal a ragged exit hole. She pressed the remaining compresses firmly onto the opening, causing the man to whimper.

"Who are you? Who did this to you? Can you speak English?"

"Jar—Jaren Pinheiro." His accent was so heavy and his voice so quiet that Jamie had to lean forward. "*O homem.* . . The man did this—*O diabo,* he make the big tower . . . blow up—"

Her eyes grew wide. "The stack! You know who blew up the smokestack?"

"*Sim!*" he gasped. "Yes. Drago... Pet . . . kov..."

Suddenly, his body went rigid as a sharp crack cut through the afternoon silence . . . as warm liquid sprayed up her chest and face, shocking her to freeze in place. Looking down, she saw the blood and gore dripping from her skin and clothing. *What?*

It took a couple of heartbeats for Jamie to realize that the sound was from a gunshot. *Oh, my God!*

She looked up, her eyes searching for some sign of the shooter, totally oblivious to her own safety, but saw nothing.

Chapter 29

The task force had set up at the empty gravel pit near the property Lucas and Jamie had scouted.

Lucas and Jamie stared wide-eyed at the bustle of stern-looking law-enforcement officers from at least four jurisdictions that included the military. There were just as many command posts, that ranged from the simple tents that the army favored, to huge forty-eight-foot RV units with satellite feeds and full lighting capability.

At least three different generators rumbled at the rear of the lot, feeding the electrical needs of the modern police forces.

Forbes, the master-spy had called them back only three hours after Lucas contacted him. Lucas and Jamie, working on less than two hours of sleep after yesterday's attack, were on shoe-string reserves.

Jamie had been driving again, and guards at a checkpoint had stopped them after the intersection of Old Cartier Road and Ministic Lake Road. Police had swarmed the vehicle until they confirmed their credentials and permission to attend the command post. Lucas nudged Jamie and tilted his head to their rear. Four automatic-rifle-toting SWAT members had them under watch in case they proved to be parties of interest.

"No sudden moves, eh?"

She bit her lip and shook her head.

Eventually, the guards waved the vehicle through. But at the entrance to the gravel pit, they once again had to go through a checkpoint and were directed to a secured area for parking. There, a soldier in green fatigues marched them to one of the command posts where Forbes was blowing steam off a mug of coffee.

"Thank you, Private," he said, bowing his head to the young soldier. To Lucas and Jamie, he asked, "Coffee?" They both accepted, and the spymaster served them himself. Lucas smiled his appreciation but waited for the reprimand he assumed was coming for his late-night adventure that had located the farmhouse.

"You are to be commended for locating the enemy's base of operations," Forbes said. "I'm extremely pleased to find that you survived the encounter." He sipped his coffee as if nothing bothered him. "However, had you contacted me the other night with your other findings, we might have avoided yesterday's attack."

When Lucas tried to defend himself, Forbes raised a hand.

"I said 'might.' We have no information how long that property has been empty. It already may have been too late. It makes strategic sense to find a new camp prior to an attack."

Lucas knew Forbes was not as pleased as he let on, but it surprised him that Forbes didn't speak with more passion. As with everything Forbes said or did, he never seemed to be troubled by what was going on around him. He accepted what he could not change and worked with the cards dealt. Lucas recalled how he had snapped at Jamie earlier this week. He could learn a lot from Forbes.

He glanced at Jamie. She avoided his eyes, yet she pursed her lips together as if she didn't trust herself not to remind him of the risk he had taken.

"So," Lucas said, directing his question to the CSIS Director. "What's the plan?"

Forbes motioned toward the military tent and walked them towards it. "We have dispatched members of the Canadian Special Operations Regiment or CSOR to do a reconnaissance of the property." He held the tent flap open for them, and both ducked into the darkened interior.

Equipment and personnel cramped the interior of the tent. A bank of computer monitors glowed with a soft radiance that lit the tent, giving those monitoring them the bloodless pallor of corpses. Lucas tried to push the morbid thought away, but it remained.

"Colonel Cameron," Forbes said, as a way of introducing them to a uniformed man who was standing at one of the monitors. "These are the two reporters who tracked our suspects to this property. Lucas Kucher and Jamie Coleman."

The officer glared at the interruption. He looked both reporters over before saying, "So you're the two idiots who thought it smart to enter what might have been an armed terrorist camp? God damn! Civilians!"

Lucas would have stepped back from the confrontation, but there was nowhere to go. As it was, the back of his head was brushing the canvas roof. He sensed Jamie's smirk of vindication, but refused to be baited. Rather, he said nothing.

The colonel stared at them before turning to Forbes in disgust.

"As I was saying, Colonel," Forbes said as if there had been no outburst, "These two found the culprits responsible for the events at Novo, even though law enforcement and intelligence entities could not. I invited them to join us today as thanks."

Lucas watched the military man's complexion turned beet red as he held in a reply. *I'm starting to really like Forbes.* The uniformed officer turned his back to them and waved at the bank of monitors.

"We have four teams of four moving towards the target buildings from different angles. They will ascertain if the property is actually vacant. If not, they will attempt to apprehend the occupants. The teams will also secure the buildings and ensure no unpleasantries were left behind."

"The colonel is referring to booby-traps," Forbes said.

"The teams also know full well how to search for any intelligence information," said Colonel Cameron, "whether it be physical, analog, or digital. If the enemy has left any indication of their new location, my teams will find it.

"These four videos are from the team leaders' body-cams," he said, indicating the monitors. "While this one," he added, pointing at the center, "is the aerial view from a reconnaissance drone we deployed."

Both Lucas and Jamie stared at the ever-changing views from five different perspectives. They were in full color, and they realized they were live feeds. Lucas felt an overwhelming omnipresence, like a video gamer watching his minions move towards their objective. He exchanged a quick glance at Jamie and found her equally absorbed in the display.

This is so cool!

THE BUSH HAD GONE DEATHLY quiet. No squirrel scampered; no bird fluttered. It was as if nature was holding its breath as killers stalked the forest.

Clad in camouflaged, lightweight body-armor, Lieutenant Cheryl Desormeaux of Team Charlie slid between two pines with only a whisper. Her three teammates followed on a parallel route, but at the four and eight positions of a 'V-pattern' so they all wouldn't get hit if the enemy opened fire.

She couldn't yet see either the barn or the farmhouse they had briefed her about. Nor could she see or sense the other three teams closing in from other directions.

The briefing had held a lot of unconfirmed information. Unknown number of enemies, possibly armed, possibly ex-military.

If these were the same people who had been attacking the Novo facilities, they were well-trained and deadly. Not having a thorough knowledge of what her team was facing was bothersome. She knew that a drone was flying reconnaissance, but it was high enough not to be seen or heard. But it reported seeing nothing other than the buildings already identified.

They were going in half-blind.

Satellite imaging showed the house empty of heat signatures, but she knew that could have changed since the last over-flight.

When she made out the peak of a building, she raised a clenched fist to signal her crew and sank to one knee. Using hand signs, she warned her teammates of what she was seeing. She double-tapped her throat-mic to inform the operations leader she was in place.

While she waited for the other teams to signal their readiness, she kept her eyes moving over the area in front of their position. Instinctively, she knew the others were watching for hostiles on either flank, while their fourth member watched their six.

Other than a light breeze that bent the tips of the trees, the only sound came from small rodents burrowing under the forest floor. She could smell the damp, earthy smell of decomposing vegetation, last year's leaves and pine needles, and it reminded Desormeaux of her own family's home in northern Quebec.

Three quick clicks in her earpiece marked the commencement of the assault. Even after all her training, her heart was in her throat, but she welcomed the surge of adrenaline. Her old friends who rode desks Monday to Friday had no concept of this kind of life. She wouldn't trade it for a second.

Rising to a crouch, Desormeaux moved forward, Colt C7A2 rifle at the ready. She could hear the furtive movements of her teammates behind her and felt secure they had her back.

The building in front of them became more distinct as the trees thinned out. It was the barn. She headed towards the rear corner of the barn so they could clear two sides at the same time.

Without being told, two of her team, Anderson and Thibeaux, scurried across the back of the structure to peek along the far side.

Her partner, Morin, gave her shoulder a tap to signal Anderson's 'All clear.'

Crouching below a window on the side of the barn, from a leg pocket she pulled out a telescopic rod with a mirror on one end. Raising the tool to a corner of the dirty glass pane, she checked the interior, but all she saw was shadows.

Nothing moved.

Moving forward to the side door, she pulled another tool from a different pocket. She unwrapped the flexible endoscope cable from the handle and energized the unit. Once the screen lit up and the green light showed that it was ready, she pushed the camera under the wooden door.

Using ambient light from the barn's dirty windows, the lens pushed back the shadows. She immediately recognized the trap. Someone had pulled a tripwire across the doorway.

Dropping the handheld endoscope, her hand flew to the transmission button at her throat, and she frantically sent three pulses followed by a second set of three across the network to signal she'd found a booby-trap.

Every soldier in the operation she knew would be frozen-in-place to wait for further instructions. If there were one trap, there more than likely would be more.

"Charlie Team, go," whispered a calm voice in her ear.

Desormeaux glanced behind her, and Morin gave her a nod to continue. He crept up beside her.

Together, they watched the four-and-a-half-inch screen as she manipulated the lens to expose the full trap. The tripwire crossed the door at ankle height, held tight to one side by a simple nail. The other side was the issue. Following the wire with the camera, she centered the fisheye lens on a Chinese Type-86P fragmentation grenade. Duct tape secured the high explosive to the opposite side of the door frame. *One hundred and TWO uses for duct tape!*

Twisting the cable electronically, she altered the camera's view and confirmed that the tripwire connected to the grenade's pin, which had been straightened for smooth release.

Beside her, Morin moved his fingers to signal they should cut the wire. She returned to the monitor and reviewed the entire trap once more before nodding.

Handing the endoscope to her partner, she reached into yet another pocket and pulled out a small pouch. Slowly undoing the zipper to reduce noise, she pulled out a tool one of her mates had dreamed up for this kind of scenario.

The gadget combined the flexibility of an extended slim-jim with the controls of a retractable pickup tool. Its outer metallic sleeve allowed her to bend it into any shape, and she manipulated it to fit under the door, then reach upward.

She exchanged the pickup adapter with a small set of cutting shears.

Desormeaux moved the tool in place, using the endoscope as her guide so that the tripwire lay in the grip of the two hardened-steel cutter blades.

She shrugged her head to Morin to pull back out of the blast area. There was no sense in both of them being killed if this went south.

Her partner wasn't having any of it, though. He gave her a smirk and flipped her the bird. The gesture warmed her heart, and she knew all the bullshit she'd put up with since her enrollment had been worth it. No matter what, she was part of something as strong as family. They had her back. So much more than her civilian life.

She crouched low, tilting her Kevlar helmet towards the building, knowing it could never protect her from a blast, but unable to help herself. She sensed Morin doing the same.

With a squeeze on the tool's double finger trigger, she cut the tripwire.

Opening her eyes, which she could not recall closing, she saw on the monitor that the wire no longer waited to pull the pin from the grenade. It lay limp on the floor.

With a sigh, she put her tools away. When complete, she turned the doorknob on the barn's man-door and pushed the door inward.

No explosion greeted them.

She sagged, feeling the dampness trickling down her shoulder blades. Worse, she caught a whiff of the acrid stench of her sweat and fear.

Through her throat mic, she clicked a three-keyed sequence, followed by two more. "All Clear."

She moved through the doorway into the barn, slowly, watching for secondary devices. Just before she took another step, a gloved hand yanked her shirt hard from behind and she fell backwards. She tensed, as her mind raced to understand what was happening. She felt sure hands lower her gently to the ground, Looking up, she saw Morin's tense features. He pointed two fingers at his eyes and then pointed towards the floor of the barn where she had been about to step.

What had he seen?

She rolled over into a crouch. His arm still pointed, and she followed the line of sight. With the light from the open door, she was able to make out three points peeking out of the dirt floor. *Land mine!* And she had almost stepped on it. Only Morin's quick action had saved her.

She risked a quick transmission. "Watch for secondary devices."

Looking at Morin, she pounded his chest twice with her gloved fist and nodded her thanks. She would definitely have to buy him a drink or maybe three after the mission.

Avoiding the hazard, she stepped through the door.

Moving to the right, she heard Morin turn left. Parked in the barn's center was a white Dodge van. It could wait. Following a predetermined search pattern that they had trained over and over, Desormeaux checked the immediate area for any signs of hazards.

While she searched, she heard the similar transmission clicks to indicate the soldiers entering the main house had also found booby-traps meant to maim or kill anyone when they attempted entry. After a time, "All Clear" signals boasted their successes.

The barn had two main doors that were held closed by a simple two-by-four held in a saddle. Light came from between and under the two doors. She checked the hinges and the simple wooden locking mechanism but found no other traps.

Confident the door was safe and needing better light to search the vast building, she pulled the long piece of wood from its cradle and leaned it up against the interior wall. She pushed the first door on the right open and swung it wide. Giving the second panel a push, it too swung open, but then hit something metal in the grass.

The unseen trigger.

Desormeaux turned in alarm when a high-pitched beeping emanated from the van behind her. She had no time to scream. No time to run.

Just time to die.

ON THE AERIAL MONITOR, the farm buildings—both barn and house—vanished in a flash of smoke and flame. The other four monitors across the tables all went black, and the technicians began hammering on their keyboards, trying to regain contact with the teams.

Jamie stood there, confused, not understanding what she had just witnessed. Lucas had gone pale, mouth slack, while Forbes' head hung as he rubbed his eyes. When he looked up and caught Jamie's scrutiny, his eyes flashed something dangerous. Something she never thought she would see in the suave gentleman-spy. Savage fury.

Seeing that expression pulled everything she had witnessed into a crystal-clear kernel of truth. She had just witnessed people dying.

The blast—the smoke was drifting away from the house—left two craters in the manicured yard. She could make out the shape of a van in what remained of the barn, and the explosion had transformed the house into a massive burn-pit. Several trees had ignited, and the pines flared as flames caught the pitch. And there, she watched her own hand raise and point—the outline of a body, stretched out on the grass. Unmoving.

The colonel spun in place and marched out of the tent, yelling orders in a loud baritone voice. Within minutes, two large army trucks loaded with armed soldiers were speeding towards the target property where black smoke marked the spot.

"We might as well make our way to the farm," Forbes said in an exhausted voice.

Forbes had gotten himself under control and spoke with his usual quiet resolve that Jamie realized, after having seen his reaction to the blast, was just a facade. He was a caring, dedicated man, but showed quiet confidence to keep others from panicking. *At least*, she thought, *he's human underneath.*

After Forbes parked in the roadside cutout that Jamie and Lucas had discovered when they'd scouted the farm, the three walked towards the charred remains of the farmhouse. They pressed themselves into the trees as one truck sped past them, a pair of medics working on what might have been a person on the rear floorboards of the deuce-and-a-half.

Entering the yard, the first thing Jamie saw was the devastation from the blast. Both buildings, house and barn, were razed almost to ground level. Wood, shingles, and glass were scattered across the lawn, while chunks of smoldering insulation hung from scorched branches like rotten fruit.

As they moved forward, all three stopped as two soldiers crossed in front of them with no apology, carrying a dull, black body bag that swung by its straps. They gently laid the slain soldier beside two companions, in a row under a clump of pines.

Jamie placed a hand over her mouth, and she reached out and grabbed Lucas's arm to steady herself. Her brain and heart had yet to truly grasp the idea that they had just watched these people die on the monitors.

They made their way to the front of what remained of the farmhouse. It was totally unrecognizable as a building that might have been someone's home. She pictured children running across the yard with clothes on the line. Not this death and destruction. Not here. Doesn't happen in Canada.

Of course, if any of her research proved anything, this was an underhanded attack by a world power whose primary goal was world domination by any means.

Suddenly, she felt the same resentment and anger that she had seen in Forbes. How dare they attack her country and people? She would write such a seething story to lambaste the Chinese—no, not the Chinese. Canada had a huge Chinese community that was completely innocent of this attack. Even the people in China had no choice but to do as they were told. The real problem was the Communist Party of China.

She didn't know how, but she would do anything in her power to expose them as the real enemy, both here and world-wide. The realization of this self-imposed task stopped her as she looked at the destruction in front of her, memorizing each charred timber, shard of glass, and body bag. These memories would motivate her in the frustrating and desperate time ahead.

This was no longer just a story. This was a life-changing quest—a lifelong mission.

She looked at Lucas, who stood off to one side, capturing the ruins and line of body bags through the lens of his camera. *What would he think? Would he encourage me or laugh at my naivety?* She felt—no—hoped that he would see himself in her assiduous pursuit of the truth.

She was eager to talk to him. To express her need to follow through with this ... crusade for justice. But Forbes called them over and she knew any such crusade would have to wait.

Lucas jogged to her side and together they walked to where Forbes and the colonel waited. A short, stocky middle-aged man in fatigues stood at ease, with his hands locked behind his back.

Forbes did a quick introduction to the soldier, Captain Terry McNally, an engineer and demolition expert attached to the CSOR.

"Go ahead, McNally. Please repeat what you've reported to me," said the colonel.

"Sir," he said with an Irish lilt and nodded sharply. "There were two devices. One in the house and the other in the van that was parked in the barn. Both were linked. I've found three definite triggers so far. There may have been more, but we'll have to dig out the debris once everything has cooled off."

He walked to the edge of the barn and pointed to the ground. "They hammered a steel rod into the ground, which was hooked up to one trigger. When the barn door, which was sheeted in metal, touched the rod, it closed a circuit, and both devices when up together. The teams would have had no warning. No time to run."

Jamie watched as Lucas's face lost its color. *It could have been him, and he knows it.*

"So," the colonel said, his face dour, "we're back where we started. Except I have ten dead soldiers and two who might not make it." He turned his dark eyes on Jamie and Lucas. "Since you are the two wonder investigators, can you do it again? Can you find these miserable worms?" He jabbed a finger at one and then the other. "But this time, *we* go in first! Understand?"

Chapter 30

The noise was like a burrowing rodent, scratching and digging into the depths of his brain. No matter how he tried to ignore the diligent bastard, it kept pawing into his consciousness. Then it stopped as suddenly as it had started and he felt relief flood his entire existence, except now he held his breath in anticipation.

When the noise returned, he almost cried out, part frustration, part fear. The gnawing became shriller, and his eyes opened to harsh light.

Without conscious thought, his hand reached out and found his phone on the bedside table. Through slitted eyes, he made out the words on the screen; and through the fog of his brain, he recognized Jamie's name.

Swiping the lens, he answered in a thick grunt, "What?"

"Up and at 'em, Lucas. There's work to do."

He groaned. The residual draw of the sleeping pill he had taken to calm his racing mind last night threatened to pull him back under.

"What happened?"

"Nothing on the Novo front, but you made me promise to get you up. You've been under for ten hours."

He sat up and put his feet on the floor, and a shiver went through him that almost knocked him over. The clothes he wore yesterday—was it only yesterday?—lay scattered on the floor. It surprised him he had managed to undress before crawling into bed.

"I'm picking up coffee and bagels and will be out front in fifteen minutes. Be ready!" she said in a far-too-energetic voice before clicking off.

With his eyes closed, he tracked down the hallway to the bathroom. After ten minutes under scalding hot water, he gradually reduced the temperature until it was cold. The contrast woke him completely, and he was dressed and locking the door when Jamie's Jeep pulled to the curb.

The smell of coffee filled the vehicle, and he ignored the burn of hot liquid as he sipped the dark roast.

"Thank you," he said, looking at the logo on the cup's exterior. "This is excellent."

"When I buy coffee, I only buy it from Espanola Roasters. Best coffee in Fox Lake. Besides, you look like you need more than one," she said with a laugh.

"You didn't get any more shuteye than I did. How come you're so chipper?"

"Good genes, I guess."

"I feel like I'm coming off a week-long bender."

"Well, maybe this will wake you up. Forbes has decided to let us run the story about Dragoljub Petkovic."

Lucas sat up straighter. "What changed his mind?"

"I'm guessing he's as desperate as the rest of us. He's even supplied a photo and what background information he has. He'll do a formal press release, but we get first crack at the story. And Felix wants both of us to write it up because our stories seem to be linked."

Lucas nodded. It made sense. The more eyes watching for the killer, the better the chances they'd have of flushing him out into the open, unless he'd already fled the country. *If I had taken down the Fox Lake smokestack, I'd be hightailing it to the nearest border. Hell, that's only three hours west of here.*

The piece took a little over an hour to put together, as they had to consult both Felix and Forbes concerning wording. At Lucas's suggestion, they omitted any reference to the assault on Amber or to the hiring of the other sex workers. There was no sense in marking them, in case the terrorist decided to make examples of them for talking to the authorities.

The story went live and was picked up nationally in minutes, and internationally not long after that.

"Now it's a waiting game," Felix said.

Lucas and Jamie exchanged a glance, and it was as if they could read the other's thoughts.

"I'm going to follow up on the property," Lucas said. "They had to buy or rent that farmhouse, so there should be a record somewhere of who did that."

"I'm sure the police are following up that lead already," Felix offered.

"Maybe, but it's better than sitting on my hands. I also want to visit Amber to see how she's making out. Now that we have a photo of Drago, we can get her to confirm that he was her attacker."

"And I want to keep digging into the Chinese connection," Jamie said.

Felix looked at both of them and said, "So, what are you doing sitting here?"

LUCAS WALKED INTO THE Amber's hospital room to find Christine talking animatedly with her. The social worker rose and hugged Lucas.

"After yesterday, I didn't know if you were alive or not. I was filling Amber in about the smokestack."

"Still here," he assured her. At first, he wondered why Christine would bring news of the superstack disaster to the girl. He figured Amber had enough stress as it was. Then, he reflected, there can't be many people who wouldn't be aware of the stack coming down.

Turning to the hospital bed, he smiled at the young girl. "And how is Amber today?"

She gave him an awkward smile, her mouth still wired shut. Much of the swelling had gone down and the dark bruises had turned that sick yellowish green that meant healing.

"It was pretty unbelievable," he said, leaning against the windowsill. Her room overlooked the snowflake-shaped science center, with Lake Ramsey stretching out behind.

"So, how are you feeling? Getting stronger?" Lucas asked Amber.

Amber nodded and grabbed a notebook off the over-bed table and scribbled a line before turning it for his scrutiny.

"Discharge in two days!" it read.

He smiled at her. "Now that's great news."

"I'm planning to have Amber move to a fresh apartment," Christine told him. "With Darcy and Rosie no longer in circulation, Amber is willing to give our program a try."

"Good for you, Amber. That's the best news I've heard in a while. Anything I can do to help, you let me know." He nodded toward Christine. "You have some great people in your corner."

The social worker glowed at the praise.

"Another reason I stopped by was to show you a photo of the man we think is your attacker, but we need you to confirm it." He held out his hand. "But only if you're up to it."

Amber looked nervously at Christine, who gave her a wink, before looking back at Lucas. Amber's fear was obvious, but so was the resolve that settled into her features before she held out her hand.

From his jacket pocket, he pulled out the photo that Forbes had supplied and handed it to the girl. She took it without looking, her eyes glued to Lucas's as if he were her anchor. She ran her lip over her teeth before glancing at the image. A shudder raked Amber's body. Her eyes teared up, and she began to visibly shake in fear.

"It's all right, Amber," Lucas said, taking back the offending picture. "He can't hurt you anymore."

Christine had stood up and rubbed the shivering shoulders in comfort. "Lucas is right. You're safe."

"I wanted to let you know," Lucas continued, "that your information helped us track this guy down." He held up his hand as her eyes widened in surprise and excitement. "He and his crew had already moved to another location; but there are a lot of resources on his trail, so it's only a matter of time until the police catch up to him."

The girl's expression changed to apprehension again, and he wondered if he should have said nothing.

She scribbled a note. "You don't think he'll come after me?"

Lucas shook his head. "First off, these people are the same group who took down the big smokestack. Christine told you about that? Good. They have every police force in the country hunting them. And we made a point of not mentioning any link between you and the other girls or your involvement with these men. In fact, they left you for dead; so as far as this guy knows, you are not an issue."

"And," Christine added, "you'll be in a new apartment in a different area of the city. I can't see how they'd find you, even if they were searching for you."

The tension seemed to drain from the girl, and she nodded with obvious relief.

Lucas glanced at Christine, and she mouthed the words, 'Thank you.' The girl had enough to worry about without the specter of her attacker haunting her.

He took in the room as she leaned back into the bed. His eyes settled on two tiny figures on a side table.

The first was a delicate yellow butterfly, while the other was a red water lily, both painstakingly folded from stiff paper.

"These are beautiful, Amber. Did you make them?"

She looked up at him in surprise before looking at the paper decorations and picking up her pad of paper. He studied the delicate sculptures while she jotted down her message.

"One man at the farmhouse gave them to us girls as we came into the house. I put them in my purse and forgot about them until yesterday. They are so pretty."

"Can you describe the man?"

"Small. No taller than me. Dark skin. Maybe Mexican. The others called him Jaren," she wrote.

He took in her form on the bed and tried to deduce how tall she was. "You're about five feet?"

She nodded.

He held up the paper figurines. "Gabby mentioned getting one of these from a guy at the party. I don't know if means anything, but can I take these, Amber? They may be evidence."

She shrugged.

Grabbing a tissue from the bedside table, he used it to gather the two figurines without touching them with his fingers. The police might pull fingerprints from them.

Amber bent over her notepad. "He was nice, but sad. He did not sleep with any of the girls."

"What do you mean, sad?"

She pointed to her eyes and mimicked a puppy dog pout, her bottom lip pushed out. She scribbled again. "The other men treated him real bad. Told him to go back to his shrine and pray. I didn't understand, but then was pulled into a bedroom to meet that one." she wrote, indicating the pocket where Lucas had put the photo of Drago.

She shuddered, and her face contorted into the now-familiar expression of pain and fear. Christine patted the girl's shoulder to remind her that she was not alone.

"You're among friends. It's okay, Amber."

The girl hugged Christine's hand against her cheek, and the gesture squeezed at Lucas's heart. He had to look away as a surge of emotion threatened to overcome his normal reserve.

After a moment, the girl pulled herself together with strength that impressed Lucas. She bent over the pad of paper before tearing the sheet off and thrusting it at Lucas.

He held onto the desperation in her eyes before looking down at the message.

"I need him in jail or better yet ... in a grave."

Chapter 31

Jamie had once again sequestered herself at the university library surrounded by every article she could find on Bao Daoming, the CEO of Fodineum.

So far, she had linked him to six subsidiary mining companies based in Africa and Pakistan. Those in the latter country were massive coal mines.

She did not miss the irony that China was closing its own coal mines to show compliance with worldwide environment pressures. To create an image of a cleaner China, Bao Daoming was opening many coal mines in other countries under the guise of the Belt and Road program. The majority of the coal was imported by China to meet their energy needs, resulting in the world blaming Pakistan and other exporters as world polluters.

She recognized the author of the current article, having read her multiple reports as a United Nations researcher. Amahle Naidoo, originally from South Africa, was highly respected in worldwide mining practices. Many of her reports that Jamie had read pointed to illegal or questionable mining practices throughout the world.

Jamie realized that speaking with the woman might unearth needed facts about Bao Daoming and other activities.

It took almost a half hour of internet surfing, mostly through the bloated website of the United Nations, before she found contact information for Naidoo.

After gathering her thoughts, Jamie left a detailed message on the woman's answering machine with a request for a phone or video call.

After another couple of hours, she pushed her chair away from the reference table and stretched. Her eyes felt gritty after reading so much material on third-world mining enterprises. She missed Tianna, the student placement, whose tenure over, had returned to school; but although she was great at finding material herself, Jamie now had to do the actual reading, so she could write from a clear understanding of the subject material.

From her explorations, what stood out was that the mining world was like the mythical US Wild West. In most countries, if bribes weren't a solution, violence was the most prevalent tool.

Many international companies ran roughshod over local inhabitants, especially if they were in isolated, backwater locations. Out of sight, out of mind.

Beatings, murder, and sexual assault were rampant, yet ignored by the country's officials, thanks to a never-ending graft. In some areas, bribes weren't even hidden.

To add injury to such insult, she learned companies would quickly set up shop using local labor at near slave-wages with no safety protocols in place. And no job training, and no compensation for injured workers.

Companies would extract the high-grade ores that created quick profit from a site, and then move on to the next claim, leaving the site without restoration of any kind. They left behind tailing ponds of toxic heavy-metals, and excess chemicals that leached into the water table—the chief source of drinking water—with absolutely no oversight.

Those downstream who were sickened by the tainted water could not find compensation or remuneration. The very resources that might have lifted these people out of poverty and helped them out of third-world poverty were gone—taken from them. The companies raped the land callously leaving generations of nationals to fend for themselves.

It sickened Jamie the more she read. What made it worse was that report after report filed with the United Nations and other world organizations fell on deaf ears.

It was as if no one cared, other than those who researched and wrote the reports. Sadly, she reflected, none of this was new. In both Canada and the United States, First Nations people had suffered similar atrocities. Companies and governments ignored treaties and land rights, and took what was not theirs at the expense of the original peoples.

Although she was searching for Bao Daoming's involvement, she could not avoid reading about foreign activities of other mining conglomerates. Especially those with ties to Canada.

Some of the biggest hitters in Canadian mining held international holdings. Safety regulations, labor relations—and profit margins—differed vastly from how these companies operated in her own country. *Mike Burgess wasn't feeding me a line.*

Legislation and regulations definitely made a fairer playing field she decided. It hadn't always been so; but over time, and, unfortunately, after many injuries and deaths, the multinational companies had been forced to improve conditions, especially in safety, impact on the environment, and—notwithstanding the recent strike—labor. And the companies still boasted record profits. It was a balance that benefited so many.

One picture she had found during her research summed up what could be accomplished if proper legislation required corporations to repair damage their processes caused. It was a comparison of the Sudbury/Fox Lake landscape. Two photos, taken from exactly the same spot, but forty years apart, clearly showed how things could change. The first photograph showed barren, acid-blackened rock, denuded of any vegetation for as far as the eye could see. A healthy forest of both deciduous and coniferous trees filled the same area in the second shot. The re-greening plan had worked, and most of the environmental scars caused by the early smelting processes had been healed. That international corporations were not doing the same in non-regulated third-world countries was proof that strict regulations kept everyone playing fairly.

It was also proof that the damage done elsewhere could be fixed if there was the political will to do so.

Her phone vibrated, and she snatched it up. The number was long-distance.

"Jamie Coleman."

"Miss Coleman, Amahle Naidoo, returning your call." The woman's voice was low and seemed to come from a much older woman.

"Thank you so much for responding so quickly, Ms. Naidoo. As I mentioned in my message, I'm a reporter in Fox Lake, Ontario, covering the terrorist attacks on Novo. As part of my investigation, I came across a name that you have written about in many of your reports and articles."

"What was the name?"

"Bao Daoming."

There was an extended silence on the other end of the line and Jamie almost spoke to check that they hadn't been disconnected. But then she heard the woman's deep intake of breath.

"Please, not over this phone," said Naidoo in a hushed voice. "I will contact you from a secure line."

"But ...," Jamie started, before she realized the woman had hung up.

JAMIE WAITED FOR OVER an hour, unable to concentrate on dry, mining reports while her mind created scenarios better suited for Hollywood blockbusters.

Finally, she gathered her notes and left the library, unsure when the woman might call.

She tried to squash the rising frustration that she could not unearth more on Bao Daoming. Not that she expected the Chinese government to be forthcoming. She had learned that in its race to become a reborn, socialist superpower, China's economy was key to its plans. Modernization of its colossal military had created a never-ending need for money and materials. Any hiccup in the economy hindered the leadership's expansion plans, even while they beat their chests decrying the presence of the Nationalist government in Taiwan, and America's interference.

The pandemic, Jamie knew, had further slowed the entire worldwide economy, China included. What made the situation worse was the country's zero-Covid policies, which had lowered numbers of cases, but resulted in lockdowns and industrial shutdowns. China's economy had stopped completely.

That situation and the growing tensions with Western governments created new challenges to a leadership that refused to accept excuses.

Okay, we think that Fodineum is behind the attack, and the intent is to lower Novo stock value so Fodineum can buy out Novo at the lowest price. Except that theory is inconsistent with ongoing attacks, because the stock prices are already low.

But why take down the giant smokestack? Novo already had plans to dismantle the chimney and had already announced its intentions to decommission the structure. And to have brought it down with such a disregard for life . . .

Cost savings?

She did not know what the financial damages the stack's collapse to the surrounding infrastructure and the community might add up to compared to the systematic tearing down of the smokestack. Any company that bought Novo would also be buying these expenses, so maybe that was the reason. If so, the attacks might be over.

She definitely hoped so. There had been enough death and destruction. The community looked like a war zone. Lord knew how long it would take the people to recover, if ever. Other than the 9/11 events, this kind of violence had never been experienced before in North America. It had always been something that played out somewhere else in the world.

She knew Forbes wasn't so sure the attacks were over. That the farmhouse had been empty when they arrived might have been routine for this particular group of suspects in order to ensure the authorities hadn't gotten a bead on them. They may have finished what they had planned, and then left for parts unknown.

But if China was involved ....

Just as she was passing the boat launch on Ramsey Lake Road, her phone began ringing. On the dash display, "Unknown caller" lit up. She acknowledged the incoming call by pressing the answer button on her steering wheel.

"Jamie Coleman."

"Ms. Coleman, this is Amahle Naidoo. Sorry for the subterfuge, but I cannot be sure if the phones in my office, and even my office itself, are secure. Any time we are dealing with hostile governments, and even some of the friendlier ones, it is much better to be safe than sorry."

"Isn't your office in the United Nations building?"

The woman let out a long sigh. "Yes. But that only compounds the issue. Bao Daoming works for a government that we suspect may even have tampered with our internal phone system. If I am correct, they now know that you are interested in their man, so make sure you are careful. In fact, please use this as a lesson to be very discreet in any future investigation of this person."

Jamie was stunned. With one phone call, she might have made herself a target. She felt an icy shiver trace its way up her spine to the base of her skull. Now, realizing this call would need her full wits, she pulled the Jeep into a boat launch on Ramsey Lake Road and parked facing the lake. She shut down the engine and pulled out her notebook, ready to record any information the woman could offer.

"Now that we've gotten the safety talk over with," Naidoo said in her thick South-African Afrikaans accent, "You wish to ask about Bao Daoming?"

"One person we suspect to be involved in the Novo attacks is a Serbian by the name of—"

"Dragoljub Petkovic," Naidoo answered for her. "Or better known simply as Drago."

"Why, yes," Jamie said in surprise.

"I'm very familiar with the man. He and another ex-mercenary, Felipe Vautour, have worked for Fodineum for decades now. Both are ruthless and absolutely psychotic. Men, women, and children have fallen—died, or good-as—to their depravity. Bao Daoming cares little how these two get the job done, as long as they produce the results needed for the circumstances. As far as I'm aware, they have never failed. However, we received a memo a few days ago from one of our agencies in Africa. It reported that Vautour had been caught between government and rebel forces in the Congo and had been killed. It has since then been verified."

"Oh, my God," Jamie blurted.

"Trust me, it is no loss. The man was vile."

"Do ... or did either of them have a ...," Jamie searched for the word, "a fetish for rough sex with women?"

The woman gave a rueful chuckle, but there was no humor in her bitter voice. "That would be Drago. The man enjoys inflicting pain. There have been countless reports of abuse by this animal. And it's not just women. There are reports of men and even children raped and murdered in many of the countries that the authorities allege he's worked in, mostly in Africa."

"In this incident, it was a sex-worker. After he finished with her, he left her for dead on the side of the road."

"As horrible as it sounds, she got off easy. Most of his victims do not live to talk about it. In fact, many just disappear entirely."

"Do you have any background information that you might share with me on Drago?"

"I do. Before I called you, I checked the website for your paper. Is the email on the site accurate?"

"Yes."

"Good, I will send you what I have. There is a lot, so I may send a few emails. I would suggest that you save them immediately to a cloud service, because I have seen electronic material disappear in the past. Especially information that is detrimental to the Chinese government."

"Thanks for the tip. Speaking about the Chinese, what else can you tell me about Bao Daoming himself? Anything not in your reports for the U.N.? Those, I have read, by the way."

"Very ambitious. The hardliners within the Secretariat of the Communist Party back him. As long as he successfully does as the Party orders, he will continue to rise. If he fails, so will his chances. Of course, depending how badly he might fail, the life and freedom of both him and his family might be at stake."

"Why would anyone want to even risk putting themselves in that position?"

The woman on the other end of the phone remained silent.

"So," Jamie continued, "he must really trust Drago and his men with these attacks."

There was a pause on the line, before the South African said, "Why would you say that?"

"Well, if the attacks are being orchestrated by China, then apparently, they have put their entire faith in this Drago and his team. Of course, what we've seen so far, that team seems up to the challenge."

Once again, the woman was silent, and Jamie again thought she had lost contact. She was about to say something, but the woman finally reacted.

"You seem to think that this attack is being controlled remotely. That this team of mercenaries is acting on a previously conceived plan."

Jamie was confused and admitted it. "How else would they be operating? It's not like a Chinese diplomat can call the shots here in Canada. That would be an act of war."

"Yes, but that's exactly what I'm implying. I know Bao Daoming. He may have been using Drago and Vautour for so-called wet work, but he is one of the biggest micro-managers in the business. If he isn't actually hiding by being a member of Drago's team, he would definitely be close by."

"CSIS believes he would never dare to operate in person here in Canada."

"They're wrong."

The woman's terse certainty struck Jamie. She seemed so sure.

"I have been tracking Bao Daoming for years. I know him as intimately as his own mother. He would not chance failure, especially where his life and position were at stake. Trust me, he is there."

"But CSIS has checked, and there is no record of Bao Daoming having entered Canada."

She heard the woman sigh heavily and felt frustration grow as the women spoke like she was talking to a child.

"Ms. Coleman, Bao Daoming uses several aliases. It's nothing for his government to supply authentic identification and passports."

Jamie felt cold at her words.

"I will send you the known aliases that I have uncovered."

Jamie muttered a thank you, but her mind was racing. *Would he still be here in Canada, or has he escaped already under an assumed name?*

"I'm guessing you've followed the attacks since they began?" Jamie asked.

"Oh, yes. Of course."

"I assumed that this entire situation was to hurt Novo, so the company's value would tumble so a Chinese company could buy it at a highly reduced price. A literal hostile takeover!"

"Where would you ever come up with an idea like that? A takeover is impossible. It would never happen."

"But Fodineum and Lhasa Ore have been buying up reduced shares since the stock has tumbled."

"That's the international company. Not the Canadian branch," the researcher explained. "Tensions between your country and China are extremely high at the moment. Your prime minister stopped the Chinese purchase of several resource companies in the name of national security. And then he embarrassed the Chinese leader at an economic summit weeks later by talking tough about trade and human rights."

"But Canada has always promoted human rights. And he can't be faulted for playing tough at trade. He's fighting for a fair share for his own country."

"I'm not arguing, but the Chinese do not consider Canada an equal to China. Between their economy, which is the second largest in the world, and their massive and growing military, they only respect the United States."

"So, if not to acquire Novo, why would they risk an international incident?"

"Because they *can*," said Naidoo simply. "By attacking your country on its own soil, China is sending a message worldwide that they can reach out and punish *anyone* who trifles with them!"

"So, this might not be over."

"I'm sorry. I wish I could tell you differently, but I don't think so."

"So, this might not be over."

"I'm sorry. I wish I could tell you differently, but I don't think so."

Chapter 32

Lucas hung up the phone and pushed back from his little-used office desk. Turning to the window, he gazed out, but didn't take in any of the cityscape. His mind clung to the series of calls he had made throughout the morning.

He'd reached out to realtors, hoping to find any trace of the terrorist group. Unless the terrorists had fled the country, they had to be somewhere in the area. There could only be so many properties that could host a small army with the seclusion they would need. He was calling in favors from a few of the real estate agents he had worked with over the years. Through both his exposés on the local businesses and live promotions for open houses, he had created a surprisingly extensive list of contacts over the years.

But so far, nothing. He needed a name or contact. Even with that information, he might hit a wall. The realtors wouldn't and couldn't just release names of property owners to the media if only for legal reasons. The police might have better legal pull, but even they might have to get a warrant to gain access to the records because of privacy laws, and the perpetual threat of lawsuits. As a reporter, Lucas didn't have that clout.

But although Lucas racked his brain, he couldn't figure what else he could investigate that might bring them closer to those who had perpetrated the attacks.

Despite many deaths, the community, he knew, had been fortunate that more hadn't died from the stack's collapse. The time of day had made the actual difference. Most of the inhabitants had been at work. Being a poor area, most inhabitants needed two incomes and had had kids at school or daycare, so most homes were empty. Not all, though. But had it happened during the evening or at night, those homes would have been occupied, with families asleep in their beds.

The strike had also saved lives. The employees were at the press conference, not on site; so they avoided becoming crushed under the falling chimney. On the other hand, had the plant been filled with workers, the terrorists might never have had the opportunity to plant the charges that took the stack down.

With the last attack, Lucas could not think what more they could do to hurt Novo. The stock in the company had dropped as violently as the massive smokestack until a freeze on stocks was put in place to save the company. Novo was already hurting from the previous incidents, and opinion in the mining world was that the company could collapse, even though the Fox Lake operation was only a small percentage of their worldwide investments.

A sharp rap on the door—the door to Felix's office—behind him startled Lucas and brought him out of his reverie. An icy shiver ran through him before he could get his bearings sorted out. He turned in time to see Jamie as she entered Felix's office.

Something's happened.

Skirting the desk he'd been working at, he followed his partner. He didn't know what she had discovered, but his pulse still jumped. They needed a break, and he knew it.

The newsroom, sharing space with national and international reporters from as far away as Germany, felt the rising excitement as they eyed the glassed office of the editor. Ignoring their inquiring glances, Lucas entered the office and closed the door, looking at Jamie for answers.

Felix had his phone to his ear, holding one finger up for silence. "Forbes, listen, Jamie and Lucas just came into my office. There's been a development. I'm putting you on speakerphone." He clicked a button on the phone and hung up the receiver. "Can you hear us?"

"Yes."

Felix nodded at Jamie.

"Mr. Forbes, this is Jamie. I was researching the Chinese angle in general and Bao Daoming in particular and came across a UN researcher named Amahle Naidoo. She has been researching illegal and unethical mine practices, mainly in Africa, but also in other areas of the world. She has written several articles that center on Bao Daoming, so I contacted her."

"I'm aware of Ms. Naidoo's research, but please go on," Forbes said, his voice tinny over the speaker.

"Yes. Well, she believes that these attacks might have nothing to do with a takeover of Novo by the Chinese, but rather are retaliation for Canada's opposition on the world stage to the Communist government. As an example, she referred to the prime minister's recent meeting with the Chinese leader during the Indo-Pacific conference, and Canada's decision to block Chinese investment in resource companies within Canada."

"I would agree that these incidents might play a part in the events unfolding; but as I mentioned before, what we know is less important than what we can prove. Was she able to offer any concrete evidence that the Chinese are behind these attacks?"

Jamie looked at Lucas, and he gave her a nod to go ahead. "She told me that her studies painted Bao Daoming as unable to fully trust his subordinates with such a mission and that he might well be in the country himself to ensure that the plan played out as the leadership envisioned."

"Again, Ms. Coleman, we have no evidence that he is in the country. Border Control has been very vigilant regarding Mr. Bao. We know of his penchant for being close to the action, so we have been watching for him very closely, even since the first attack at the smelter."

She leaned in her seat, so she could be closer to the phone, and gave Lucas a malevolent smile. He knew she had been holding her ace for the last round and he admired her cool. *Never, never play poker with this lady.*

"Mr. Forbes, Bao Daoming has four aliases that Ms. Naidoo has ferreted out through her research." She winked at Felix. "She has passed them over to me."

There was silence on the line and Lucas figured Jamie had just broken Forbes' cool demeanor. He recovered quickly, though.

"That is big news, Ms. Coleman. You are to be congratulated. Although I would not be surprised that he would travel under an assumed name, there are no known aliases in his file. Can you fax those names to me, so I can have them confirmed?"

"Fax? Not email? Certain—"

Felix cut her off. "Should we then assume that it will be Jamie who will get credit for this breakthrough and not one of the agencies involved, when this all gets out in the open?"

Jamie looked from Felix to Jamie as laughter issued from the speaker. "Ever protective of your people. I like that, Mr. Cameron. And I have no problem giving credit where it's due. And yes, fax, please, Ms. Coleman."

Felix smiled and leaned back in his chair. Lucas felt a sense of pride in Jamie and was glad to be there to share her moment. He gave her a nod that was part bow.

Her blinding smile said it all.

FORBES CALLED BACK in less than an hour. Bao Daoming had arrived in Canada under the assumed name of Huang Liu, a week before the first attack, but days after the infamous party that saw Amber beaten nearly to death. Lucas wondered aloud if the night with the women would have even occurred under the watchful eye of Bao.

The Forbes phone-voice said Bao had used another of the aliases in mid-January, and it was under that name that he had purchased the farm. "A private sale, and he paid the entire amount by wire transfer. No mortgage, no inspection, title passed along in a lawyer's office. Therefore, very little paperwork. Less chance of being noticed. We're now looking for similar transactions in case the group has gone to ground somewhere nearby."

"But that was long before the Indo-Pacific Conference and the canceling of the resource purchases Fodineum was trying to acquire."

"It's possible they were going for an economic hostile takeover originally but altered their plans with the new circumstances. Until we can grab one of the hostiles and question them, we are only working on theories."

If you can get them to talk. If the Chinese Communist Party would sanction an assault on Canadian soil for a perceived insult and a trading disagreement, what would they do to someone who really pissed them off?

"So where does that leave us?" Jamie asked.

"Same as before," Forbes said, clear tiredness in his voice. "We need to find where these people have gone to ground. Or where their next target is. There is no record of Bao Daoming leaving the country, under any of his aliases. And that tells me that this is not over."

"Or he has other identities we're unaware of."

"Granted," Forbes said from the phone.

The three in the office exchanged looks that expressed the stress of the situation. They needed to end this before another attack.

"I have another bit of information to pass on," Forbes said. "We confirmed the individual Ms. Coleman encountered the day of the stack's collapse to be Jaren Pinheiro, a Brazilian from the Minas

Gerais area. In case you're not familiar with the place, it was where the Novo tailings pond collapsed earlier this year. Mr. Pinheiro lost his daughter and his mother-in-law to the flooding."

"Do you think the Chinese recruited him to attack Novo?" Jamie asked.

"I think that might have been the plan; but of course, we are way beyond that point now. The local police found the spot where Mr. Pinheiro first was shot and left to die, we're guessing by his co-conspirators, possibly to lead us down some sort of false trail. How the man could drag himself as far as he did over the rubble is a case of superhuman determination. He trailed a lot of blood over yards of broken ground. It would have killed anyone else a lot sooner."

"The women who had taken part in the sex party mentioned him, but that he wanted nothing to do with the festivities that night. In fact, one woman mentioned that he seemed sad."

"Maybe he was being used as a scapegoat," Lucas said. "Without the Chinese angle, had we found this man, all our attention would be on a Brazilian group looking for payback."

"Regardless, he's another mystery in this picture," Forbes said.

"What can my people do?" Felix said, his voice directed to Forbes via the phone, but his eyes moving from Jamie to Lucas.

"Keep doing what you're doing. Both of you have uncovered good information that regular investigative tactics have failed to find." He chuckled in his refined manner. "Careful Felix, I might have to recruit these two."

"You'd have a fight on your hands," Felix countered, smiling.

"I'd imagine. If I hear anything else, I'll drop you a line." With that, the phone clicked off, leaving the three journalists in a strange silence that seemed like the calm before a storm.

"You heard the man. Follow any idea you have, any hunch. This is no longer just a news story. It seems our country is being attacked by a foreign national, regardless of whether he has the endorsement of his masters. We are at war. A quiet, private war."

Chapter 33

Lucas slid two iced teas across the table, before dropping heavily into the chair opposite Jamie. "How come I feel like I'm coming off an all-night bender and you look like you're ready for a morning hike?"

She gave him a tight smile. "Don't feel bad. Makeup covers a lot. I'm as exhausted as you. When this is over, I plan to take a nap in my tub."

"Nice image."

Her smile brightened up as she eyed his obvious attention. "So much for being too tired."

He shrugged but said nothing. He might be interested; but except for that one brief kiss, she had revealed nothing. The last thing he needed to do was misread her intentions. It would make for an awkward working relationship.

They's stopped for sub sandwiches. Unwrapping his, he grabbed half and took a large bite, oblivious to all but his hunger. When he looked up, his chewing slowed when he looked at Jamie.

She'd unwrapped her sub and bent the paper so that it lay neat and tidy. She then had taken a small bite and was carefully chewing with her mouth closed, dabbing at the corner of her mouth with a napkin.

He slowed his intake to appear less urgent. And more civilized.

Suddenly, he felt way out of his league. She was a lady, prim and proper. He, on the other hand was, comparably, a slob. He considered his own words just minutes ago, about her being fresh and looking presentable.

His own appearance was not something that had ever really concerned him. Until now. There was no way to hide his wrinkled shirt, and he was conscious of the fact that he had worn the same pair of jeans three days in a row. He'd have to do better if he ever thought about asking her out for a proper dinner.

When the hell did I decide to ask her out? Man, I must be tired.

Needing a break from the story, they talked small talk through the meal, mostly about her schooling and some professors she'd enjoyed. He listened politely, asking questions when appropriate. It occurred to him he was genuinely interested in how she felt about a lot of issues and wasn't just letting her carry the conversation.

Having finished her lunch, she folded her trash as if she planned to use it again, compared to his, which was balled up for a slam-dunk to the trashcan.

While they talked, she pulled a small figurine from her purse and began fingering it on the table. Lucas saw it was a paper figure that resembled a lizard with a red-tipped match head for a tongue. An origami.

He looked up, surprise registering across his features. "Where did that come from?"

"This?" she answered and then saw the look on his face. "Eh, when I surveyed the damage to the Acid Plant after the original explosion, I found it off to the side."

His eyes grew large at her words.

"Why?" she asked.

"Amber and at least one of the other girls, Gabby, were given similar origami figures from a man who sounds like your Jaren Pinheiro." He pulled over his bag and rifled through it for a minute before pulling out the tissue that held Amber's two origami figurines. He laid them on the table. "I was supposed to drop these at the police station in case they could pull fingerprints, but it slipped my mind after Forbes called."

Jamie leaned forward and studied the delicate folded papers, marveling at the intricate detail. She looked back at the paper lizard in her own hand before glancing over at Lucas. "You don't think ..."

"What ...?"

But she wasn't listening. Her entire attention was on the tiny creature in her hands. He watched as she used her long, tapered fingernails to pull at the folded paper, taking care to follow its bends, before lifting it apart. One part opened slightly, and she had to twist the entire figure in her hands to follow the next seam. Slowly, she teased the paper apart, so as not to tear it. The lizard lost its shape and become a larger piece of crumpled paper that seemed to lack stiffness because of countless bends and creases. With painstaking patience, she finally could pull the last folds apart and carefully spread the paper flat onto the tabletop.

Across the sheet of rumpled paper in blue ink was printed 'CHAMINÉ DE ATAQUE.'

"What the ... that's not English," Lucas said.

Jamie shook her head. "But neither was Jaren Pinheiro."

"Brazilian," they both said together, which caused both to smile inanely at each other. She beat him to her phone and searched up a Portuguese to English translation of the phrase.

"Attack chimney,'" she said under her breath. Her eyes fly up to meet his. "Attack chimney—attack on the smokestack. Could he have been sending a warning?"

Lucas pushed the tissue containing the other two origami figures, the yellow butterfly and the red lily, towards her. "Try these two. I'd tear the damn things apart with my thick fingers."

Once again, after a moment of study, she used her mint-colored nails to worry apart the delicate folds of the paper. The butterfly was simple and came apart after a few minutes. It carried the same message, 'CHAMINÉ DE ATAQUE.'

The water lily, being so small, with multiple petals, proved to be more of a challenge. Jamie had to tug gently until the little puzzle revealed its secret. Once she realized how it was folded, she easily unfolded the creases to reveal a different message.

'ATACAR PLANTA ÁCIDA'

"Something Acid Plant," Lucas said excitedly.

Referring to the online translator, Jamie nodded, "Attack Acid Plant."

"You're right. He *was* trying to send a message. Jaren passed out the origami to each of the girls who attended the party, hoping that one of them might unfold the paper to find the message. He must have dropped one near the acid plant when they were setting up the explosions, still trying to tell someone."

"It must have been the only way that Drago and the other mercenaries would not catch on to what he was doing. They would have stopped him, had they known."

"Maybe that's why they killed him? I know Forbes thinks it was to send everyone on a wild goose chase, but maybe ..."

"You said that he gave each of the girls one or two of these when they arrived at the farmhouse?"

"Yes, Gabby mentioned it and, of course, Amber had these two."

"Then we need to find the others. He might have been warning of another target. His messages," she tapped the two sheets of paper, "warned of two that we know of. If there was another planned, wouldn't he have tried to get the word out about that target as well?"

"Grab your bag. We have to get to Christine's and try to get a hold of the other women."

IT TOOK OVER SIX HOURS to track down the other women. With Amber in the hospital and Gabby staying at an undisclosed apartment, trying to make a clean break from the life, they were missing only two. Lucas drove while Christine rode shotgun, pointing the way to the various locations where she knew the women worked or hung out.

Even with Darcy and Rosie off the streets, Lucas understood that since the women had no other means of income, they'd probably continue to ply the trade that helped supply them with needed drugs. Cravings didn't take a break, so Christine felt they'd take a chance and try to work freelance.

Of the six sex workers, only three still had the origamis Jaren Pinheiro had handed out. When they carefully dissected the three new figurines, they found similar warnings of attacks on both the stack and the acid plant. Liquid had damaged the third origami, a more traditional swan. The powerful odor of rot-gut whiskey filled the vehicle as Jamie unfolded the booze-soaked figure. Lucas had to roll down a window.

"All we need is to drive through a spot check," Christine said, trying to keep a straight face.

The paper, stained a honey-brown, when pried apart, was unreadable, its blue ink having run together into a soggy mess.

"We haven't heard from Jewel yet," Lucas said. "Does Gabby have any idea where we might find her?"

They were sitting in Lucas's car at a busy corner that usually had at least one worker trying to entice customers to part with their money for a few minutes of pleasure. It was a usual haunt for Jewel, and Christine thought it best to wait, rather than drive around aimlessly.

"Gabby is reaching out to Jewel. I texted her earlier." She expelled a tired sigh. "Jewel could be working or whacked out on her latest score. We have no choice but to wait to hear from Gabby."

They sat in silence, knowing that time was not on their side. Another attack could come at any time. Stale coffee and greasy takeout had not helped their dispositions, nor had long hours sitting in the vehicle.

Further up the street, a gray Rav4 had pulled to the curb. The passenger door swung open and a tall, thin woman with jet-black hair emerged. She leaned back in to say something to the driver, before tapping the roof and shutting the door. As the car pulled away, she pulled down on her short skirt, so it hung evenly.

"That's Bella," Christine said. Without waiting for a reply, she threw her own door open and walked towards the woman. With a look over her shoulder to check for traffic, Christine crossed the street and called out a greeting to Bella. The streetwalker's shoulders slumped at the interruption, and with her hip pushed out at an impatient angle, she stared as the social worker approached.

Lucas and Jamie watched the two women talking, their body language saying more than their unheard words could. Christine was obviously imploring the other woman to help, but it seemed the other wasn't interested. Lucas caught Jamie's eyes in the rear-view mirror. "Now, you'll see why no one can say no to Christine."

As if they had choreographed her actions before he spoke, Christine's arms crossed in a stubborn challenge. Even though they could not hear what was being said, the raised middle finger of the sex worker toward Christine as she strode away left nothing to question.

The woman began waving at vehicles that passed her corner, calling out encouragement. As a car slowed down, Christine moved closer; and using her cell phone, snapped photos of the vehicle's license plate before aiming at the driver. The car roared off as both Lucas and Jamie broke out in laughter.

This time, the ensuing conversation between the Christine and Bella *could* be heard, but only because of the volume. Both strutted towards each other like wildcats, looking for an opening, Christine with her phone's flash bouncing off windows of passing vehicles while both of Bella's middle fingers were telling the world that Christine was number one.

Finally, the young street walker bounced on her high heels like a child having a meltdown. She opened her purse and turned it upside down, scattering the contents of the small clutch onto the sidewalk. When she pointed at something on the ground, Christine took a chance and snapped up two items from the clutter, before retreating, not daring to turn her back on the nearly hysterical woman.

Lucas was wiping the tears from his eyes when Christine yanked open the door. "So, you think this is funny, do you? Fuck you too, Lucas!" She looked back at Jamie who was trying hard to keep a straight face. "And you!" Slamming the door shut, she tossed two paper figurines at Jamie. "At least, I got results."

Jaime cupped her hands, trying to catch both without crushing them. One fell to the floor, as she latched onto the other. She reached down, gently feeling around the dark floor for the second one.

"Why did she give you such a hard time?" Lucas asked.

"She said that she had to make up for all the money Darcy and Rosie had stolen from her before some other pimp took over the neighborhood."

Lucas burst out again, slamming the steering wheel. This time the social worker smirked, "You're such an asshole, Lucas." But she was laughing now too.

"Turn on the light, Lucas."

Still laughing, he did, brightening the interior of the car.

Turning the first origami over in her hand, Jamie spied how the folds ended and pulled the tip of the paper from its position; and within minutes was pressing her hand across her thigh to flatten the paper.

"Different message. It says, ' PLANTA DE NIGUEL CARBONILO DE ATAQUE.'"

"Nickel Carbonyl...Plant...," Lucas tried to translate by the familiar-sounding words. Jamie tapped the words into her phone's browser.

"Attack Nickel Carbonyl Plant," she read. Her eyes snapped to the mirror. "Where's that?"

"I'm guessing the nickel smelter. They use nickel carbonyl to separate or purify the nickel. Bad stuff, if memory serves me right. Real bad."

"It's a new warning," she said as she began to work on the second origami.

In minutes, her shoulders slumped. "Another warning about the acid plant."

"It might be enough for Forbes. The other warnings came true, so why not the carbonyl one?"

"I suppose. I would have liked to get one more to clinch it," Jamie said.

"Christine, can we give Gabby a call? She might have heard from Jewel, but she has one of the origamis from that night. She mentioned it in her notebook the other night. It's how I know about it."

She nodded and pulled out her phone. It took seconds before she directed them towards the north end of the city. "I'm sure I don't have to remind you that this place is a secret. We can't have anyone knowing we stash the girls at this house." Both reporters nodded their understanding.

As they pulled in front of semi-detached duplex, Gabby stood up from the stairs she had been waiting on. She walked to the car and bent over to gaze into the window. "Hope you don't mind, but I couldn't just sit here and wait. I took it apart, and it has something written in Spanish or something. I couldn't make it out."

She passed the limp sheet to Christine, who turned it over to Jamie in the back seat.

"We have a match!"

Chapter 34

The noise in the EOC, the emergency operations center, was almost deafening. Lucas had to raise his voice so that Jamie could hear him over the many other conversations. "How can anyone think, let alone make decisions with this kind of noise?"

She replied with a look that agreed.

Three rows of desks, normally filled by city department managers in the event of a city disaster, now held provincial and federal representatives whose many organizations created a complicated alphabet soup of acronyms. Locally, only police and fire departments were represented.

The military had taken over command of the city's EOC, but there were so many other agencies present, the place overflowed. CSIS had sent Forbes, who waved a greeting from a desk near an exit.

Lucas had toured the facility when it had first opened, but it was his partner Jamie's first visit. From her wide eyes, he knew she was a surprised by all the activity. And noise!

Four massive LED screens covered the wall at the front of the room. The far left showed a weather radar screen similar to that on the Weather Network.

The second screen had a satellite image of the nickel smelter that was located west of the North Shore Complex by only a few miles. Superimposed were highlighted key-access routes and lettered labels for the different components of the facility.

Technicians had broken the third screen into three images. Highly detailed floor plans of the plant exposed its interior to show hazardous-materials, storage-tanks, staircases, control rooms and offices, all clearly identified.

Comparing the images, Lucas knew that the true size of the nickel refinery could not be gauged without actually visiting the site. It was a vast complex with a lot of places to hide.

The last screen held a close up of Bao Daoming, his features soft and fleshy, right next to a portrait that emphasized the hardened and cruel features of his subordinate, Dragoljub Petkovic. From the information Jamie had procured, though, Lucas knew each man was ruthless in his own way.

He felt Jamie's hand give his arm a squeeze. He followed her gaze to where Forbes, accompanied by the same Army officer who had been in charge of the Recon division at the farmhouse, Colonel Cameron, moved towards the front of the massive room. More distracting, Jamie left her hand on his arm.

Forbes had left his desk, crossed to the center of the room, and raised a hand. The simple gesture, quieted a sizable number of people, and they turned their attention to the front. But many who were still turned away either didn't see the signal or were too involved with their conversations.

Colonel Cameron showed less patience. His wide chest expanded, and he bellowed with a parade-ground voice, "Quiet!"

Lucas exchanged a grin with Jamie, as even Forbes flinched at the command. It did, however, get the desired results.

"Thank you, Colonel," said Forbes, nodding at the officer, who glared at the assembly as if daring them to resume their conversations.

"Thanks to our colleagues in the Fourth Estate," Forbes said, pointing to where Lucas and Jamie stood against the back wall, "we believe we have identified the next potential target Bao Daoming and his men might attack."

Both Lucas and Jamie nodded self-consciously as most eyes turned towards them.

Forbes drew attention back to the front of the room with an invitation. "I've asked Dr. Steve Wheaton, a senior chemist with Novo, to explain in layman's terms the hazards associated with the refinery, especially with its use of nickel carbonyl, which we feel is the terrorists' next target."

A tall, bald man stood and turned towards the room. He raised one hand in a nervous gesture, as if assuring everyone that he was who Forbes had said he was. His nervousness quickly disappeared as he began talking about subject matter so familiar to him.

"First of all, nickel carbonyl is identified by UN #1259, which is an identification used throughout the world and managed by the United Nations for hazardous materials.

"Novo uses what's called the Mond process to refine the nickel. In the process of extracting and purifying our nickel, we heat raw material until the metal becomes a molten liquid. Then we introduce carbon monoxide to the impure mix, and that gives us nickel carbonyl in a vapor state. Two different processes are used to separate the nickel, creating either nickel-covered pellets or pure nickel powder. We have used the process for over a century.

"The issue that we have is that nickel carbonyl is quite nasty to deal with unless you are properly protected with the right safety equipment. It is highly toxic, a known carcinogen, and it does not mix with water. It's also highly flammable and heavier than air, so will follow and settle in low-lying areas. And oh," he said as if he had forgotten, "although it is an inhalation hazard, it can also be absorbed through bare skin.

"It has a musty smell—most carbonyls stink—think urea, for example—but it is so toxic that smell provides no warning for getting a lethal dose. Someone once said of hydrogen sulfide that your first sniff is your last; well, nickel carbonyl is pretty much like that."

There was a stunned silence in the room.

Off to one side, a soldier broke it. "And you work with this shit?"

The scientist laughed and nodded. "Yes, and we have since the 1800s. Of course, we have strict safety and operating protocols to protect both our people and the environment. In the past thirty years, there has only been one accident with it that I can recall. Our people have a healthy respect for safety."

An arm went up, like a child in a classroom. The man wore the uniform of the fire-service chief. When the scientist acknowledged him, the man asked, "So, if the worst happens, how do we deal with the leak or a fire?"

Wheaton tilted his head in thought. "Honestly, Chief, if it's on fire, get the hell away. At the very least, stay upwind from the site. If it *is* a major gas leak, heaven help anyone downwind. Especially if it reaches a residential area.

"We've sent out material to local doctors about the signs, symptoms, and treatment of nickel carbonyl exposure, but what we have was only intended to treat individuals; employees involved with our operations. If this becomes a public event, I have no idea whether any hospital would be prepared for it. We can deal with leaks and have done so before, but we never have planned for an armed attack."

The entire room erupted in a hundred different conversations and questions as the risk became apparent. There was no plan to deal with a potential disaster of this size. The fire service, the police, and even the military were without plans for this.

Lucas gave Jamie a worried look. "I don't think I've ever wanted to be wrong so much. God, we're still mopping up from the collapsed stack—and now, this!"

Jamie nodded.

Lucas watched her eyes dart across the room. He looked over his shoulder. A short man was trying to get Forbes' attention but went unheard because of the pandemonium of all the voices. Frustrated, the man stepped on his chair, maps trailing from his arms, and *yelled* over the din.

The colonel, seeing the man, startled the crowd once more with his baritone voice. "Listen up!"

As the group became silent, everyone turned to the man on the chair, who had suddenly found himself at the center of everyone's attention. "Ah—," he stammered. "We have another problem. As I'm sure the local authorities know, most winds here come from the north-west. The upcoming weather could cause hazardous materials to spread to the towns of Chelmsford, Lively, or even Sudbury. All are residential."

He stood there, frozen on the chair standing over the assembly, before stepping down.

"Not only that," said the fire chief. "But all our resources are on the other side of the Main Street corridor, which means anything we need would have to take a round-about detour to avoid a contamination zone."

"Okay, then," Forbes pushed forward. "We have a lot of barriers to overcome. Does anyone have any solutions?"

The room was silent as each contingent looked at their partner agencies with blank expressions.

"Colonel?"

The army officer looked over to Forbes.

"Can you and your people protect the refinery to prevent an attack until we find this group?"

"Given enough time, armament, and personnel, we could secure it to anything but aerial bombardment. But not with the limited personnel on the ground available to us, and not dealing with such a large complex. After our losses the other night, we have fewer than thirty soldiers on site. Ottawa is sending replacements, including a full CBRN response team; but at this time, their ETA is unknown, but should be soon. Canadian Forces Base Gagetown also has an entire convoy on the road headed here—complete with one of their field-hospitals—in case the gas hits the city, but that's fifteen hours by road. But we're also bringing in air support, and that, at least, should be here soon as well as soldiers from local army reserve units.

"I know it sounds like we're turning this into a war zone, but we've studied the satellite photos and floor plans, and there are just too many ways to infiltrate that site. And if that gas gets loose . . ."

Lucas leaned forward and whispered a translation to Jamie, "CBRN stands for Chemical, Biological, Radiational and Nuclear."

She nodded.

"Thank you for your candor, Colonel." Forbes said with a nod.

Colonel Cameron tipped his head to Forbes. "My people are getting settled around the complex in case the enemy does something blatant. We'll work to secure it with what we have."

"Should we begin evacuating the affected areas?" Police Chief Dillard asked.

"That is the question of the hour," Forbes said. "The fact we do not know for sure if Bao Daoming and his crew are in the area, or whether he is actually planning this attack, and that's troublesome. If we play it safe and evacuate, they may just stay hidden until people return to their homes before executing an attack. On the other hand, if we do nothing and the worst happens, we lose the opportunity to save a lot of lives."

Forbes looked towards Lucas and Jamie. "You two have managed to unearth a lot of what we know. Any thoughts about what comes next?"

Lucas exchanged a long, silent exchange with Jamie. He nodded at her.

Jamie turned to Forbes. "I think we have to assume the worst."

Chapter 35

Dillon Fox leaned into his spotter scope and viewed the barren ground from the top of the copper-refinery, near the perimeter of the metals complex. He was spotting for Romeo Baptiste, who lay prone beside him on the refinery's roof, and who was the shooter today—they took turns on alternate mission days. They were taking twenty-minute shifts viewing the surrounding area to keep themselves sharp. Eye and mental fatigue could spoil the easiest shot. Rotating tasks and short shifts had become routines that had developed over seven years of working together. Baptiste lay beside Fox in the shadow of their hide, eyes closed, breathing steady.

It never ceased to amaze Fox how quickly his partner could fall asleep. Close his eyes and he was out. Fox on the other hand, had to perform breathing exercises just to calm his mind enough to get some shuteye.

"Guilty conscience," Baptiste would tell him when the topic came up.

Fox's reply was always the same. *Next to nothing in that thick skull of yours that needs to calm down.*

There was nothing fancy about their blind, their 'hide.' A huge sheet of rusted, corrugated steel had been leaned against and fastened to the outer wall of the stairwell roof-access. Another sheet closed off the interior opening, so they were in constant shadow. A couple of Novo maintenance guys had slapped it together in the middle of the night. Before dawn, Fox and Baptiste had climbed the grated-steel stairs and hunkered down, prepared to stay for however long the mission took. The roof was scattered with exhaust stacks.

What was being exhausted, Fox didn't have a clue; but the immensity of the complex impressed him. He had patrolled the North Shore facility, and it spoke to the amount of money this company had spent just to facilitate the process of refining the raw material. It was mind-blowing.

He suppressed a grin that he and his partner were able to stay in their standard, baggy, yet comfortable, CADPAT combat uniforms rather than the chemical suits the others deployed were ordered to wear. Because nickel carbonyl is so much heavier than air, their hide at a higher elevation was deemed sufficient to keep them safe from any exposure risk.

Water and IMPs (Individual Meal Packs), the Canadian version of American MREs (Meals Ready-to-Eat) would be delivered sometime during the night, according to their briefing. *It's not like it's Afghanistan. If they've going to deliver meals, why not just send out for pizza?*

Fox scanned the dry brush and black barren rock that stretched behind the refinery. The horizon was a mixture of dwarf brush and acid-scarred stone. Satellite photos had shown a lake on the other side of the low mountain to their south, but they could not glimpse it from their vantage point.

Fox kept the tripod-mounted scope moving from west to east. Stopping to inspect every shadow and every clump of grass or brush, he watched for anything that stood out.

Directly south was a vast area of mining waste that covered the high ground. It had been groomed; and even from this distance and height, Fox could see signs of the heavy equipment that had spread waste over the rough rock.

Below their position, Fox knew that the Novo people were building reinforced steel walls in front of the two massive, vertical containers of pressurized gas. Their briefing had identified these storage tanks as most probably the enemy's main targets. There was no way that he and Baptiste could see the work being done to shield them, but the sounds of steel on steel carried over the wind.

Army ground-units, mixed groups of full-time soldiers and local reserves, were spread across the complex, both around and inside the structure, and were expected to counter any attack by an outside force. Both Fox Lake and Sudbury SWAT teams backed them up. And, although Colonel Cameron had called it overkill, but hadn't nixed it, six militia members from Sudbury's Second Irish Brigade—a mortar brigade—were also in position to help defend the plant. With their mortars!

Because how he and Baptiste had been positioned, Fox knew they were expected to at least catch sight of intruders before they became a danger.

He shifted the scope and began to move it in the opposite direction. He squinted as a flash of harsh light filled the lens. Pulling back, he checked the area with eyes only, but saw nothing to alarm him. Bending back to the scope, he examined the ground around where he had seen the reflection of light.

Nothing.

Did I imagine it?

Moving beyond the area to the west, he retraced his line of sight until he caught the flash again. Something was reflecting the summer sun and bouncing light towards his position. The light filled his scope as he locked onto the source. Without looking away, he reached over and tapped Baptiste on the back. His partner came awake instantly, ready for anything.

"I've found something in the bushes four hundred yards out that I can't make out. Need a second set of eyes," Fox said.

Baptiste pulled himself around to use the scope of the heavy caliber rifle that lay propped on its bipod.

"Point me."

"Eleven o'clock. Five hundred and thirty-five meters. Long clump of trees running east-west in front of some kind of cargo container. Look for a flash of light."

Baptiste studied the area, adjusting the zoom on the scope to check detail. For minutes, nothing changed. Then a flash. He zeroed in on the spot and studied the surrounding vegetation. He slowly scanned the entire clump of brush, looking for any sign of a threat.

"I got notting," Baptiste said, Quebec-French accent strong. "Radio it in."

Fox nodded and tapped his throat microphone. "Penthouse to Command. Over."

"Command. Go ahead Penthouse."

"Spotted a flash of light at …" he looked down at his compass to read a bearing, "One, eight, three degrees. Five, three, five meters out. Brush in front of white sea-can."

"Copy. Stand by."

TOGGLING THE CONTROL arm, Natalie Drummond launched the drone, mission-named "Wasp," using a pneumatic launcher. "Wasp to command. Airborne. Do you see my feed?"

"Roger, Wasp. Good video. Recording," said an emotionless voice in her headphones.

"Roger," she said. "Commencing."

She'd had countless hours with the RQ-21 Blackjack and loved the sleek little plane. Unlike most drones that worked like a helicopter, the Blackjack could not hover and was better suited for larger areas.

With her eyes on the surveillance video from the flying machine, she manipulated its controls to send the little fellow skyward. Rather than 'hopping' over the building for a look-see at the spot where

Penthouse had seen something, she took a high-angled circular route. By coming in from a totally different direction, she hoped that the versatile machine would remain undetected. The higher, the less chance of the enemy hearing the whine of its engine or spotting it with the sun behind it.

She followed a reverse bearing of three degrees, stood off from the indicated spot, and allowed the machine into a coast on an east to west bearing. Using the incredible lens on the camera, she was able to pull right into the brush that flanked the large shipping container that Penthouse had identified as a white sea-can.

Movement caused her eyes to narrow as she leaned into the four-inch square screen.

"Command, are you seeing this?"

"Roger. Try to find source."

"Affirmative."

What she had spied was a rectangular piece of glass that jumped from the dry bed of leaves, hung for a moment, only to fall again. *Someone's playing games.* She zoomed in tighter on the chunk of glass and followed the string that was hung from the branches of the brushes. Seeing nothing under the nearby trees, she continued to trail the tawny-brown twine across the acid scarred rock of open ground to another clump of trees.

BINGO!

From under the foliage, two pairs of camouflaged legs poked out.

"Command. I have two bogies, both decked out in digies," said Drummond, meaning digitalized camouflage.

"All units, this is Command," announced a new voice over the network. "Anyone out there is to be considered hostile. We have two Tangos hiding in the bushes in front of the storage container. Does anyone have a shot?"

When no one answered, Drummond keyed her microphone. "Sir, the Wasp is equipped with the Ukrainian grenade." There was a pause in the radio traffic. She had studied the many improvisations the Ukrainian military had applied during their desperate fight against Russia. And the collection of destroyed tanks and dead soldiers was testament to their ingenuity.

The Wasp was now similarly equipped, thanks to a simple trial-and-error system to determine weight and height. A second camera mount on the undercarriage of the Wasp held a homemade bomb put together with an M69 fragmentation grenade and a simple tail so it fell straight.

"Command to Wasp. You have a green light. Fir..."

The command was interrupted by the report of a heavy caliber rifle-shot.

Below the drone, its camera picked up the puff of dust created by the concussion of the shot.

DIXON FOX FELT NOTHING. One second, he was searching the brush through his scope for anything that looked man-made. The next, he was dead.

Because of the speed of the bullet, he might not have even registered the muzzle flash that erupted from underneath the dense brush. The bullet leaped from the hidden rifle and took Fox in the forehead. His head exploded; the bullet continued to bounce repeatedly around the steel walls of the hide.

His partner, Baptiste, was painted in blood. He swung his own rifle towards the ball of dust pushed up by the heavy enemy rifle, but before he could find a target, four more rapidly fired rounds crashed into the hide. He was not immediately hit, but took two impacts from the ricocheting chunks of lead. One hit him in the back of the neck, tearing half of his jaw off as it exited his body. The other struck the inside of his thigh, rupturing the femoral artery.

Neither injury killed him outright. Bleeding out did.

DRUMMOND DIDN'T HESITATE, except to ensure she was within the required height. She released the grenade and watched as it fell in what looked like slow motion. While it fell, more blasts from the heavy rifle pushed dust and leaves ahead of the sniper position. She willed it to drop faster.

"Now! Now! Now!" she panted under her breath. Her fellow soldiers were under fire.

The grenade slipped past the first branches of the stunted tree when it exploded. Leaves ripped from the branches, exposing two figures, one prone, arms and legs askew; the other withering in pain. His movements slowed and became still as she watched.

"Wasp to Command. Two Tangos neutralized."

"Good work, Wasp. Rearm and stand-by."

Pulling back on the small arm of the control panel, she pulled the agile drone straight up and circled back. She kept the plane positioned so anyone searching for the drone would have to look directly into the sun.

"Command to Penthouse."

Drummond watched the landscape on the monitor slip by as she plotted an alternate route to remain undetected.

"Command to Penthouse."

Drummond heard the dispatcher's nervousness and instinctively turned the drone's camera to the refinery's rooftop. She centered on the metal lean-to where she knew the sniper team had set up the night before. With a push of a lever, the camera zoomed closer. She could see the still form of one of the snipers, but as good as her equipment was, it could not infiltrate the deep shadows of the hide.

"Wasp to Command." She said, trying to keep her voice professional. "I have eyes on Penthouse. I can only see one team member. He's not moving. Do you want me to close in?"

There was a pause over the network.

"Negative, Wasp. Continue to rearm and standby. Thanks for your report."

Drummond swallowed hard and concentrated intently on the small screen. Every time her mind tried to visualize the two snipers she had trained with, she pushed the thought away to a far corner.

She had to stay sharp. This was far from over.

Chapter 36

"**G**oddammit!" roared Colonel Cameron. He stormed across the front of the room in a futile attempt to bleed off frustration.

Forbes stayed still, his eyes on the monitor that displayed the video feed from the military drone over the nickel refinery.

Lucas had no quick comeback to the colonel's anger this time. From the shocked expressions around the room, everyone was affected by what they had witnessed. The feed from the Wasp had shown for all to see the deaths of the two enemy soldiers and the carnage on the refinery rooftop, all in high-definition video.

Jamie's fingers had dug into his arm, making him flinch. Her eyes glossed with tears at the horror of the scene; but like Lucas, she didn't turn away.

For him, it was almost mesmerizing. He couldn't have looked away if he had wanted to. Part of it was his usual search for the truth, but part of it was to acknowledge the sacrifice these soldiers had made. But then, if he was really honest, he, like many people, was fascinated with death and violence. It seemed shallow, even sick. But many who called the ancient glory of gladiators barbaric were often the biggest fans of boxing, mixed martial arts, and the gory headlines Lucas knew well. These deaths didn't even seem real. It was like playing a video game like *Call of Duty*.

The colonel turned on his heel and barked, "Bring up the latest satellite imagery."

Two military technicians bent over their laptops and hammered at the keys. "Sir, we're piggy backing a British satellite that will be overhead in ninety seconds. Standby."

The center screen went black, and then hissed to a grayish nothingness.

Lucas gave the room a quick glance and noted that not one head was turned away. Everyone stared unblinking at the LED screen.

"Thirty seconds."

The grayness began to produce a fuzzy image. Within seconds, it materialized as the familiar refinery building that lay far below. The area of the shot took in not only the complex, but an area much farther out, exposing the Spanish River to the west.

"Zoom in on us," ordered Colonel Cameron.

The picture closed-in on the buildings of the metals complex as if the satellite was descending like a helicopter. As the image pulled closer, Jamie released Lucas's arm and stood straight up.

"Stop!" She was pointing at the screen. "Please! There!"

Heads swung at her voice.

"On the road leading up from the river. That looks like a line of men!"

Risking later discipline, the technician adjusted the picture. The image reared upwards and then pulled to the south, exposing a group of camouflaged soldiers moving at a run up the roadway. Behind them, three boats floated near a pump house beside the river from which they'd come.

"EOC to Copper Command. Be advised; we are tracking a group of hostiles south of your position. Twelve of them. They appear to be heavily armed."

"Copper Command, Roger."

Oh, my God. This is turning into a real-life war-zone.

Not ten seconds later, the mortars proved their worth as two plumes of white smoke blossomed to the right of the main building.

As detailed as the feed was, the satellite image could not show the traveling mortar shells, but the reaction of shells impacting ahead of the column of men was clear enough. The group of mercenaries scattered at the first impact so they wouldn't be caught in a tight group.

The little group of local militia at the plant first fired mortar shells in a pattern, then adjusted their aim based on the highly detailed satellite feed.

Lucas hoped for direct hits on the terrorists, his hands bunched into fists as each round exploded. He felt Jamie's eyes on him, and he reluctantly turned from the screen to catch her wide eyes, then looked back at the screen. Guiltily, he pulled out his notepad and scratched down his thoughts and feelings on paper without looking away from the action in front of him.

Smoke covered the entire hillside that faced away from the refinery. There was no visible movement. The mortar rounds walked up the roadway and across the lower half of the waste-material mound.

But then, a brilliant flash appeared from out of the smoke. It speared across the pale topsoil covering the waste material towards the refinery building. And there it crashed with a massive explosion, sending up a flash of fire and debris.

"Rockets!" Forbes hissed. "They're aiming for the storage tanks."

From both the rear of the extensive building and on either side of the waste mound, the Canadian special forces opened a deadly crossfire. As the smoke around the waste dissipated, the image showed both the dead and those still returning fire. Two enemy soldiers scrambled on hands and knees to load another round into a shoulder-held RPG launcher. The man wielding the weapon rose to one knee and took aim towards the refinery.

Multiple bullets from different defenders struck the man, and almost everyone in the room gasped. As the man fell back, the rocket screamed skyward. The exhaust, which should have blown backwards over his partner, angled downward when the weapon fired. The second man took its full impact and disappeared into a ball of flames and smoke. They watched as the rocket sailed gracefully over the building and over the highway to the north to explode harmlessly against the side of a mountain.

With all firepower on the dying RPG team, no one noticed the second rocket team advance over the rough terrain. With a flash, another rocket screamed across the open ground to hit the steel guard that the Novo welders had been installing. The round bent the guard, but it held and protected the pressurized containers. However, the next round found its target, tearing through the damaged metal, releasing the gas. The explosion ignited the volatile chemical, causing a huge fireball to rise over the refinery.

From either end of the building, white-clad figures moved towards the enemy position as mortar shells continued to 'walk' across the hilltop. Lucas realized the soldiers were wearing chemical suits. Air tanks bulging on their backs, protected against inhalation hazards but Lucas knew that they gave no protection from bullets.

Both groups moved forward in well-practiced maneuvers so that one team covered the other. The barrage of mortar shells stopped as if on cue, and the hazmat-suited infantry rolled over the rise, firing at anything that moved. There was little resistance. Those still alive were rolling in the dirt, mouths wide open like fish out of water as the nickel carbonyl that they had fought so hard to release took its due.

"THANK GOD, THAT'S OVER," said Chief Dillard, the police chief. He had removed his tunic and rolled up his shirt sleeves because of the room's heat from over-crowding and the stressful anxiety of the decision makers.

"It's not," replied Dr. Wheaton, the Novo scientist, his cellular phone pressed to his ear. He covered its mic and told the room, "One tank exploded, but the explosion damaged the other at its base. We have a high-pressure leak with no chance of containment."

"What are our options?" Forbes asked from the front of the room.

"The tank will bleed out. The gas is heavier than air, so will follow the contours of the land. If it hits an ignition source, the entire cloud could ignite. If the tank is still leaking, the flames would run right back to the tank, and we could have another explosion."

"I understand all that," Forbes said, his voice tight with forced patience. "But I repeat, what are our options?"

"My people had set up sensors along the low areas leading to North Shore Creek, which flows around this mountain," Wheaton said, pointing at the expanded satellite map. "We're pretty sure the gas will flow along the rail tracks, but may collect in this low area," touching on an area that the map showed as swamp. "We issued an evacuation of personnel from West Mine and the main office building when the shooting started, so at least those people are safe. But it may cross the highway here and enter this residential area of North Shore." He tapped the satellite photo that showed a seven-story apartment block that stood in front of a subdivision of row housing.

Forbes turned to the room until he spotted the fire chief. "Initiate an evacuation of that area in North Shore. This stuff hangs low, so move everyone you can to higher ground. And Chief, start moving your people in through the back way into North Shore, through Novo property, so there's no chance they'll breathe that crap—or have your own vehicles set off the gas. I would also suggest you call in extra resources and have them stand by on Lorne Street. If this cloud ignites, we could end up dealing with multiple structure fires. And even if it doesn't, it's going to poison anyone who is near it."

To his credit, the chief didn't argue or question the order. He gathered his phone and left the room to start moving equipment and personnel.

Chief Dillard motioned to Forbes. "My people will shut down Main Street and close the highway upwind of the Copper Refinery. We will be standing by when you need us."

Forbes nodded and turned his attention to the colonel. "You should have your people fall back to higher ground, Colonel. No sense risking anymore lives. Compliments to your group. "

The stern-faced officer nodded his thanks, did an about-face and marched out of the EOC.

Lucas leaned close to Jamie. "This is our chance. While he's busy planning, you and I can head towards North Shore so we're on-hand to witness the evacuation and any explosion, as it happens. Felix will expect photos."

She gave him a tight nod. "You go first, and I'll follow in a moment, so Forbes doesn't think we're abandoning ship." She handed him the keys to her Jeep. "If we have to do any off-roading, the 4x4 will come in handy."

He nodded. "I'll be just outside the main entrance." He watched to see Forbes' attention focus on someone on the far side of the room and then glided out the exit in the room's rear. He took the stairs two at a time, wondering where this story would end up.

LUCAS PUSHED JAMIE'S sporty off-roader's speedometer well beyond the limit. As he raced along the four-lane highway leading into the main part of Fox Lake, Jamie had her phone plastered to her ear, updating their editor, Felix. The Jeep having been stripped of roof and doors, wind noise was overwhelming; so her other hand

covered her other ear, and she bent away from the Jeep's open doorway.

With both wind and road noise, Lucas could barely hear the
one-sided conversation, so he kept his attention on driving. The
highway was busy with commuters, many of them miners returning
after work from the cluster of mines in the town of Levack, twenty
miles north of the city. With all that had happened locally, he was
surprised at the numbers on the road; but he also knew that earning
a wage was a priority when you live hand-to-mouth. And, of course,
today's events still hadn't hit the news.

The traffic lights leading into the back end of the North Shore facility and town were in sight when Jamie disengaged from the phone.
She looked up, saw where they were, and turned to Lucas. "I don't
think this jeep ever saw that kind of speed before."

His grin was fixed as he swung behind a fire engine that had
come from the city. He kept Jamie's Jeep tight on the truck's rear
running-board as the emergency vehicle was waved through the controlled gate to Novo's property. They were through the entrance before the security guard could wave them off.

"Nicely done!"

"I do have my moments," he said. "What did Felix have to say?"

"Basically, that if you get us killed before filing the story, he'll
give all this credit to a person in sales."

Lucas's laughter ceased as he maneuvered around potholes that
threatened to swallow the Jeep. The two bounced and shook like
mad bobble-head figurines.

"Jesus! With the profits they posted last quarter, you would
think they could fix the damn road."

"You could slow down. It's not like you're going to pass the
bloody fire truck."

He didn't retort, but let off the gas pedal. It gave him more time
to avoid the biggest holes. They passed the enormous Jessup Mill and

North Mine in a blur. The parking lots were filled to capacity, evidence that the work had barely slowed down regardless of the threat.

Ten minutes of bouncing along the pot-holed road, they crested the hill leading into the town and could see that the green space that made up North Shore Park was covered with a small city of tents.

Jamie pointed. "Looks like they're getting ready for the worst."

"It's better than waiting until after the disaster. Oh, my God, they're working fast!" Lucas said, pointing at the old nursing home where he had helped recover the bodies from the smokestack collapse. The tip of the stack had already been broken up and removed. Scaffolding covered the outside of the nursing home, tradespeople repairing the damage despite this new threat. He pulled Jamie's Jeep to a stop and took out his camera. Standing between the Jeep's roll-bars, he clicked off a couple of photos before dropping back into his seat. Handing the camera to Jamie, he dropped into gear and floored the accelerator.

"No wonder Felix loves you."

He blew a raspberry. "He's got a new favorite now."

Jamie's head came around. "Are we back on that again?"

He laughed. "No. You've earned you way to the table, but don't think that'll slow me down. You'll have to fight me for any story I find."

She smiled. "You're on." But then, her expression turned shrewd. "Or we can team up against Felix and tell him we'll only work together."

His mouth dropped in shock. "You'd stand up to the old man?"

Her eyes narrowed. "Watch me!"

They both laughed.

Even over the sound of the wind and the engine, they both heard the long wail of emergency sirens that the mining company had scattered around the community. The citizens of the area were familiar with the weekly testing of the system that was meant to warn of a chemical leak. Jamie gave Lucas a worried look. "I'll never hear those sirens again without thinking about today."

Lucas nodded. "Yeah. I've heard them most of my life, but I'll never ignore it again."

They slowed for the barricade ahead. Unlike the previous gate to the Novo property, the military manned this one, their suspicious glares made more threatening by deadly-looking rifles that hung by straps from their necks.

"Authorized personnel only, Sir."

"I'm Press," said Lucas, showing his credentials. "If you check with Colonel Cameron or Darren Forbes, you'll see we are allowed. We just left the EOC."

The soldier took Lucas's creds and moved to a tent set off to one side of the roadway. His companion kept steely eyes on the Jeep and its occupants. Minutes later, the guard returned and handed Lucas's documents back to him.

"Sir, Mr. Forbes would like you to call him ASAP."

"Thank you, Corporal. Stay safe."

Lucas drove forward as the soldier moved aside and then pulled the Jeep to one side, so he was not interfering with the traffic. He turned and gave Jamie a wink. "Time for a spanking."

Her giggle turned to a snort that she tried to cover with her hand.

He thought the snort was adorable. On impulse, he kissed her. And she returned it, but with much more passion. He was breathless when their lips parted.

"Wow!"

She gave him a saucy grin. "Let's finish this story so we can explore this further."

When he hesitated, she said, "C'mon. Call Forbes."

Lucas made the call and placed it on speaker so they could both hear.

"Forbes.

"There's just no slowing you two down, is there?" Forbes' voice dripped with sarcasm. "Must I remind you that that gas is invisible and *deadly*? You go snooping around and you could very well end up dead."

"We know, but we have to see the story to report the story. We'll keep to high ground and, like the Irish blessing, keep the wind at our back."

"Listen, Forbes," Jamie said. "I was thinking about those enemy soldiers showing up at the refinery like that. They had to have arrived by boat since the roads had been closed. Is there any way of back-tracking their movements from past satellite passes? It might show you where they were based. The Spanish River flows south to Lake Agnew and there are a ton of homes and cottages on the south side with access to the Trans-Canada highway."

Forbes' laughter issued from the phone. "You two keep amazing me. You sound like operatives. Yes, I have my people looking into that as we speak. Preliminary data shows they came from the south, and followed the river system. Hope to have something more conclusive soon."

"Have you figured out how you're going to deal with the gas?"

"Once it has stopped leaking, if it hasn't settled in residential areas, we plan to ignite it remotely. We've got people watching the monitors that the Novo scientists deployed to see just where the cloud is moving. Had you stayed put, you'd see the modeling on the screen in real time."

Lucas gave Jamie a tight smile. If that was the worst Forbes was willing to dish out for their being here instead of there, they were getting off easy, and each knew it.

"If we see anything on our end, we'll let you know."

"Do that." He said almost sternly, but then his voice mellowed. "From the initial report we've had from military personnel at the

nickel refinery, none of the combatants were Drago or Bao Daoming. So, they are still out there. Be careful. Both of you."

Chapter 37

The two made a quick stop to allow Lucas to photograph the mini-city that had sprung up across North Shore Park. It looked like controlled chaos.

Medical staff in gowns led people and supplies into a military tent with a white square with a red cross on it—the field hospital from the base at Gagetown. The symbol was brilliant against the drab, army green. Lined up in neat rows across the grounds of the park were the Command structures and vehicles from a multitude of agencies. The array of communication antennas and portable satellite dishes was a poor substitute for the magnificence of the smokestack that no longer filled the eastern skyline. To Jamie, the lack of the smokestack made the sky seem so much larger somehow, especially when homes and trees hid the smelter complex. It felt surreal not to see the structure that had stood vigilant over the community since before she was born.

As they watched, a line of vehicles followed behind a Novo security car, leading from the suburb, past the park, and up the hill that they had recently descended. These were the people who were being evacuated from low-lying neighborhoods. "I'll bet the people of North Shore will be happy when this is over?" Jamie said and recognized her own understatement.

The affected residents were being escorted right out of the area, to ensure their safety, and, she surmised, to keep them from being underfoot while the threat remained. Children were leaving happily on a new adventure, while their parents looked concerned and worried; and Lucas photographed it all. One SUV drove slowly past; and when the two boys in the rear seats spotted Lucas taking pictures, they offered the peace sign and goofy faces. Lucas captured their antics with a series of photos, smiling as he did so. Police and military personnel, their expressions grave, ushered the refugees through the town.

"I'm betting a lot of these folks will find somewhere else to live. As far from the mines as possible."

She glimpsed another tight community of vehicles at the far end of the park, pushed tight against the empty school grounds. An alphabet of letters and numbers announced their affiliation with some of the larger news outlets both in and out of the country. Canadian news agencies CBC, CTV and Global News were just a few of the logos that were printed on the panel vans. But already, NBC and Fox had appeared to represent the US, and a leased van with the BBC logo on it was just pulling in.

A mixed group of reporters was gathered around a small contingent of police officers, and Jamie realized it was a press conference. For a moment, she felt a sense of panic at not being among them in case some tidbit of information was released that might help lift her story to another level. Then she laughed at her own paranoia. She and Lucas were at the center of the story. In fact, they had both nailed information that had scooped both Forbes and the all the other so-called professionals. *Damn*, she thought, *it feels good*!

Lucas ran back to the Jeep. "I've got some great shots." He tossed her keys to her. "You drive while I upload these shots to Felix."

She started the vehicle and turned to him. "Where to?"

He craned his head out the window and pointed. "We should be able to see everything from up there. The gas is heavier than air, so we ought to be safer up near the water tower."

"How do we get up there?"

He pointed back the way they came. "Take the street at the old hospital."

Jamie turned the vehicle around and slowly made her way to the street Lucas indicated, driving on the lawn because the roadway was still full of evacuees.

At the corner, she eased her Jeep over the curb and turned down the road. She turned the wheel down an access road that Lucas pointed at. It passed by the stately building that was the North Shore Club, which was where formal Novo functions were held. Beyond the building, she saw the open gate that led to the tailings area.

She knew that the area had been used to deposit waste material ever since the opening of the first mine over a hundred of years ago. In the past few decades, the Cities of Fox Lake and Sudbury had worked hard with Novo to rejuvenate the area by planting massive numbers of trees. Not long ago, the area had looked like a moonscape because of acid rain, and from deforestation for smelting furnaces over the past century. Today, much of that damage had been healed.

The road quickly turned to gravel, and she had to gear down to take the steep hill around the back of the mountainside. The plant's enormous water tank reared over the landscape and Jamie parked the Jeep next to the structure. She and Lucas got out to rush to the mountain's edge.

The town of North Shore stretched out in front of them. Military and first-responder tents lay at their feet while the subdivision stretched southward toward the highway. Lucas pointed to the southwest.

"That bigger white building up behind the others is the nickel refinery where the tanks were hit. The ditch next to the rail line is the path the gas will have taken to the low area opposite Westview Apartments, according to the scientist."

"It all looks so peaceful."

Lucas gave a rueful chuckle. "What you can't see can kill you."

She nodded. She was fully aware of the danger this chemical release posed for the people of North Shore.

Her phone buzzed, and she pulled it from her pocket. "Coleman."

"Are you and Lucas somewhere safe?" asked Forbes.

"Yes," she assured him. "We're at the water tower overlooking the town." She turned on the speakerphone so Lucas could hear.

"Good. You're over a half mile away from the cloud. The show is about to begin. We have the green light to ignite the gas. Tell Lucas to get his camera ready. He'll only get one shot at this."

"How are they going to ignite it?"

"We're using one of the military's Griffon helicopters. They'll shoot flares into the area. The chemists tell us that once the cloud is consumed, the risk to the community will be over."

"Which way will they come from?" Jamie twisted around, searching the skies.

"From Sudbury airport; so, southwest of you."

"Okay, we'll watch for it." She tapped Lucas's arm and pointed to the general area to the west.

"Stay safe." Forbes said before terminating the call.

Within minutes, they could make out the growing form of a drab green helicopter racing toward them. Lucas crouched to hold his camera ready, while Jamie held her phone out, already zoomed to its highest setting in video mode.

The sleek machine slowed and hovered over a section of grassland near the apartment complex, opposite the low area across the highway. Four crescent streaks left the helicopter and angled downward.

It was all the warning they would get.

The entire area erupted in a massive fireball. Growing rapidly outward, it seemed to boil back towards the refinery. A drainage ditch that ran along the low area carried the flame under the highway, only to shoot out the culvert like a torch, igniting the tall dry grass. The fire swept across the ground growing in intensity as it sought the source of the volatile spill. But the flames stopped alongside the rail line more than football field length from the refinery building.

All that fire, yet no heat.

From where they stood, Jamie heard a deep rumble as the flame crackled across the landscape, even as the clicking of Lucas' camera raced on like a snare drum.

Fire mushroomed and boiled over itself as it ignited the deadly gas until there was nothing left for it to feed on. Small flickers of flames ignited by the major fire lit up in pockets of gas separated from the larger cloud.

The colossal cloud of flame went out as fast as it had burst to life, leaving charred grass and smoking brush in its wake. The suddenness of its ending shocked Jamie, and it took her a few seconds to register that she was still filming.

Lucas stood, his mouth slack and eyes wide. "That was fucking unreal!" he whispered. He shook himself from shocked stupor and immediately uploaded the photos to the paper's cloud service. Jamie followed suit and then called their editor.

"Felix, the crisis at the nickel refinery has been averted. Video and photos are already in the cloud. It's like nothing you've ever seen."

"Great work! Send me some copy, too, just as soon as you can. We'll be uploading this to the digital paper. This is world-breaking news!"

Jamie realized that Felix was right. And she had played a central role in the story. Her emotions threatened to overwhelm her. Her sense of accomplishment joined the excitement of the moment; and as she held her hand out in front of her, her fingers shook. Ready to burst, she swung her gaze to Lucas and saw he had on a shit-eating grin and was staring at her. He looked like a kid let loose in a chocolate factory, and he was practically bouncing.

Without conscious thought, she was in his arms. Both were breathless, bodies crushed again each other, and she felt giddy. She pulled back enough to find his mouth. Lips crushed in a fierce play of emotions, she, as aggressive as he. All the excitement, danger, and thrill of the story released new emotions she had failed to recognize. Right there, right then, she wanted—no, needed—to feel him inside her. She wanted to share these overwhelming sensations with Lucas and never have it end. She let her hand snake down his chest to cup his groin, surprised to see he was equally aroused.

He released a groan, and so did she.

She tugged at his shirt but was cut short as a gust of wind suddenly buffeted the two of them. They pulled apart, although not letting go of each other. They looked for the source of the wind, and to their amazement, saw a military Griffon helicopter descending towards them. In the windshield of the bird sat a grinning Forbes. He held a microphone to his lips.

"Are you two too busy to take part in the endgame?" blasted them from the mounted bullhorn on the copter's frame.

Jamie felt blood rush to her cheeks. She covered her eyes to avoid the dust the machine was stirring up, but also to hide her expression. Lucas released her, but took her hand instead, pulling her towards the craft as it settled onto the black rock of the mountain.

The side door slid open, and a crewman helped them into the craft, where they sat on canvas-covered seats. The crewman handed headsets to each of them after they had buckled in.

Forbes' voice crackled in her headset. "Your idea of following the boat worked, you'll be glad to know. We were able to identify both Bao Daoming and Drago. You will have heard by now that Vautour was killed in Africa, so at least he's out of the picture.

"We're following the creek system to the west. This waterway flows right past their other camp off Agnew Lake Road. But they must have had a second property nearby. It must have been how they entered the city unseen during their other attacks."

"Are they there now?" Lucas asked.

"No. It's still a long distance, but we are keeping track of their progress. We still don't know where the new camp is situated. But once they go to ground, we'll hit them with everything we have!"

Chapter 38

D rago was livid.

Most, if not all, of his people had been killed in the attack. How had the enemy known of their plans? The attack had been simple enough, except the element of surprise was stolen from them. And once the Canadians started lobbing mortar rounds on top of his men with pin-point accuracy, he knew the ambushers had been ambushed.

However, he felt satisfied that they had at least destroyed one of the chemical tanks. The explosion and fireball had been massive. It must have taken out both the Canadians soldiers and his remaining men. At least they would not be alive to betray him.

His hand squeezed hard on the little boat's throttle, but the engine was moving as fast as it had been designed. All he was accomplishing was causing his hand to cramp. He wanted to hit something—or rather, someone. He thought back to the women a few weeks ago. Beating the woman had been satisfying. It made him feel totally invincible. When he was finally clear of this mission, he would have to find another woman, just to help him relax.

He eyed the Chinaman in the bow of the boat. Then again, he didn't have to wait. Man, woman; what the hell deference did it make? It would also show the smug bastard that he and his Communist goons were not superior to anyone. It's being the strongest dog in the pack that makes you the Alpha, not some stupid ideology.

The call he received last night gave him the final orders in the event the mission failed. He knew that Vautour was dead, so the call was from a stranger—a stranger with an Asian accent, but all the right ID codes. The voice had told him that the Chinese government could not allow Bao Daoming to be captured alive. If the Canadian authorities interrogated him and proved that the PRC was behind the attacks, they would face a worldwide backlash. It would set their international plans back for years. So, Bao was living on borrowed time.

But nothing in the orders said *how* he was to be killed.

As if he could feel the threating thoughts aimed at him, Bao Daoming swung his legs over the metal seat to face the rear of the boat.

"What is our next move?" asked Bao Daoming, not looking directly at Drago.

"Make our escape!" His eyes narrowed. "Why do you even ask? We've discussed everything. The carbonyl plant was our last target. Escaping the country was always going to be the next move." As Bao turned to look at him directly, he stared at the man's dark, expressionless eyes. "Unless you know more than you've shared."

His voice had tightened, but if the Communist noticed, he did not let on.

"I have left nothing out," Bao replied. "Everything we planned has gone forward with barely a hitch. My superiors are impressed. The Canadians do not know who is behind the assault on their country. If they suspect, they'll think twice about criticizing or interfering with China. And Novo will not survive the fallout of the damage to their facility. When we buy out their North American division, we control most of the world's iron supply—and price."

Drago said nothing as he aimed the boat towards the narrows, which would lead to the next lake in the water system. Having made the journey many times during the past few months, he knew they would arrive at their latest camp in less than an hour. He would deal with the pompous ass then. Drago knew he could kill the man now. He need only flip the boat and let him drown. His fear of the water had been clear since their first trip up the river. He had even volunteered the fact that he had never learned to swim.

But where would the fun be in that?

"With only the two of us left, should we alter our escape plans?" Bao asked.

"We stand a better chance if we take different routes. There is no escape using regular transportation. They will be watching roads and airports very closely."

"As we planned, your best bet is to get yourself to either your embassy in Ottawa or one of your consulate offices in Toronto, or even Calgary. They can put you on one of their official jets, where you won't have to worry about a check by customs or border agents."

Bao Daoming nodded.

"For myself, I'll make it out of the country by land. Both Interpol and the UN have a file on me, so I would probably be picked up through facial identification if I try to leave through a big airport. It's why I arrived here by similar means to your own."

Drago motioned with his chin. "Here come the rapids."

Bao Daoming's turned toward the bow of the boat. Seeing the drop in the water's surface made the man's complexion pale. He turned his back on the rapids and tilted his head as if in prayer. Both hands gripped the gunwales so hard that Drago could see the man's knuckles turn white. It was all Drago could do not to laugh out loud.

He tilted the motor so that the propeller was just under the surface. Keeping to one side of the chute that he knew to be deeper; he rode the bouncing and bobbing boat with a child's glee, enjoying his companion's terror. As the boat shot out the other side of the rapids, he tilted the motor back to its normal depth.

"That was fun!" He said in a mocking tone.

Bao Daoming glared at him before turning around again to face the front of the boat.

Oh, I can't wait to see the fear in your face when you realize you are about to die. You'll have a real *reason to be scared!*

JAMIE'S HAND FELT GOOD in his own, even in the surreal surroundings of the interior of the Griffin helicopter. His emotions were still rolling from her kiss and the not-so-subtle move of telling him what she wanted. He wanted it too, but would never have had the nerve to express it so openly. It was refreshing, and, he had to admit, damn sexy. He loved her enthusiasm and determination. She never seemed to second guess herself and always knew exactly what she wanted.

She noticed him staring at their hands and gave his a quick squeeze.

He pulled off his headset, covered the microphone, and leaned into her. She pulled back her own earphones.

"Is this going to make it weird for Felix?" He had to yell to make himself heard over the machine's rotor-wash.

"He'll have to learn to live with it," she said with a wicked expression. "In fact, if the paper doesn't want to hire both of us full time, we can hire out as a freelance team. Or set up a website for local news. Not much he can do about that."

"He'll lose his mind."

She shrugged. "If he thinks we might become the competition, he'll get over it."

Lucas pointed to the front of the cockpit where Forbes sat. "Or the alternative."

Her mouth opened wide as she laughed at the thought of becoming a spy, and he joined her. Forbes turned in his seat at the loud bark of laughter. He gave each of them a hard look before shaking his head and turning back.

Moments later, their headsets crackled, and Forbes advised them, "They've gone to ground." He passed a tablet to them. "Satellite shows them on the south side of the Spanish River, just up from the chutes. We'll be standing by until the Colonel's team clears the area. If I got you killed, your boss would have my butt."

They both laughed.

Lucas studied the high-definition image. With his fingers, he widened the screen to show the town of Whitefish to the north. Into the mouthpiece of his headset he said, "We're not all that far from their old position. Panache Lake Road is just off to the west." To prove his point, he spread the screen even farther and pointed at the farmhouse where the recon team had been killed a few days earlier.

Forbes nodded, his eyes hard as iron. The spymaster reached to the front console and retrieved a different microphone. He spoke into it. "Red Fox to Team Leader."

"Team Leader here," came over their headphones. Lucas recognized the gruff voice as Colonel Cameron's.

"You are clear to attack, Team Leader. If possible, take Bao Daoming alive, but only if it's safe to do so. We've lost enough people."

"Acknowledge, Red Fox. Attack commencing."

Lucas shared a nervous look with Jamie as the helicopter wheeled in place, nose dipping as it surged forward.

Chapter 39

One minute, their chopper had been hovering over a canopy of mixed forest; the next, it dipped down into a river valley. Lucas felt totally lost. He knew the area well, but he wasn't sure where they were now, and tried to compare their immediate surroundings to the satellite photos displayed on the tablet that he still held between Jamie and himself.

He craned forward, trying to follow the rush of the river. They came to a set of chutes, water of the rapids cresting a line of rocks that stretched diagonally across the river before falling into churning water. The machine began to hover, waiting for a signal to advance.

The chutes!

He glanced down at the tablet and found the white water downriver from where Forbes had said the terrorists must had made shore. The helicopter had moved in from the west. With his location finally assured, he felt less disconcerted; but his nerves felt like they might snap at any moment. Beside him, Jamie stared ahead intently, her hand squeezing his leg. Although she looked calm, her grip on his leg said otherwise. But then again, who wouldn't be nervous? Neither of them was trained for this kind of situation.

Far ahead of them, cruising just over the water's surface, Lucas spied three more Griffins like the one they were in, sun reflecting off their windshields. Jamie's arm came up and pointed as she saw them. He nodded and raised his camera to capture the attack.

With a practiced manoeuvre as graceful as a dancer's, the three machines rose together and slid over the forest canopy. Even before the machines had settled into a hover, Lucas could see bundles being kicked out on either side of each of the machines. The distance was too far to distinguish what was being thrown earthward, but in the next second, soldiers dropped from their choppers, sliding on ropes, three on each side.

Then the three helicopters rose together, still trailing ropes, and fled from the drop site.

The radio crackled into life.

"Alpha on site, no sign of enemy. Advancing."

"Bravo on site. Covering Alpha."

"Charlie on site. No contact. Standing by."

"GO, GO, GO," URGED the copilot over the interior speaker even as Bravo Team's helicopter flared into a hover.

Bravo Leader readied himself, breathing shallow, heart tripping like a jackhammer.

The crewmen pushed three rope sacks off either side of the chopper, followed by the special forces' soldiers who slid in an almost dead drop, with quick jerks to control their fall through the trees to the forest floor. They slowed before impact, tossing ropes clear so it they wouldn't catch when the helicopter retreated to a safer location. The team dove to the ground or ducked behind natural cover while arming their weapons.

Bravo Leader thought the descent took forever, fearing they'd be shot from the sky.

He knelt, his Colt C7 pointing forward while his team moved into position around him. In his ear, he heard the double squawk from Team Alpha, signifying they were moving forward. Once they had moved into cover, another squawk signaled him. Using hand signals to his own team, he moved forward through Alpha's position under the protection of Alpha's guns. The two squads leapfrogged through the forest towards the terrorist's camp, one protecting the other.

He couldn't see them, but knew that Charlie company was moving into a flanking position, so that when they got into contact with the enemy, they would have the terrorists in a crossfire. It would also stop the enemy from retreating to the river if they hoped to escape.

Moving in a crouch, weapon at the ready, his team surged forward. He caught sight of a cluster of lean-tos, simple shelters built with branches and leaves. Raising a fist to signal a stop, he whispered into the throat mic, "Camp ahead. No movement."

He sensed rather than heard Alpha team move in behind them. When he felt a tap on his shoulder, he signaled and together they rushed the camp, eyes alert, and weapons swinging back and forth, searching for a target.

Nothing moved.

Even the birds and animals were keeping out of sight, instinctively knowing that death was at hand.

His eyes caught a flash of white, and he aimed at it. As he moved forward, his eyes darted everywhere, but always returned to his target. Then, his mind told him what he had found, but he was having trouble understanding why.

He crouched next to the body. Stripped naked, the man, an Asian, was covered in vicious knife gashes. Bravo Leader, having served two tours in Afghanistan, was no stranger to barbarity, but had to swallow hard at the sight of the man. His tormentor had castrated the poor bastard before slicing his throat wide. Blood was no longer flowing, which told him the fellow was beyond help.

He took off a glove and touched an unbloodied spot on the man's arm and found it still warm.

We interrupted something. The sick son-of-a-bitch has to be close by.

LUCAS REALIZED HE WAS holding his breath as he waited desperately to hear anything from the teams who were on the ground in harm's way. Forbes had been right. Drago and his men had hurt or killed enough people. He didn't want to hear the screams of the dying, but resisted the urge to tear the headphones off his head.

"Bravo to Team Leader."

"Team Leader, go."

"We've found Bao Daoming. He's DOA. Someone carved him up pretty bad, though. No sign of his partners. Camp is clear."

Forbes turned and glanced back at the two reporters to see their reaction. Lucas felt nothing for the Chinese national. He had orchestrated an attack on Canada, his country. Helped kill a lot of Canadians, his people. But now, apparently, he'd answered for that.

For Lucas, his concern was centered on Drago. Having seen his brutality up close, Lucas knew that if they didn't stop him, he'd be free to continue to hurt others.

Beside him, Jamie had stiffened when the report of Bau's death came over the radio; but she nodded to herself, knowing her research had just been confirmed.

IT DID NOT COMPLETELY surprise Drago that they'd discovered his camp. After all, he and his men had made multiple trips up and down the waterway. Not that it mattered, but he wondered if someone living on the river or adjoining lakes had reported them, or if a satellite had spied them.

He could have used another hour with Bao Daoming, but he'd at least enjoyed himself while he could. He'd been right. The man's suffering and fear had been very satisfying. Even better than that cheap whore a couple of weeks ago.

Now he'd just fade into the bush until he found a way to cross the border. But first, he had to create a little more chaos, so the pursuers would hesitate to get too close.

From his backpack, he pulled out a detonator; and with no further thought, armed the unit and pressed the trigger button. A string of explosions echoed through the forest, some close, some farther away. He tossed the detonator away, hiked his backpack into place and swung his leg over the powerful motocross bike that had been leaning against a tree. A long, black gun-case hung along the side of the bike. Turning the key, he kick-started the big bike, and revved it to warm up the engine.

He dropped the bike into gear and twisted the throttle. The bike jumped with power, and he laughed as it tried to buck him off. He could never get enough power or speed. It was almost as exciting as killing.

He raced out of the forest on a faint trail beside a small, swampy pool of water. Suddenly, with a rush of chopper blades overhead, the terrifying rip of a Mini-gun capped the animal growl of the bike. Leaves and chunks of bark struck him; yet miraculously, no bullet found its mark and the chopper moved off.

Following the old trail, he skirted the wide marsh that split the forest. At the far end, he could just make out the entrance to an old logging road. Heavy foliage covered the road, so it looked like a green tunnel. He aimed for that spot.

When the helicopter appeared before him, he gunned the motorcycle and drove right under it before it could lock its heavy machine-gun on him. The mouth of that dark forest was mere feet away when he heard the whining rip of the chopper's Mini-gun reaching out for him again. As soon as he entered the cover of the forest, he launched himself sideways off the bike, landing in a roll. The bike continued onward, twigs, leaves and branches raining down on it. Riderless, it toppled over; the engine returning to a rough idle.

He carefully rose to his feet, testing to ensure he had broken nothing in his wild jump. He winced at the pain in his shoulder. The helicopter had flown over his position, and it sounded like it was circling. Well, this time he would be ready for the attack.

He ran to the bike, and with a grunt, flipped it over to clear the black nylon weapons-case. Ripping open Velcro flaps, he pulled out the deadly tool.

THE HEAVY, HOLLOW CRUMP of explosions was unmistakable, even over the noise of the helicopter. They felt as much as heard them. Smoke billowed from the forest's canopy and the pilot looked at Forbes for orders.

The radio crackled. "Bravo Leader to Command. Multiple explosions. We have people down! Request Medivac."

"Team Leader to Bravo. Calm down, son. Tell me exactly what happened."

"There was a string of explosions throughout the camp. Must have been a remote detonation. We have many people down, sir. Those left standing are helping the others, but we need these people pulled out of here. We're unable to pursue the enemy at this time. Sir."

"Understood. Can you clear some trees so we can drop a basket for extraction?"

There was a pregnant pause, and Lucas hoped the man hadn't been one of the wounded.

"Affirmative, Team Leader. We have enough det cord to clear you a full landing zone."

"Good job, son. Get to it then. Help is on its way."

The helicopter rose and moved towards the smoking canopy. Lucas felt totally helpless. He tried to take pictures, but his hands were shaking—from fear, or the chopper's vibration, he couldn't say.

The radio blurted again.

"Bravo to Team Leader. We just heard a dirt bike starting, and it's moving south of our position. It might be our guy."

"Right. We'll get on it. Now, just worry about your people, Bravo."

"Roger, Sir."

Forbes didn't hesitate. He ordered the pilot to move south of the enemy camp to cut off the fleeing enemy. "That has to be Drago!"

The helicopter banked hard, throwing Jamie against Lucas' side. Only their belts kept them from falling through the open door. They were looking straight down on the tops of tall pines before the craft leveled out and flew across the treetops. Tree tips whacked on the skids. The machine rose and crested a small rise before dropping to an oxbow lake that was closed off from the main river by a shallow sandbar. The sides of the small body of water dipped deep, following hard granite cliffs. At the far end of the lake, a flash of bright light danced through the trees; but before Lucas could call out, Forbes pointed to the fleeing terrorist.

"There! That's him."

The door gunner, the one who had helped Lucas and Jamie into the helicopter, didn't have to be told twice. He triggered the Dillon Aero M134D Mini-gun. The helicopter vibrated violently, and up-range, the foliage was torn apart. The Griffon slid sideways as the Gatling gun raked the forest near and ahead of the fleeing bike, shredding leaves, branches and decapitating entire trees.

Then, with no more clear shots, the pilot pushed the throttle, and the craft jumped ahead in an arc, so they were in front of the terrorist. Below, the all-terrain motorcycle sped right at the approaching aircraft. Before the gunner could get off a shot, the bike ducked under the chassis, racing for the far side of a small, dry marsh. With a sickening twist that pushed Lucas onto Jamie, the pilot pivoted the helicopter and spun to face the opposite direction.

Once again, the roar of the Mini-gun shook them, digging a line of destruction that followed the fleeing terrorist into the forest. The object of their hunt disappeared into the canopy of vegetation. The machine tilted as it throttled up, reaching for more sky. There was no sign of their prey.

Forbes circled his finger, and the machine started a wide arc, its nose pointing towards the last spot they had seen the motorcycle entering the forest.

Without warning, a flaming trail lifted from within the dark foliage and rose towards the helicopter. The pilot must have seen the threat, because the craft pitched over to flee the approaching rocket.

Jamie was on top of Lucas again, arms tight around his chest. He had time to cover her head with his hand before an explosion rocked their world.

Lucas would later recall an echoing blast that blocked out all other sounds, a flash of fire, and jagged metal that seemed to peel effortlessly from the craft, even as it rolled them over.

The gut-plunging fall as the machine lost power and plunged earthward.

Then nothing.

Chapter 40

The thump of her heart told her she was alive. But it felt like the steady tempo came from her head rather than her chest. She drew in a deep breath and gasped at the pain in her side. The pain made her whimper, and she panted shallow breaths.

A confusing sight greeted her as she blinked open her eyes. It took her groggy mind a few moments to realize she was hanging upside down. Beside her, the limp form of Lucas dangled, arms hanging limply towards the chopper's roof. The machine had fallen and rolled just before it hit the ground.

"Lucas," she said. It came out as a gurgle, even to her ears. She tried to clear her throat, but found her mouth full of blood. Using her tongue, she examined the inside of her mouth, and found a raw gash on the inside of her cheek. *Bitten myself.* She spat a mouthful of blood and tried again.

"Lucas." Much better.

Mindful of the pain in her side, she pulled an arm around her chest to find the source. Her fingers found a sharp sliver of metal protruding from between her ribs. Even that careful inquiry caused searing pain to radiate through her. *How deep is it in?*

Lucas stirred beside her, and she almost cried in relief that he was still alive. She forced herself to look forward, checking for Forbes and the pilot. Both men hung inverted. But neither man moved. From the pilot's helmet dripped a stream of blood into a pool beneath him. There was no sign of the gunner.

Lucas groaned as he gained consciousness.

"What the fu—?"

"We crashed. We're upside down."

She felt him turn as he took in his surroundings.

"You, okay?" he said, grabbing her hand.

"I have a chunk of metal in my side. Even breathing hurts."

"Okay, first things first." With that, he pulled the lever on his seatbelt. Without the restraint, gravity did the rest. He dropped hard to the helicopter roof with a grunt, causing the craft to shift.

"You, okay?" she asked, her voice tight with worry.

"I'll be feeling that for a while." He pulled himself to his knees and worked himself around her to examine her wound. The expression he made when he eyed the wound told her all she needed to know.

"That bad, eh?"

He looked at the seat she was tied to and how she hung. "I can lessen your fall, but this is still going to hurt, especially with your wound. And I'll have to turn you as you fall so that chunk of metal doesn't get driven deeper. But we have to get you out of here. I can smell fuel. There's no telling if it'll catch fire."

She bit her lip and nodded at him.

"I'll brace you, but you'll have to undo the seatbelt when I tell you. Once you're loose, I'll roll you into a sitting position away from your wound. From there, I can drag you out of here."

She nodded, her eyes tightening at the pain that would come. *There was no point in false bravado. She was scared shitless.*

He tucked his shoulder into her belly and wrapped his arm under her knees.

"Okay, release the belt."

It was harder than she thought. She had to wiggle her hand between his shoulder and her gut. With him pressed to take her weight, there wasn't much room. When her fingers touched the clasp of the belt, she stiffened in readiness of the pain.

"Go limp. It'll be easier to roll you."

It took all her resolve and blind trust Lucas would do his best not to hurt her.

She pulled the lever.

Her weight settled on Lucas's back. The pain did come, but nowhere as bad as she had imagined. He turned her body towards the entrance.

"You okay?" he grunted.

"Yep."

"I think I can walk right out of here like this. It'll save dragging you over the uneven ground."

She swallowed hard. "Do it." Keeping her eyes closed, she gritted her teeth in anticipation of more pain.

Lucas duck-walked her out of the machine and as soon as they had cleared the doorway, she felt breeze on her damp neck. It might well have been the most pleasant sensation she ever experienced.

But it didn't last.

The blinding torment in her side came so fast that there was no way she could brace herself. It washed over like a tidal wave, taking everything that was her, with it.

Which was a mercy.

LUCAS FELT HER GO LIMP as he laid her on the forest floor. Clumps of grass and moss were the best kind of bed that he could find. He examined her wound, seeing bright crimson leaking from the around sharp, jagged metal. He dared not pull the shard out. It might be all that was keeping her from bleeding out.

He had to get help. And fast. He could hear the thumps of helicopters in the distance and realized that help was on the other side of the mountain. Colonel Cameron was busy medevacking the wounded soldiers at the enemy camp. Would Cameron know that they had gone down? He couldn't remember the pilot radioing their position or that they had taken enemy fire.

He had to get the word out.

Leaving Jamie, he strode back towards the crumpled chopper. The pilot's door was crushed in on itself, and he didn't think he could force it open.

Entering the rear compartment, he knelt down to check Forbes, who still hung upside-down. The man was breathing, but had a deep gash across his forehead. Turning to the pilot, Lucas felt his stomach rebel. He had to swallow hard as he took in the poor man's injuries. Even with the helmet, which looked intact, it was obvious that man's skull was distorted, bent in ways no living soul could endure. He'd probably died instantly. At least Lucas hoped so, for the man's sake. But that was another life that Drago had taken. The sudden thought of the murderer made Lucas scan the forest through the broken web of safety glass that stretched across the cockpit.

Looking between the dead man and Forbes, he spied the Forbes's headset wedged between the man's hands. He reached between the seats, pulling on the spiral cord to pull the headset towards him. The cord had become tangled around Forbes' arm, and he had to patiently untangle it before pulling the headset towards him.

Clicking the transmit button, he said, "Mayday. Mayday. Colonel Cam . . . ah . . . Team Leader. Forbes' helicopter is down. Hit by rocket fire. We need help."

The radio crackled, and he heard the colonel's gruff voice over the headset. Before Lucas could relay any more information, someone yanked him violently backwards by his belt. As he fell, he careened off the sliding door frame and his vision exploded in a sea of stars.

He collapsed to the ground on his stomach, face slamming into a bed of decaying leaves. Lucas tasted damp, earthy soil. He could still hear the colonel's voice through the helicopter's speakers, demanding information.

Before he could roll over, a boot connected with his ribcage, and he let out a hard *woof* as air exploded from him, leaving him gasping. He was in a world of pain, but deflected a second kick with his hand, the boot snapping a finger, and he yelled. He rolled away from his assaulter and staggered to his feet.

The man was a monster. Over six feet with shoulders half as wide, his heavy brooding features made his smile more menacing than any frown. But what he carried in his hand scared Lucas even more.

It was a black-bladed tactical knife. The man held it low and menacing. He began to circle, forcing Lucas to move in the opposite direction.

Lucas cast his eyes over the area, looking for anything that he could use to protect himself. Holding his ribs with his injured hand, he circled away from the deadly terrorist. The movement pushed him towards the tail of the helicopter. *Is he trying to pin me against the fuselage so there's nowhere to escape?*

The big man lunged, but it was only a feint. Lucas jumped back, and his shoulder came in contact with the helicopter's tail piece. Drago laughed harshly.

Lucas ducked under the tail, his eyes never leaving the mercenary. Drago didn't hesitate. He lunged towards Lucas, knife extended to gut him. As he jumped back to save himself, Lucas grabbed the tail rotor blade and spun it away from himself. His timing was nothing more than miraculous. The opposite end of the blade rotated just as Drago extended his arm to stab Lucas.

Instead, the tail rotor cashed across Drago's wrist. The snap was audible. A tortured scream followed immediately. The knife flew from his injured hand to land in the rotting humus. Rather than step back, the mercenary stepped forward, reaching with his good arm for Lucas' throat. His eyes were wild.

Lucas fell backwards, hitting the ground hard. Drago dropped onto Lucas, landing on his chest with his full weight. Once again, the wind gushed from Lucas's body, leaving him lightheaded and weak. Drago pinned Lucas's arms with his knees and grabbed him by the throat with his good hand.

Lucas' eyes bugged out of his head as Drago applied pressure. Lack of air was killing him. Spots flickered through his vision as his oxygen-starved body tried desperately to thrash back and forth. But there was no give.

As the light faded, he felt the hands jerk from a sudden impact, the force causing the pressure on his throat to ease. Over the horrifying fury of the terrorist's blood lust, Lucas thought he saw a shadow rise and strike at the big man's back.

Air entered his battered throat, and as the spots cleared, he felt another tremor.

Lucas made out the dark braids of Jamie's hair as she pulled the black blade of the discarded tactical knife out of Drago's back and plunged it in again. And again.

The big mercenary was like a monster tree. His fall started slowly as he toppled away from Lucas's throat, fell across his legs—and lay still.

Jamie knelt over him, bloodied knife clasped in both hands. Tears and blood mingled across her face as she cried uncontrollably.

Lucas and Jamie sat there unmoving, Jamie crying and Lucas gathering his breath, while the dead man lay across his legs. When he could, he pushed the corpse off him and got up—then he crouched in front of Jamie.

He reached out and carefully pulled the bloody knife from her hands, dropping it into the grass. He pulled her into his arms and buried his nose in her hair. She shuddered.

"I guess now that you saved me, you're going to want your name ahead of mine in the by-line?"

He felt her shoulders bounce as her sobbing stopped and she began to laugh.

"Jerk!"

"Yeah, but I'm *your* jerk."

Epilogue

Lucas pushed Jamie's wheelchair through the door into the dark room with difficulty. His broken-fingered hand hung in a cast from a sling. The deep, dark bruising surrounding his throat was beginning to turn sickly yellow.

For her part, Jamie seemed fine, but Lucas knew the truth. The shard of metal had pierced her lung and cut through one rib. As suspected, keeping the metal in place was the only thing that had saved her life. Where she had gotten the strength to rise and attack Drago, even the doctors could not or would not contemplate.

He pushed her beside the hospital bed, where Forbes lay propped up with a generous supply of pillows. His leg hung from a harness where stainless steel rods held his pelvis together, a result of the crash. He wore red-lensed glasses.

"Nice mood-lights," Lucas said. 'Do they help when you have to drive in fog?"

Forbes grunted a weak laugh. They all knew that concussion was the cause of his light sensitivity. "Doctors have prescribed photophobia glasses to help with the harsher light, but I've been sidelined for a couple months from any screen time because of the screen's blue light. It's rather annoying, if I do say so myself."

Jamie looked at Lucas and then back at Forbes. With a conspirator's smile, she said, "I have the name of a co-op student that might read your reports to you. She's a pretty smart investigator in the right library or database."

"I might have to take you up on that. Unfortunately, the enemies of our country will not allow me the grace to convalesce. It would really help if you two would consider my offer."

Lucas laughed. "Oh, you're smooth!"

He held up his hands. "You can't blame me for trying, Lucas. Most, if not all, progress in this situation was because of both of you."

"Coming from you, that is high praise, Darren," Jamie mumbled. "And we both appreciate it. But both of us honestly believe in exposing the truth no matter the cost, while government picks and chooses what information is released because they don't think the average citizen is bright enough to understand. We both understand the idea of playing your cards close to your chest so an enemy can't use sensitive information against us, but there has to be a time to allow the public to know the truth."

There was a difficult silence among the three.

Lucas broke it. "Do you plan on releasing Bao Daoming's identity?"

Forbes stared back, but answered honestly. He shook his head. "We know you are announcing that information in your newspaper's upcoming investigative report, but the government itself simply cannot confirm, or deny. Through you, China will be put on notice that challenging Canada will have consequences, and that we are ready for them. They won't blindside us a second time.

"By our *not* confirming, we give the CCP a face-saving win. If we don't do it this way, we're asking for a more hostile attack—maybe an economic one next time—that we cannot protect ourselves from." He clasped his hands in his lap and sighed deeply. "It's all part of a larger game, one we cannot afford to lose."

The two journalists exchanged a look. "Thank you for your honesty, Forbes," Lucas said, reaching out to shake the man's hand. He pushed Jamie's chair forward so she, too, could shake the hand of the country's master-spy.

"Take care of this big lug," Forbes said with a wink. "And if either of you needs my help, don't hesitate to reach out. If it's not against the country's best interests," he said with a grin, "I'll do what I can."

The three exchanged smiles and then Lucas backed Jamie out of the room, ensuring the door closed off the bright light from the hallway.

They were both silent until they entered the elevator. They were alone.

"Well, what do you think?" Jamie asked.

"I think he was as honest as we can expect. It's up to us to dig up the truth, but for him to use that truth or a version of it for the next move in his great game. I'm glad we don't have to make that decision. The truth works for me."

She patted his hand. With that thought, they were way ahead of the game. Theirs, as well as Forbes'.

LUCAS AND JAMIE SAT on the couch in the quiet office of Second Chance. They were waiting for Christine to arrive with a special guest. The minute they'd arrived, Christine had been adamant that she gather her flock to hear the news that the reporters had come to deliver.

Lucas and Jamie had sat talking quietly, enjoying each other's company. Lucas felt numb. They had spent two full days writing their exclusive into a complete account of the attacks on Novo. Lucas had also done a full write-up on Drago Petkovic and his late partner, Felipe Vautour, with a little unofficial background help from Forbes.

Jamie was able to trace Bao Daoming back to the Chinese government and used her research to outline Chinese maneuvering in other parts of the world. Felix did very little coaching before she agreed to write a full exposé on the Belt and Roads program. He planned to make it a national story if not farther-reaching.

In their story, they also explained how one of the conspirators, Jaren Pinheiro, had tried to stop the attacks once he realized he had been duped. He'd thought that he was just fighting to get justice for his family's deaths.

Lucas did a separate story about the in-fighting among the sex traffickers, and how Darcy and Rosie had been arrested for forced confinement of a minor and sexual interference, on top of human trafficking charges. Although mentioned in the article, no one had made contact with Gabriel Kebede since his release from the hospital. The rumor was the pimp had left town. Or had been *taken*. *Good riddance.*

This visit to Christine's was the last on their list. Within an hour's time, they were planning to leave the city for a well-deserved break. Lucas had rented a cabin for a week on a lake where there was no internet connection or phone service. They planned to rest and get to know each other away from the world.

He smiled and stood as he heard excited female voices coming from outside the storefront. Even through the plywood 'window', he could recognize Christine's enthusiastic voice. He held a hand to Jamie and helped her gingerly to her feet just as the lock disengaged and five women burst in, laughing and talking excitedly.

Seeing Lucas and Jamie, the conversation stopped as the former sex-workers recognized the reporters.

"Come on, grab a seat. Lucas has news, and I can't promise not to break the news myself if I have to wait one more minute," Christine said, waving at the chairs.

Amber, her jaw no longer wired shut, gave Lucas a shy smile as she sat, while Gabby and Jewel sat on either side, perched on the chair's cushioned arms. One woman that Lucas recognized, but couldn't place, stood behind the couch.

To Christine, Lucas said, "I figured you were bringing Amber over. I didn't expect a full audience."

"Lucas, I don't know if you recognize Terry. Terry was my first success story—which you are definitely going to want to write a story about. After joining our program, Terry returned to school and earned a degree in Social Work and has just agreed to join Second Chance as a councillor.

Lucas shook Terry's hand. "Hi, Terry. Now I remember you. And you're right, Christine, I would love to write that story. Congratulations on your new position. And now that you're working here, I guess I know how to find you."

Terry nodded.

Stepping back beside Jamie, he turned to the others and drew a deep breath.

He smiled at the women. "I made a promise last week—was it just last week?" he said, looking at Jamie in surprise. So much had happened. "I promised I would find who had hurt you, Amber, and that I would do my best to make sure he'd never do it again. Jamie and I are here to tell you that you're free. That man can never hurt you again. He's dead, so you never have to worry about him."

Amber's eyes went wide. "You killed him?"

"Not me," he said, looking at Jamie.

All eyes turned to Jamie, and she nodded. "He didn't give me a choice. His days of hurting people are over." She took Lucas's hand in hers.

Lucas saw Christine catch the movement and also noticed the drop of her shoulders. There was no avoiding it. Better now than to draw it on.

"So, with Christine's help, you'll be completely free of the past. And like Christine, Jamie and I want you to know we are there for you, if you need us."

Amber stood and gave Lucas and Jamie a hug, tears flowing freely. Even Lucas had to swipe at his eyes a few times. They spoke to the women for a few minutes before they left. Christine gave each of them a hug, but not with her usual energized self. "Thank you, again. You two made a difference to these women."

"Not as much as you do, Christine," Lucas said. "You're the real hero to those women."

In the Jeep, Jamie said, "She seemed to take it well."

He shrugged. "She's hurting, but it was inevitable. She's like a little sister. And besides, I'm off the market."

"Good. Then it's time to negotiate our byline."

THE END

I hope you enjoyed The Origami Deception. Reviews are the lifeblood for authors and please complete a simple review; even a couple of words about your experience at www.goodreads.com[1] or wherever you purchased this copy.

Thank you,

David

---

1.   http://www.goodreads.com

Don't miss out!

Visit the website below and you can sign up to receive emails whenever David Wickenden publishes a new book. There's no charge and no obligation.

https://books2read.com/r/B-A-NTFJ-CHJRD

BOOKS 2 READ

Connecting independent readers to independent writers.

Also by David Wickenden

Laura Amour Thriller
Deadly Harvest

Standalone
In Defense of Innocence
Homegrown
For Heaven's Sake
The Home Front
The Origami Deception
The Origami Deception

Watch for more at davewickenden.wixsite.com/dave-wickenden.

About the Author

After 31 years in the Fire Service and attaining the rank of Deputy Fire Chief, David Wickenden retired to write thriller novels full time. He has published six thrillers and one YA Fantasy since 2018. David is a member of the International Thriller Association, International Screenwriter Association, the Writer's Union of Canada, and a board member of the Canadian Crime Writers. He has adapted five books for feature films and his Laura Amour Vigilante series into a TV Pilot. His last novel, The Home Front, placed as a Finalist in the Global Thrillers Award hosted by the Chanticleer International Book Awards. He is currently working on a thriller dealing with firefighting.

Read more at https://davewickenden.wixsite.com/dave-wickenden.

www.ingramcontent.com/pod-product-compliance
Lightning Source LLC
Chambersburg PA
CBHW071553030726

47593CB00001BA/145